HER LAST BREATH

A WOLF LAKE THRILLER

DAN PADAVONA

GET A FREE BOOK!

I'm a pretty nice guy once you look past the grisly images in my head. Most of all, I love connecting with awesome readers like you.

Join my VIP Reader Group and get a FREE serial killer thriller for your Kindle.

Get My Free Book

www.danpadavona.com/thriller-readers-vip-group/

1

Erika folded the john's money and tucked it between her hip and thong. His footsteps shuffled away until she didn't hear them anymore. These were the moments she cherished. The alone time inside the motel room before the staff kicked her out and the next guests bustled in.

With a yawn, she swung her legs off the mattress and dangled her feet over the salt and pepper carpet. A hard spot congealed in the fibers. She grimaced and tried not to imagine how it got there. A door slammed in the next room. Voices rose as a man and woman argued through the walls. This used to be a nice motel. When she was a kid, tourist families stayed at the Wolf Lake Inn. It was a destination spot. You saved money all year to afford a resort like this one. Five years ago, with the local economy in the toilet and the inn on the verge of closing, the family who owned Wolf Lake Inn sold to an outside bidder. The new inn developed a rundown, shady look to it—warped and peeling shingles, chipped paint, and a gaudy neon sign with two letters dead to the world. This room used to cost two hundred a night during the glory years. Now it was fifty-nine with a coupon, and if you knew the owner by name, you could rent it by the hour.

Erika padded to the bathroom and tucked brunette locks behind her ear. The carpet made brittle, crunching noises beneath her feet. She wished for a thick pair of socks or slippers. But those wouldn't match the stiletto heels. She flicked the light and squinted. According to the mirror, she was eighteen going on forty-five. Skin draped off her face like a Shar-Pei's. Her flesh looked like the paste the teacher handed out in third-grade art class. She ran the water and splashed her face. The caked on makeup ran in black and red streaks until she scrubbed her skin clean. She wouldn't be working again tonight, not with this face. Thank God, the john got it over with quick. He'd outweighed her by a hundred pounds and had a back full of hair that made it seem like she caressed a bear. She held her breath while he finished, and her ribs still ached from his girth.

She slogged to the bed and fell on the mattress. The room was hers for another forty minutes. Erika set the alarm and closed her eyes, her sore, exhausted body slipping into sleep. A second later, an angry fist pounded on the door.

"Go away," she said, piling the extra pillow over her ear.

"You leave room," said Ryo. She recognized the innkeeper's voice. "New guest stays all night. Housekeeping come in ten minutes. You be gone, or I call police."

Right. Ryo wouldn't call the police. Girls like Erika kept his inn afloat. More pounding on the door got her moving.

"All right, all right. Hold your scrotum and give me a minute to get dressed."

Erika ripped the shirt over her head and stepped into her skirt, the hem almost high enough to reveal the thong. Her feet protested the second she pulled the stilettos on. Outside the door, someone dragged a rolling suitcase. She was almost to the door when she remembered the money. The folded bills sat on her hip until it became one with her sweaty skin. She pocketed the money and shielded her eyes from the gaudy neon sign. Ryo glared from the office. She wanted to flip him off.

But she needed Ryo as much as he needed her. Her purse strap hanging off her shoulder, Erika clicked across the blacktop and angled toward the sidewalk. The money felt thin inside her pocket. A cold thought dripped into her chest before she ripped the money from her pocket and counted the bills. Dammit. The john had ripped two bills in half. The scumbag stiffed her. A helpless tear clouded her eyes as she imagined what Troy would do. Troy Dean ran the 315 Royals, the Harmon gang surrounded by whispers of white supremacy. Their rivals, the predominantly black Harmon Kings, controlled the west side of the city, the Royals ruling over the east, including the city's red-light district. Hence, the 315 Royals ran Harmon's prostitution. The Kings wanted in on the Royals' business, and tensions rose between the two factions. Last week, a Royals member shot into a club owned by the Harmon Kings, a message to back off their prostitution business.

She wouldn't call Troy. The last time she came up short, he blackened her eye and promised the next time would be worse. Her stomach growled. She hadn't eaten since breakfast, and it was ten minutes until midnight. How would she get back to Harmon? The city sat five miles north of Wolf Lake, and she couldn't afford a taxi.

"I told you to leave," Ryo called from the doorway.

"I'm on the sidewalk."

"You bad for business. You go."

Swallowing a sob, Erika turned her head and stomped down the concrete walkway, past the closed dress shops. Though spring arrived in upstate New York, winter's breath returned at night, as though the cold hid within the shadows and ventured out after sunset. With the scourge of the Wolf Lake Inn behind her, the boulevard gave way to quaint village homes. Wolf Lake drowned in old money. She could get used to a place like this. In her fantasies, she owned a little home beside the water with a garden in the backyard. Grapes snaked up a trellis along the side of the house. With no better plan, she turned north, the darkness too thick to make out the street signs. She didn't have the strength to walk all the way back to Harmon, and the sheriff's department sat two miles from the inn. If a deputy caught her walking through the village, she'd spend the night in a cell. Troy would kill her if he needed to bail her out.

Flashing headlights brought her head around. She was ready to step out of her heels and run. But it wasn't a sheriff's cruiser. A white SUV crawled along the curb. The driver flashed his lights again. The SUV slowed when it caught up, the driver pacing her as she followed the walkway. He drove a Chevrolet Trax. She recognized the make. A 315 Royals member named Flacco bought a used model last winter.

The stranger's buzzed hair appeared white, as if he dyed it. His head lingered close to the SUV's roof, his muscles rippling beneath his t-shirt. A good-looking guy in his middle or late twenties. Red splotches marred his face. Like he fell into a patch of poison ivy or had an allergic reaction to a bee sting.

"You want a ride?" the man asked after lowering the window.

Ignoring him, she walked arrow-straight past the sleepy residences, many with gated driveways.

"Long way from home, aren't you? Come on. Hop in, and I'll take you someplace warm."

"Not interested."

"Hey, I won't turn you in. You're not supposed to be in Wolf Lake. Climb in, and I'll buy you a late dinner. Then who knows? We could go back to my place."

She scoffed.

"I don't need your charity."

Except she did.

"Who said anything about charity? Look, I know the game." He lowered his voice and scanned the neighborhood conspiratorially. "I'll pay, all right? Whatever you get per hour, I'll double it. Then I'll drive you home so you don't have to pay for a cab. From what I can see, I'm your only ride back to Harmon."

Erika slowed her pace. She still felt sore from the bear-man and couldn't escape his stench. This client was her ticket home, and Troy wouldn't know she worked again. If she agreed, she'd be able to pay Troy and pocket the rest. Hell, she could afford to buy breakfast tomorrow morning. Still, something about this guy sent a shiver down her spine.

He paused at a stop sign, then followed Erika after she crossed a side street and continued northward.

"Look, my wife walked out on me a month ago. I'm not some creep who pays for sex all the time. I'm lonely, and I don't want to spend all night drinking and watching sports highlights. Tell me what you make per hour."

Erika glanced at the guy. His head hung out the window, one strong forearm resting against the sill. Red lights flared as he tapped the brakes, bathing the leafless trees in bloody colors.

"Two-eighty."

Who the hell was she kidding? She hadn't commanded that price since she turned fifteen and ran away from home.

"No problem. Tell you what. One hour in bed, another hour talking over a late dinner. Or an early breakfast. Your choice. Barbecued chicken or waffles with maple syrup. Like I said, I could use the companionship."

Was this guy serious? This would be her best payday of the year. She'd pay Troy and keep four-hundred for herself. But she didn't trust this john. Lots of guys threw around money when they laid eyes on her long legs and high cheekbones, but came up short when it was time to pay.

"Show me the money, Jerry MaGuire."

"I'm good for it."

"You want two hours? Show me the bills, or I walk home."

The man stopped the SUV in front of an old Victorian home with a wrought-iron gate. Shadows from the tree branches hung over the sidewalk like the claws of some faceless beast. As she tapped a nervous foot, he wrestled the wallet from his pocket and flipped it open. She fought to hold her poker face. A thick wad of bills stretched the black leather wallet to the seams. For all she knew, the bills were singles. But when he pulled a fistful of twenties and fifties out, a happy butterfly fluttered inside her chest.

"We good now?"

She nodded.

"Then get in before a sheriff's vehicle catches us."

Erika rounded the vehicle. Shaking off the cold, she wiggled against the warm seats when he blasted the heat. The Trax left the curb and shot into the night. A minute later, they put the village behind them as Erika cast a wary eye at the mirrors.

"Where are you taking me?"

"Home," he said, not pulling his eyes from the road. The dividing line swept at them in a blur. "Not far now."

Her eyes lingered on his knuckles. They were raw and cut. A spiderweb tattoo wound around his forearm. She'd been around the block enough times to recognize a prison tat. And if he did time, he might have gang affiliations. Shit. Was he in the Kings? Rumors circulated about the Kings murdering escorts to hurt the Royals.

"Hey, I'm having second thoughts. Why don't you drop me off here, and we'll call it even?"

The man ignored Erika and stared through the windshield. His fingers tightened around the steering wheel. Sensing something was wrong, she reached for the door handle before he engaged the child safety locks. The Trax revved faster. Stars flew at the windshield as he stomped the gas.

Fumbling in her pocket for the phone, Erika didn't see the fist before it slammed her cheek. Her head smacked the window. She screamed before a second punch dislodged her jaw. Tires screeched as the SUV jerked to a stop. Momentum whipped her forward before the seatbelt yanked her back. As Erika's eyes rolled back, he set a video camera on the dashboard and aimed it across the seat.

Two meaty hands circled her throat and squeezed. She flailed her legs and struck him with an ineffective punch, the seatbelt pinning her back as memories hurtled through her mind. Her father dying in a car accident when she was four. Mom's new boyfriend sneaking into her bedroom at night when she turned twelve. Running away at fifteen to escape the rapes. Her mother following her to the red-light district of Harmon, braving the Royals as she begged Erika to come home.

Somehow, she knew prostitution would be the end of her from the day she left her mother. Starlight reflected off the knife as Erika fought to draw her last breath.

The remorseless night faded to black.

2

Thomas Shepherd pushed the button and waited at the crosswalk until traffic cleared. Even after the last car motored through the intersection, he refused to step off the curb until the sign read *WALK*. The sign changed, and he looked both ways. Twice. Always twice. Then strode across the thoroughfare and hopped the curb, flinching when a distant horn bayed.

Across Lagoon Road, the red brick edifice of the Nightshade County Sheriff's Office hid behind two leafless maple trees that wouldn't bud for another few weeks. The walk from the municipal parking lot took two minutes, five less than he'd budgeted for. Since returning to Wolf Lake, he kept noticing how small everything seemed. The houses, the roads. Even the football field behind the high school, where he ran track during his teenage years, appeared shorter than he remembered. Moving home from Los Angeles could do that to you.

He finished his bagel and tossed the napkin in the trash container as butterflies fluttered inside his chest. Interviews always set him on edge, though his resume was solid. How many times had he sat across the desk from a prospective employer and lost the job because the interviewer worried Thomas wasn't interested?

Before he stepped inside, he checked his reflection on the dusty glass door. Nothing he could do about his unruly tangle of chestnut hair. Since he was a child, his mother had referred to it as the rat's nest. Uncertainty nudged his heart rate. He'd always been too small and slight of build for law enforcement. The deputy crossing the hallway appeared twice his size.

Rusty hinges shrieked when he pulled the door open. He hadn't taken two steps before a woman with orange-brown hair removed her reading glasses and stood behind her desk. My God, Maggie was still here. Maggie Tillery had been the administrative assistant for the sheriff's department when Thomas was a kid.

"Well, I'll be darned," Maggie said. She crossed the entryway and drew Thomas into an embrace. "I haven't seen you in...what has it been? Five years?"

"I moved to California a decade ago," Thomas said, causing Maggie to draw a breath and cover her mouth. "Ten years, two months, and eleven days." He cleared his throat. "I mean ten years."

"Where does time go? You kept your California tan," Maggie said, holding Thomas at arm's length. "Around here, you don't see the sun between October and April. But you remember how it is. How are your parents?"

Thomas cleared his throat. He hadn't talked to his parents in two years, except after his mother called about the shooting. He imagined how they'd react when the rumor mill alerted them their son lived two miles from their estate.

"You haven't spoken to them. Nothing worse than a rift between family," she said, shaking her head. Advice hung on the tip of her tongue before she waved it away. "Not my business, and I'm holding you up. The sheriff is expecting you."

"Thank you, Maggie." He turned away and stopped himself. "It's good to see you...again."

"This is so exciting, having you back. To think after all these years you'd return home as a sheriff's deputy."

"This is just an interview. I'm certain there are plenty of qualified applicants."

Maggie touched his forearm and gave him a wink.

"If you say so. It's good to see you again, Thomas."

Maggie sat at her desk and pressed a button on her phone. The relic phone was the same one that slumbered on her desk when she first started. At least it was touch tone and not rotary.

"Sheriff, Thomas Shepherd is here for the deputy position." Thomas struggled not to roll his eyes. "Yes, sir. I'll send him right in."

Maggie lowered the phone and motioned him down the hall.

"Sheriff Gray will see you now."

Florescent strip lighting buzzed overhead as Thomas passed two offices on his way to Sheriff Gray's at the end of the hall. Inside one office, a tall deputy with his hair cut military-short leaned over a desk, sifting through papers. This was the man Thomas saw through the glass doors.

Stewart Gray, Nightshade County's venerable sheriff, wore the same whitish-gray shriek of hair he'd donned ten years ago, though a few more lines creased his features. Blowing out his big, puffy mustache, Gray looked like a caricature from a black-and-white western. Standing, Gray offered his hand.

"Welcome back to Wolf Lake, Thomas. When did you get in?"

Thomas sank into a cushioned rolling chair and fidgeted, wrapping his ankles around the wheels so the chair wouldn't glide forward on its own.

"Five days ago."

"Heard you bought Truman's old house beside the lake. Fine home, and a good place to put down roots."

"Ironically, the family who purchased my uncle's house moved to California. That's strange, isn't it?" When the sheriff didn't respond, Thomas wiped his mouth. "We traded places. I came from California, and they went to..."

Gray raised his hands.

"I get it, I get it. "How's your back healing?"

Just hearing the sheriff mention the bullet wound forced Thomas to slip a hand around his back.

"Better. Six months of rehab did wonders."

Gray gave Thomas an unconvinced nod and leaned back in his chair, resting his chin on a steeple of fingers.

"The newspaper said it was a gang shooting."

Thomas dug his fingers around the wound. Realizing what he was doing, he set both hands in his lap and clasped them together.

"It was a matter of wrong place, wrong time. Random chance. Our task force targeted a drug house. The second we stepped out of the vehicle, a rival gang drove past and shot the place up. We got caught in the crossfire, and I took a bullet in the small of my back."

The sixty-year-old sheriff winced.

"These damn gangs don't give a crap if there's a police car at the curb. They do whatever they want these days. From what I heard, you got off lucky. Not that taking a bullet is getting off easy."

"The bullet missed my spine. Another inch or two to the right, and I'd never walk again. If I survived. So yeah, the percentages prove I got off lucky."

Gray's fingers slid to the khaki hat on the corner of his desk. He touched the rim as he considered his words.

"Someone looked over you, son. The important thing is you

lived to fight another day. They ever catch the bastard who shot you?"

Thomas bit his lip.

"The attack happened too fast. Nobody got a look at the shooters."

Gray grunted.

Thomas's eyes drifted to a framed picture perched on the corner of Gray's desk. He recognized the sheriff's late-wife, Lana, in the photograph. The photo depicted a younger Gray and Lana on vacation someplace tropical. She held a margarita in one hand, and a palm tree climbed into a deep blue sky in the background. Gray followed Thomas's gaze to the photo and rubbed his eyes.

"I'm sorry about Lana," said Thomas. "I should have come home for the services."

Gray waved a hand.

"No reason. She wouldn't have known the difference."

Thomas had sent a card and called to express his condolences. Four years ago, Lana Gray lost control of her car on icy roads and slammed into a tree two miles from the lake. Whispered rumors suggested Father Josiah Fowler of St. Mary's church ran Lana off the road. He was a heavy drinker and had no qualms about getting behind the wheel. One witness claimed Father Fowler's car swerved over the centerline a mile from the crash site. But the sheriff's department couldn't prove Fowler caused the wreck.

"I'd like to say you came home for the peace and quiet. But thugs are everywhere these days. We're dealing with two gangs in Harmon. Nothing like that in Wolf Lake, but Harmon is only five miles away. There's a rumor the gangs use the lake to transport drugs after dark. Since you bought Truman's place, keep your ears open and your eyes peeled. This isn't the home you remember, Thomas. "

"The only constant is change."

Muttering, Gray drew out his desk drawer and found his glasses. After he slipped them on, he opened a manila folder and rattled several papers. Thomas recognized his resume.

Scanning the documents, Gray said, "Criminology degree from SUNY Cortland, class of 2009. Joined the LAPD in January 2010, made detective in March 2017."

Gray licked his fingers and flipped to the next page as Thomas sat in silence, fighting the urge to squirm. Over the papers, the sheriff studied Thomas the way he would a flower sprouting from the center of a January snowbank.

"Collaborated with the DEA on an LA-based drug task force. Various commendations and too many recognitions to mention." Gray sighed and dropped the papers on the desk. He scrubbed a hand over his tired face and squinted at Thomas. "One problem—you're over-qualified. A county deputy? You should have my job, Thomas. Hell, with this resume, you should run for mayor. You sure this is what you want? State police are hiring."

Before Thomas could reply, Gray tapped a pen against his desk and met Thomas's gaze.

"I shouldn't question your interest. Truth is, I only have two active deputies, and the three of us can barely cover Nightshade County. But I don't want you committing to a position and regretting it."

"There won't be any regrets."

"You realize starting salary for a sheriff's deputy is thirty-nine thousand?"

"Yes. Money isn't important to me."

Gray glanced at the papers fanned across his desk.

"Given your experience, I can sweeten the pot and offer you forty-five per year. With mortgage payments on a lakeside house, that won't leave you enough money to eat. But it's the best I can do."

Thomas nodded. He didn't tell Gray he paid for Uncle Truman's former house out of pocket, and the previous owner sold at a discount, desperate to escape the slow life of upstate New York.

"Well," the sheriff said, clasping his hands in his lap. "If you're sure, I'll have Maggie draw up the contract."

Thomas straightened.

"So I have the job?"

Gray snickered.

"I could interview a hundred more candidates, and I'd never find one with a quarter of your experience. If this is what you want, the job is yours. Nightshade is fortunate to have you."

Thomas rose from his chair, wiped his palm on his shirt, and shook Gray's hand.

"Thank you, Sheriff. You won't regret this."

"I'm certain I won't. When can you start?"

Thomas shuffled his feet. He hadn't expected Gray to offer him the job on the spot. Truthfully, he'd taken an enormous risk moving back to Wolf Lake without guaranteed employment. If the deputy position had fallen through, he'd have to accept a position at his father's firm. Though Thomas saved enough money to afford Uncle Truman's place, the tax bill alone would bleed Thomas dry without a steady paycheck.

"I can start today."

Gray shook his head.

"Nah. Take the weekend to acclimate yourself and check out what's new around the village. I'm sure you have plenty of work to do at the house. How about Monday morning at eight?"

"I'll be here at eight o'clock. This opportunity means the world to me."

Thomas had a bounce to his step that didn't exist when he

arrived this morning. On his way out, Thomas paused at the door after Maggie called from the filing room.

"Your papers are ready," she said. "Sign them now and save yourself another trip this afternoon."

"You drew up the contract during the interview?"

"Was there ever a doubt you'd get the job?"

Actually, yes, Thomas thought as he scribbled his name.

And there it was. He was an official deputy for the Nightshade County Sheriff's Department. No turning back now.

The April sun blinded him on the sidewalk. Returning to the intersection, he pressed the button and searched his pockets for his car keys while he waited for the light to change. The traffic light turned red, and the crosswalk read *walk*. Looked both ways twice. He hopped off the curb and strode halfway to the centerline before a motor growled and pulled his head up. Thomas lunged back as a red Dodge pickup ran the red light and shot through the intersection. An angry horn assailed him, the driver extending his middle finger out the window.

Thomas's breath flew in and out of his chest. Not only because the bumper missed him by inches. He recognized the driver. After all these years, the bully who made Thomas miserable during high school still lived in Wolf Lake.

Ray Welch.

3

The cherry wood A-frame grew halfway up the swaying pines. Glass frontage covered both floors, just as Thomas recalled from his childhood, and a weathered deck stretched across the front of the home. A smaller deck in disrepair sat off the back, accessed by a sliding glass door. All this glass and sunlight, Thomas thought as he plopped another box in the entryway. He needed blackout drapes for the bedroom so he could sleep after late shifts. Did they make blackout curtains long enough to cover all that glass?

Uncle Truman's A-frame featured an open design on the first floor, the plans drawn up long before open designs became vogue. He crossed the Persian rug in the living room and cut to the kitchen where he opened the refrigerator and removed a bottled water. Wiping sweat off his brow, he guzzled the drink until the plastic crinkled.

Ray Welch. Thomas had almost forgotten about Ray. Before Thomas grew into his bones, he'd been a gangling boy with a forehead full of acne. The bigger kids caught his scent and bullied him, but no one had been as vicious as Ray. He recalled the boy shoving Thomas inside a locker after gym class and clasping the hinges with a padlock. He'd never forget his humiliation when the gym teacher asked a janitor to cut the lock with bolt cutters. Ray left him alone during their senior year after Thomas returned from summer vacation two inches taller and twenty pounds heavier. The extra pounds were wiry muscle, forged at Uncle Truman's house. Ray still towered four inches over Thomas and outweighed him by fifty pounds. But there was no greater kryptonite for a bully than the quiet confidence Thomas developed.

Truman taught Thomas construction and remodeling, and together they erected the guest house in the backyard. Hours of climbing roofs, hauling wood, and installing floorboard worked magic on Thomas's physique. He liked to work with his hands. It calmed him, kept his mind from leaping to-and-fro.

Which reminded him. A cursory glance at the guest house during the inspection revealed the previous owner hadn't cared for the property. Pulling a baseball cap over his head, Thomas descended the back deck and crossed the yard. The guest house seemed to tilt as he neared the structure, as though it feared a berating for not maintaining itself. In the next yard, a young teenage girl in a wheelchair struggled to get the wheels moving. Recent rains left the yards soggy.

The door opened without issue. Then the mold walloped Thomas's nostrils. One look at the warped floorboards told him he had a leak on his hands. Following the hallway which branched to a bedroom on the right, a bathroom on the left, and ended at a small sitting area, he lifted his eyes and confirmed the sagging plaster. He made a mental note to add roofing materials to his purchase list at the hardware store. Good thing the A-frame was in tip-top shape. He'd have his work cut out for him once he tackled the guest house.

The walls echoed with the voices of forgotten ghosts. How many nights did he sleep in the guest house after a fight with his parents? He wrangled a shiver out of his shoulders as he recalled his father screaming at him over the B Thomas pulled on his economics exam. Nothing but A's would ever do, and even then his father grilled him over missed questions.

Not that Thomas didn't love his parents. He did. But they didn't want the best for Thomas. They wanted what was best for them. According to his father, Thomas would major in business at Union like his parents, then join Dad's project management firm and take over the business when Dad retired. Except Thomas wanted to help people in ways his parents couldn't comprehend, and he'd developed a taste for law enforcement after Sheriff Gray brought Thomas aboard as a student intern during high school. Thomas had figured his parents would be proud. The internship earned him three college credits before he attained his high school diploma, and he finally had a focus in his life.

His father berated him after Thomas applied to a state school and declared his major.

"You think you'll make it in the world, working as a deputy in a Podunk county? You don't appreciate how cruel and unforgiving the world is."

Uncle Truman and Aunt Louise took Thomas in as always. Truman was Mom's brother, and he'd worked as a prison guard in Auburn, New York, though the man's sleepy eyes and easy going demeanor made him a better fit for a librarian job.

"Don't take it to heart," Uncle Truman had told him, sitting beside Thomas on the twin mattress as Aunt Louise carried an armful of sheets and blankets from the house. "They love you."

"They have a funny way of showing it."

Truman sighed and patted Thomas's knee as though he was still in grade school.

"Your father built a successful business from the ground up. He was never good with his hands, and he couldn't have built this." Truman motioned at the ceiling and walls. "One method of building isn't superior to the other. But he only comprehends one way. When he sees you, he doesn't understand what you're becoming, because he can't picture himself doing anything other than what he's doing."

"I don't care about project management and software design. It's boring."

"There's nothing wrong with your father's path. When the time comes, he'll understand his son needs to find his own path and not follow his footsteps."

Now Thomas's throat tightened. Despite Uncle Truman's prediction, his father never changed. Which is why he took a law enforcement job on the other side of the country, as far from Wolf Lake as the map allowed.

As he exited the guest house, a chainsaw buzzed across the lake. Thomas tried not to stare while the girl fought the soggy lawn. One wheel sank two inches deep into the mud and muck. Sweat glistened his brow.

He couldn't watch anymore.

"Need some help?"

He waved over his head and prayed the gesture appeared friendly. The girl blew the straight brunette hair off her forehead and pushed her glasses up her nose in frustration.

"I shouldn't have come this far after it rained. The wheels get stuck when the ground turns muddy."

The girl caught her breath as Thomas's long strides carried him into the neighbor's yard. Thomas had yet to meet his new neighbors, and they hadn't lived here when Uncle Truman owned the A-frame. The neighbor's house was a white, nondescript two-story with a patio off the back.

"Where are you trying to get to?"

The girl lifted her chin toward a stand of trees in the backyard.

"To the lake. I want to sit by the shore since I can't see the water from the patio."

Thomas estimated the distance at a hundred yards. Too far for the girl to wheel herself through the mud.

"How about I help you back to the patio?"

The girl lifted a shoulder.

"I guess. At least I'll have a picturesque view of a leafless hemlock tree. I'm Scout, by the way. Scout Mourning."

She squinted up at Thomas and offered her hand. He took it.

"My name is Thomas Shepherd. I just bought the place next door."

"The last owners didn't talk much. I've already talked longer with you than I spoke to them last year. Where are you from, Mr. Shepherd?"

"Right here in Wolf Lake." He swallowed and gestured at his house. "This was my uncle's home when I was a kid."

"That's cool that you bought his old place. Where did he move?"

Thomas shoved his hands in his pockets and scuffed at the dirt with his sneaker.

"Uncle Truman died eight years ago while I lived in California, and my aunt passed a year later. I never thought about buying his place. Then circumstances changed, and I moved home." He was talking too much. In his head, he heard his mother's advice. Let the other person speak. "How about you? Are you from Wolf Lake?"

He stopped himself from asking about the wheelchair, not wanting to act insensitive. Better to let her broach the subject.

"Ithaca originally. We moved to Wolf Lake after the accident."

Scout appeared ready to tell him more when the back door opened. The woman edging onto the patio looked like an older version of Scout. She wore faded blue jeans and a heavy gray sweater, her arms wrapped against the April chill. Even with the sun shining, the wind coming off the lake cut through Thomas's bones. The woman eyed the stranger hovering over her daughter.

Thomas gave her a disarming nod.

"I'm Thomas Shepherd, your new neighbor. On my way through the yard, I saw your daughter get stuck. I hope I didn't frighten you."

"You bought the Fleming's place?" the woman asked, tilting her chin at the A-frame.

The Fleming's place. Faces changed, and time refused to stand still. Truman and Louise had been Wolf Lake staples when they lived next door. A decade later, did anyone remember them?

"Yeah, I bought it from the Flemings."

"Just you living there?"

The pointed question inferred he wasn't married, and a single guy in his thirties was a bigger threat than a family man. She edged a step closer to her daughter.

"Just me. I'm a deputy with the county sheriff's department."

The tension drained from the woman's shoulders. Scout glanced at Thomas as if seeing him for the first time.

"Cool beans," the girl said.

"My daughter loves reading mysteries and watching all those television crime shows. I'm Naomi Mourning, and you already met Scout. Welcome to the neighborhood." Naomi's glare moved to her daughter. "And why were you pushing the chair through the mud? You'll rust it through and tear up the yard."

Scout lowered her eyes.

"Sorry, Mom."

"Don't tell me you were trying to get to the lake again? It's too dangerous for you to sit beside the water without supervision."

Scout's eyes flicked to Thomas with a combination of embarrassment and frustration.

"It doesn't make sense. Who buys a lakeside house with no view of the water?"

"You know we can't afford to take those trees down, not with all our bills."

Thomas wondered if Naomi meant her daughter's medical bills. And where was the father?

"I could take the trees down for you," Thomas said, drawing Naomi's eyes. "Or trim them so you have a water view."

"I can't ask that much of you, Mr. Shepherd."

"It wouldn't take long. A half-hour per tree, times four trees. That equals two hours." Naomi's eyes widened. "Give or take. And please, call me Thomas."

Naomi's lips pulled tight in consideration as she took in her daughter's hopeful stare.

"It's not a priority. But if we take the trees down, I'll pay you a fair price."

"No charge, Mrs. Mourning. We're neighbors now. Removing those trees would give me a better view of Wolf Lake from my deck."

"I'll think it over." A vehicle crawled down the road, its engine rumbling. Naomi gave the car a wary glance. "We should trade numbers."

Numbers? It took him a second to process she meant phone numbers. Naomi and Thomas pulled out their phones and updated their contact lists. As Thomas crossed the yards and scaled his deck, he overheard Scout lobbying Naomi to invite him to dinner.

4

Night perched at the window, and the moon played hide and seek as it slipped in and out of clouds.

Thomas's shoulders throbbed and his knees ached. Kneeling in the master bedroom, he sanded a splintered rough spot where the beam met the floor. After he sanded the beams, he needed to refinish the floor if he planned to restore the A-frame to its original glory. His uncle built the home himself. Thomas recalled the eye rolls as his father discussed Truman's project over dinner.

"He'll never finish it," his father laughed, crumbling crackers into his chowder. "I know a good builder in Harmon. We installed his company's software. I'll make a call after Truman throws in the towel."

Truman never quit. It took him eighteen months to build the house. Thomas rode his bike across the village and sat at the edge of the curb for hours, transfixed by the progress. Then his uncle handed him a hammer and told Thomas to knock in a few nails. A simple task, but Thomas caught the fever. Construction and remodeling were part of his blood now.

As his eyes moved up the beam, Thomas caught a name

carved into the wood. Andy. He moved the sandpaper over the name and stopped. Looks like the Fleming's son wanted the house to remember him. Who was Thomas to erase the boy's presence? Ten years ago, he would have sanded the name away, unable to accept anything but perfection. With a smile, he sanded around the name and fixed where the boy made errant scratches with the knife, keeping his signature in place.

The long day rekindled memories. It started with his first trip to the sheriff's department since he was a student intern. Then Ray Welch almost flattened him with his truck. Did Ray recognize Thomas? Fourteen years had passed since high school, and Thomas continued to grow after graduation. Ray still looked the same. Truman's house held memories around every corner. Thomas floated through a never ending state of deja vu.

And that got Thomas thinking about *her*.

Thomas thought he and Chelsey Byrd would always be together. All high school romances struck like kismet, but most flamed out after a few weeks or months. Not Thomas and Chelsey. He met her during their sophomore years at a Friday night football game.

She'd shivered beside her friends in the stands, fashionably wearing a pair of torn jeans and a sweatshirt with no hood, her hands buried inside her pockets as she bounced on the balls of her feet to stay warm. Girls didn't talk to him because he was different. For some reason, Chelsey did. It had been cold for a September evening, and Thomas, who sat on the metal bleachers with his friends, noticed Chelsey's teeth chattering and offered her his hooded sweatshirt. The connection was immediate and turned his legs to jelly. By halftime, they'd moved away from their friends and sat hip to hip, ostensibly to fight off the cold, though both knew the real reason. By the fourth quarter, the stands cleared out as Wolf Lake High built a commanding lead. Thomas and Chelsey held hands until the teams left the field, both shocked the game ended while they rattled on about their favorite teachers and music they listened to. He could still picture her—brunette hair whipping in the autumn wind, button nose pink from the cold, eyes darting to his as if drawn by magnets.

For three years, Thomas and Chelsey beat the odds, surviving the stares and whispers. Why would a popular girl date a boy their classmates called a freak? As their senior year raced toward spring, attitudes softened, and his classmates accepted Thomas. His peers voted Chelsey and Thomas most likely to marry after college. It felt inevitable. Chelsey would attend SUNY Cortland while Thomas earned his criminology degree. And maybe that's why she left him.

On a dreary May morning, Chelsey came into school late and kept her eyes glued to the floor for the rest of the day. She snapped whenever Thomas questioned her, and before the day ended, she broke up with Thomas without explanation. She was drowning. He'd read enough about clinical depression to recognize it in his girlfriend. Why wouldn't Chelsey allow Thomas to help her? She locked him out, refusing to take his calls. According to her friends, she'd dug a hole and hidden herself from the world. Thomas caused her depression. He was sure of it. If he'd been like the other boys, if she hadn't fought her friends, parents, and everyone who told her she could do better...

In August, Thomas left for Cortland. Chelsey remained in Wolf Lake. His stomach sickened with guilty remorse. Did she rescind her scholarship to avoid him?

He never got over Chelsey. For years, friends kept him abreast on his old girlfriend. Then her name faded away as though she didn't exist. Someone told Thomas at their five-year reunion Chelsey lived in Albany. Another friend argued she'd moved to Toronto. No one had seen her, and she wouldn't show her face at school reunions.

With a heavy breath, Thomas set the sandpaper aside and sat against the beam, his eyes following the sparkling lights across the lake. The day hung heavy on his body. He was about to prepare for bed when a branch snapped outside the open window.

Straightening, Thomas moved to the screen and cupped his hand over his eyes, blocking out the light. Someone was outside the house. In his yard? The trees stretched around the water and climbed into the state park on the east side of the lake. He pushed the window all the way open and flipped the lights off. Now he could see into the woods. A shadow passed behind a tree and descended the ridge, heading toward his house. Sheriff Gray's words flickered in Thomas's head—the Harmon gangs use the lake to transport drugs after dark.

Thomas grabbed his gun and a flashlight. He took the stairs two at a time and slid the deck door open. The backyard slept in shadow. The lake sloshed against the shore. Hopping from the deck, he stayed low and jogged toward the trees. The footsteps came closer now. Unwanted memories of the gunshot kept him on high alert.

The shadowed figure cut across a trail, agile for a big man.

"Who's there?"

The man stopped upon hearing Thomas's voice. As Thomas touched the gun in his shoulder holster, the unknown figure raised his hands.

"Don't shoot. I'm Darren Holt, the ranger for Wolf Lake State Park. Sorry if I crossed your property line."

Thomas let out a breath when the man edged out of the darkness. The imposing figure stood a few inches over six feet. Black stubble on his face matched his short hair, partially hidden beneath a baseball cap.

"You must be the new deputy in town," Darren said, stepping into the light. "Someone told me you were a hometown guy."

Thomas wasn't surprised. The rumor mill was always active in villages like Wolf Lake. How soon before word got back to his parents?

"I'm Thomas Shepherd."

"Hope you don't mind me stopping by unannounced. But it seems you heard me coming first." Darren wore a dark green ranger's jacket. The way his eyes shifted around the lake told Thomas this was more than a courtesy call for the ranger. He was looking for someone. "Deputy, you hear anyone pawing around in the woods tonight?"

Thomas shook his head.

"I was upstairs working all evening."

His mouth tight and grim, Darren set his hands on his hips and scanned the water.

"The park closes at sunset. But I swore someone was out in the woods and moving toward the water. I followed the footsteps toward your place."

"Until you came through, I hadn't seen another soul tonight. But I'll keep my eyes open." As Darren turned away, Thomas added, "Don't take this the wrong way, but you don't look like any ranger I've met since I joined the force."

A wry grin curled the corner of Darren's mouth.

"You have a trained eye, Deputy. I worked for Syracuse PD until last year, then I tired of the overnights and rising crime rate, so I threw my hat in when the ranger position opened at Wolf Lake."

Having an ex-cop working in the state park had its benefits, if the rumors about drug trafficking were true.

"I worked with the LAPD for the last decade. Guess I felt the same as you. Too many problems to solve, too many sleepless nights. I mean, that's what many police officers face. Not saying you did too. It's not right to make assumptions about others."

Darren eyed Thomas as he might a zoo animal with four heads. A splash across the lake drew the ranger's attention.

"Yeah, I came here for the solitude too. But trouble has a funny way of finding everyone."

5

On the southern edge of Harmon, where urban blight encroached on rural conservatism, Jeremy Hyde loomed over the Save Mart buffet bar. At nine o'clock, the only remaining entrees were fried fish in congealed grease and macaroni and cheese. A fly buzzed around the bar and lit on the fish, so Jeremy scooped the macaroni and cheese into a Styrofoam container and eyed the people milling around the produce section. Bundled inside a fur coat, a woman in her sixties picked through the lettuce and sniffed, dissatisfied with the selection quality. A box boy wheeled canned goods through the produce aisle and vanished around the corner.

Jeremy filled the container and pushed the top down until the brittle locks snapped together. He glanced at his hand and bristled at the cheese smeared across his palm. Jittery, he searched for something to clean the mess, then settled on a plastic produce bag hanging over the radishes. He yanked down on the plastic as fur coat woman studied him through her glasses. He wanted to tell the bitch to turn around and mind her own business. But a manager type in a shirt and tie strolled past the lettuce in a hurry. Jeremy turned and shielded his hands with his body. After he wiped the cheesy muck off his palm, he dropped the bag in the garbage can and slipped a bottle of hand sanitizer from his coat pocket. Squeezed the goo onto his palm and rubbed his hands together as if warming himself beside a fire. Then he slid the hand sanitizer into his coat and rummaged deeper for the antibiotic ointment.

Before he applied the ointment, he raised his palm to his mouth and flicked his tongue against the skin. Did he taste blood? He couldn't be too careful. One tiny cut, and germs would clamber inside his body. He squeezed the ointment over the unblemished skin and massaged it in. Were he at the apartment, he would have covered his skin with a bandage. Just to be sure.

The checkout boy had a face full of oozing zits. It was enough to turn Jeremy's stomach and make him wish he'd purchased the fish. He held up his hand when the boy reached into the cash register for change.

"Keep it," Jeremy said, snatching the container before the boy protested.

The automatic doors hummed open. Night struck his face like an open-handed slap. The cold made him feel alive, reminded him of last night.

He turned the key in the ignition and set the food container beside him. A dry chuckle escaped his lips and careened around the SUV. Blood soaked the passenger seat. He'd spent hours cleaning the mess before he gave up and covered the massacre with a blanket. The interior stank of copper and fate. And nobody knew.

On his way back to the apartment, motoring through the vacant city streets where only shadows moved, he slowed the vehicle when he approached the whores. One woman clicked toward him when he paused at the stop sign. She leaned over and motioned for Jeremy to lower the window before he kicked the gas and turned the corner, tires screeching.

A gym bag rested beneath the glove compartment. Plastic crinkled inside. He giggled at the irony. The prostitute had approached his vehicle, not knowing her dead friend lay inside. Well, part of her, at least. He spit laughter and swiped his forearm across his lips.

When he checked the mirrors, the whores' shadows strutting on the distant corner, he was surprised no police cruisers rode his bumper. No flashing lights or screaming sirens. He'd taken Erika forever, and nobody caught him. The murder took months of careful planning. It had been so easy.

As the Chevrolet Trax crept between the dark buildings, he missed Erika. He couldn't say what attracted him to the young prostitute. Perhaps it was seeing her every day, her long, sensual legs beneath the short skirt, the way the cold brought the pink out of her cheeks and made her look even younger than her teenage years.

Easter had passed. The cold wouldn't last forever. Soon, every woman in Harmon would embrace spring and show skin. He liked it when they displayed just enough to pump his blood. And spring meant endless possibilities.

There was always another Erika. He needed to find her.

6

Silver light from the overcast morning bled through Scout's bedroom window while she loaded the internet browser on her laptop. Outside, hammer struck nail as the new neighbor worked on a deck behind his house. She'd been curious about Deputy Shepherd since he helped her across the lawn. The Flemings hadn't paid attention to Scout, though they were cordial if she started the conversation. It was nice to have someone next door who waved and asked how your day was.

She typed his name into Google and scanned the results. Lots of Thomas Shepherds. Narrowing the search to Wolf Lake, she discovered a story from six months ago in the *Bluewater Tribune*. LAPD Detective Thomas Shepherd of Wolf Lake, New York, was shot in the line of duty during a raid on a drug house in South Los Angeles. A joint task force between the LAPD and DEA coordinated the raid. Shepherd, who was diagnosed with Asperger's syndrome as a child, rose through the LAPD ranks...

A detective with Asperger's syndrome? Scout's eyes moved to the window. In the next yard, Thomas pried an old board off the deck and laid a new weatherproof plank. Despite the midmorning chill, the man used his sweatshirt to dab sweat off his forehead. Her heartstrings pulled when Thomas reached behind him and touched the small of his back, favoring the old wound.

Mom hadn't told Thomas the whole truth about her interest in crime. Yes, she read mysteries and watched television crime documentaries. But she'd also taken to amateur sleuthing since the accident. Being stuck inside made her edgy and curious, and the concept of solving a mystery in front of her computer lent her a fire and drive she hadn't had since she lost her ability to walk.

"It's not nice to stare."

Scout flinched, not hearing Mom descend the carpeted stairway. Usually the floorboards moaned overhead and gave Scout fair warning to minimize her browser window. Mom supported Scout's curiosity, but she wouldn't approve of the crime scene photographs Scout acquired from private sleuthing forums.

"I wasn't staring, just watching him work. He seems like a nice guy, right?"

Mom crossed the bedroom and laid a hand on Scout's shoulder.

"We just met Mr. Shepherd yesterday. I realize you want to trust him, but fourteen-year-old girls should be careful of strangers."

"But he's not a stranger. He's a deputy with the sheriff's department."

Naomi uttered an unconvinced grunt. Scout's mother was about to turn away when her eyes locked on the laptop screen. Shoot. Scout should have closed the lid. Now Mom knew she'd been snooping for information on their neighbor.

"An LAPD detective with Asperger's," Naomi said, inching closer to the screen.

"Now do you agree we should trust him?"

But Mom wasn't paying attention. She skimmed the article and turned her gaze on Thomas, slaving over the deck.

"Shot in the line of duty. Worked on a joint task force with the DEA. What's he doing in Wolf Lake?"

"Mom, when is Dad coming to say hello?"

An injured look struck her mother's eye. Scout didn't mean to upset her mother, but it had been months since Dad visited.

"Your father is busy with his new job," Naomi said, scratching her nose as she turned her eyes away. "I'm sure he'll visit when he can. Why don't you text him?"

Naomi's chest tightened as she watched Thomas through the window. Her daughter needed Glen, but Naomi's ex-husband was never the same after the accident. Yesterday, she'd grown uncomfortable as Scout carried on with the new neighbor. She recognized something was off with Deputy Shepherd, and she felt stupid for not recognizing it. He seemed like a decent man, and having a deputy next door might be a good thing. Perhaps Scout's idea of inviting Thomas to dinner made sense.

She wiped down the counters and tossed the sponge in the sink. After she dried her hands on her apron, she checked her hair in the window, untied the apron, and straightened her sweater.

"I'll be next door for a few minutes if you need me," she called down the hall.

Scout muttered acknowledgment and clicked away on her computer. Probably solving another cold case, Naomi thought with a grin. Thomas looked up and set the hammer down when Naomi crossed the yard. With the sun behind the clouds and a chilling wind whipping off the lake, it seemed like February. Condensation clouds puffed from her mouth.

"Good day," she said, rubbing the chill off her arms.

"Mrs. Mourning, I hope I didn't wake you."

"No, I've been up since sunrise." She ran her eyes over the deck. "You work quick."

"I like to finish projects."

"When the Flemings were here, I worried the deck would collapse, it sagged so much in the center."

"Old deck. It was time to replace the boards."

He motioned her to sit on one of two Adirondack chairs off the deck. She fell into one. He turned the second to face hers as she gazed at the water. From Thomas's yard, she could see Wolf Lake. When the wind came from the north like today, waves piled against the shoreline, and a cold spray wet the land.

"You have a beautiful view."

He nodded and looked toward the water.

"I find it peaceful. When I was young, I'd sit here for hours until my aunt and uncle called me in for dinner."

She noticed Thomas talked about his aunt and uncle with reverence, but never mentioned his parents.

"Sounds wonderful."

"You can have the same view, you know?"

"About your offer to cut down the trees. That was kind of you, but that's too much work."

He removed his gloves and set them on the chair arm.

"It wouldn't take long. A sunny afternoon is all I need, and you can keep the firewood." He set his hands in his lap and assessed her. She got the impression Thomas was good at reading people. "You and Scout are welcome to use my yard anytime. I'll finish the deck by tomorrow evening. I'd like to have you both for dinner, if you like barbecue." He lowered his gaze. "The deck. That was insensitive. I don't have a ramp for your daughter. We would sit in the yard, of course."

She flipped her hair behind her ear.

"Let me talk to Scout. Speaking of my daughter, thank you for helping yesterday. I worry about her pushing herself around when I'm not there to supervise. That's not the first time she got stuck."

"Happy to help. She seems like a nice girl."

"She is, and she's maintained a good attitude since the accident."

He leaned forward and set his elbows on his knees.

"Accident? Sorry. I assumed she had always…never mind."

Naomi's throat constricted. Sometimes the memory overwhelmed her. She could still see the look on Glen's face as his eyes shot to the mirror, still felt the truck motor rumbling through her bones before impact. She brushed a tear off her eye and stared at her lap.

"We were driving out of Ithaca two years ago. A tractor trailer lost its brakes. The impact crumpled the rear of our car, and Scout was in the backseat when it happened." She swallowed as her eyes misted over again. "The doctor told us Scout would never walk again. I keep praying for a miracle."

Naomi dug a tissue from her pocket and wiped her nose. Thomas's face remained stoic, but she caught a flicker of emotion in his eyes.

"Anyway," she continued, crossing one leg over the other. "Glen, Scout's father, blamed himself for the accident. There's nothing he could have done. We both saw the truck flying at us. Glen says he should have punched the accelerator and shot through the intersection. But there was another car. He's not remembering the incident accurately. My husband couldn't live with himself after Scout lost her ability to walk. A chasm formed between us, and he stopped being a father or husband and crawled into a shell."

"How's Scout handling all of this?"

Naomi glanced over her shoulder. She expected her

daughter watched from the bedroom window.

"My daughter hides her feelings well. But I know it's killing her. Before the crash, she had so many friends in Ithaca. The kids in Wolf Lake don't know how to approach her. They make her feel welcome in school. But when someone organizes a sleepover, they conveniently forget Scout. It doesn't help that her father is missing in action."

"So you separated from your husband?"

"Yes. We never divorced. But it's been two years since we lived together, and Scout doesn't see her father more than once a month." Naomi pressed a fist against her teeth. "And the time between visits keeps getting longer."

For a long time, they sat without speaking, the April wind shrieking over the water. Thomas narrowed his eyes in thought.

"What if I built a path through your backyard? Something that wouldn't bog down every time it rained."

"You keep offering so much, yet we just met. I'd be overstepping boundaries if I agreed."

He waved her concern away.

"I could dig the path in a day, then fill it with concrete. Let it set for forty-eight hours, and Scout can get around the yard without worrying about mud."

"Correct me if I'm wrong, but wouldn't that cost a few thousand dollars if I hired a contractor?"

"Most of the cost comes from labor. Give me two days of clear weather, and I'll trade you straight up—my labor and concrete for a couple steaks."

Naomi played with her ponytail.

"You strike a hard bargain, Deputy Shepherd."

"Please consider the offer. When my uncle built this house, his neighbors were his family." He stared at his hands. "That was forward of me."

"Not at all. Neighbors should be like family."

7

When the clouds cleared after sunset, the night turned colder. Thomas was tempted to turn the heat on as he walked around the upstairs, shutting windows. A knock on the door brought him down the stairway. Except for Naomi, he hadn't had a visitor since returning to Wolf Lake. He spied Darren Holt, the state park forest ranger, at the front door. A surprise on his face, Thomas pulled the door open.

"Hope you aren't here to tell me I have another stranger sneaking around my backyard."

"Ha, nothing like that. What's your work schedule like this week?"

"First day is tomorrow morning at eight. I fall asleep at ten and wake up at six."

Darren shook off his confusion and jiggled his car keys.

"I'm bored out of my skull. You up for a beer at Hattie's?"

Thomas shoved his hands in his pockets. The last place he wanted to visit was a bar, but he talked a good game about meeting his neighbors and hadn't left the house in twenty-four hours.

"I'll grab a jacket."

He eyed his wallet and reminded himself to stop at the bank tomorrow. Slipping a Mets cap over his head, he followed Darren out to the midnight blue Silverado parked in the driveway. The engine roared when Darren turned the ignition. Thomas turned his head toward Darren as they pulled onto the road.

"Who were you looking for last night when you came through my yard?"

Darren returned the glance.

"I'll wager Sheriff Gray spoke to you about the drug trafficking rumors."

"Gangs come down from Harmon."

The ranger nodded, his strong hands wrapped around the wheel as he navigated toward the village center.

"That's the theory. I'll let you in on a dirty little secret. The high school has an opiate problem. But don't say that too loud in the village center, unless you want someone to shout you down. Wolf Lake buries its problems and keeps them secret."

"Who's supplying these kids?"

"Two gangs run the streets in Harmon—the 315 Royals and the Harmon Kings. The Kings push more opiates than Walter White. There's a kid named LeVar Hopkins. He's the muscle behind the Kings. Drives a black Chrysler Limited. You can hear the music thumping from his speakers a mile away. Twice in the last month, I spotted LeVar cruising Wolf Lake. Now why would a banger like LeVar frequent a sleepy resort village five miles from home? I doubt he's checking out the real estate."

Thomas stared out the window. Residences lined the road, and a child's bike lay on its side in a front yard. People in Wolf Lake didn't worry about crime, and some old-timers still left the doors unlocked.

"Okay, but why would LeVar sneak around the state park grounds after dark?"

"Two nights ago, I saw him driving along the lake around nine o'clock. Moving real slow, like he was looking for an address. The engine cut off a mile west of your place, and I lost sight of him. A half-hour later, someone crossed the trail." Darren stared across the car. Thomas hadn't made the connection. "If you head due east from the park, you'll hit Wolf Lake High. This winter, the sheriff's department chased off a group of kids, congregating out by the football field at midnight. Everyone scattered before the deputies caught them. The theory was the department broke up a drug sale."

Thomas scratched his chin. He'd keep an eye out for LeVar Hopkins. But he wasn't convinced a drug trafficker would cut through the state park to reach the high school. Wouldn't it be easier to drive to the school?

Darren pulled the 4x4 truck into Hattie's parking lot before Thomas could reply. Music from a cover band pounded through the doorway as Thomas and Darren leaped from the cab. Several patrons mingled outside Hattie's. Two men in flannel work shirts eyed Thomas as he crossed the lot.

Hattie's reminded Thomas of every rock-and-roll club he'd stepped into during his adult life, usually responding to an altercation. A stage sat opposite the bar, separated by a hundred feet of floor space. The staff pushed tables along the wall to make room for dancers. Mostly, people stood in front of the stage and bobbed their heads to the beat, bottles hanging at their thighs. The band butchered an ACDC song as the singer strained on the high notes, and the guitars sounded out of tune. A sarcastic clap followed when the set ended. After Darren chose a table away from the crowd, the waitress brought them two bottles to start. Thomas twisted off the cap, wiped the top on a napkin, and took a sip.

"When I'm upstairs, I see a light at the top of the park, shining through the trees. Is that you?"

Darren drank from his bottle.

"That's me. There's a row of cabins along the ridge line. Mine is on the end."

"Anybody rent this time of year?"

"We get a few campers on the weekends. Business won't pick up until the summer tourist season. You should stop up. I have five pavilions and a dozen grills to myself."

Thomas picked from the bowl of pretzels the waitress set on the table.

"What's it like living in a state park year round?"

Darren cocked his head in consideration.

"It's about what I thought it would be. Relaxation interspersed with bouts of extreme boredom. We had a family of black bears knock a cabin door down last autumn. That was exciting. What about you? What made you leave the glitz and glitter of LA?"

He touched his back. After a heartbeat, he considered what his LAPD partner, Mick Harlan, would say. He'd make a joke.

"Besides waiting tables for ten years, expecting Hollywood to call?"

"Don't forget earthquakes, fires, and runaway property taxes."

"Yes, the taxes are high," Thomas said, leaning back in his chair. He wondered how much Darren knew about the ill-fated raid. The story made the local papers. "They pay for infrastructure and social programs. But California was too busy, too frantic a pace. I couldn't imagine spending the rest of my life there."

"Anything in particular bring you back to Wolf Lake?"

Just as Darren asked his question, a woman with shoulder-length black hair crossed the room and took a seat at the bar. Thomas's chest turned to ice. It couldn't be her. She sat beside an athletic looking black woman with long braids down her back. They clicked bottles and shared a laugh. Damn, it looked like Chelsey Byrd. But he would have heard if Chelsey returned to Wolf Lake.

As the woman turned her head and reached into her purse, Thomas saw her face. His stomach dropped. She wore her hair a few inches longer than he remembered. Otherwise, she seemed caught in a time warp. Chelsey hadn't aged a day since he last saw her before high school graduation.

Darren followed Thomas's gaze.

"You know her?" Darren asked, knocking Thomas out of his haze.

"From a long time ago, yes."

Glass smashed behind him when someone dropped their beer. Chelsey and her friend turned to look. Thomas ducked and covered his face, feigning a headache. He prayed she hadn't seen him. He hadn't processed Chelsey being in Wolf Lake. What would he say if she recognized him? He exhaled when she turned to her friend.

"I know that look," Darren said, setting his bottle down. "Let me guess. Old girlfriend."

"It's a long story."

"I'll bet. You don't seem excited to see her. Hattie's isn't the only bar in town, if you'd prefer a change of scenery."

His racing pulse told him to get the hell out of Hattie's before a yell from the doorway brought his head up. Dammit. Ray Welch strode into the bar, accepting slaps on the back from friends. Suddenly, Thomas starred in a nightmarish episode of *This is Your Life*. Bad turned to worse. Ray sauntered over to the two women at the bar and pinched Chelsey's backside. Thomas rose from his chair, wondering if he was about to defend his old girlfriend from the jerk who terrorized him through his teenage years. To his shock, Chelsey grinned and kissed Ray on the cheek. What the hell was Chelsey doing, dating a guy like Ray

Welch? He caught a scowl from the ebony-skinned woman as she sipped her drink. Apparently, the friend wasn't as high on Ray as Chelsey.

"You know, I wouldn't mind a change of scenery."

Darren gave him a knowing wink.

"Let's get the hell out of here."

8

He stood below the deputy's window. Darkness curled around his body like an old friend, making him one with the night's shadows. An electric current buzzed inside his body. He'd gotten away with murder. It didn't seem real.

Since Friday night, Jeremy had expected a sheriff's cruiser to screech to a halt in front of his apartment building, lights flashing. No one came. Did they even realize the whore was missing?

Above his head, the A-frame pointed skyward and divided the starlight. So many windows. If Deputy Shepherd had been home, he could have watched the officer through the glass without the man knowing. He'd read about Thomas Shepherd in the newspaper. The idiot threw himself in front of a bullet to save another fool. And now he'd returned to Wolf Lake as a supposed hero.

He knew the real reason Shepherd came home. The man was a coward, running from his fears.

Behind Jeremy, the skiff bobbed with the waves. It had been a struggle to yank the boat from the state forest to the deputy's shore, but the effort had been worthwhile. He'd drop his first victim's headless corpse into the lake, steps from Deputy Shepherd's home. The concept sent giggles rippling through his body.

His only regret was the deputy hadn't been home tonight. The A-frame's windows were no match for the glass cutter inside his pocket. The tool made an effective weapon in a pinch. But he preferred the serrated survival knife sheathed at his hip.

The urge to kill grew as he remembered the murder. The whore's blood had appeared midnight-black beneath the starlight, and he longed to see it again.

A door slid open on the neighbor's house as Jeremy edged away from the A-frame. He crept beneath a tree and watched from the shadows as a woman stepped onto a patio and cupped her elbows with her palms. A ramp led from the patio to the sliding glass door. Yet she wasn't wheelchair bound. The breeze carried her scent. She smelled like wildflowers and desperation. His fingers curled and uncurled as the woman stepped off the patio and wandered into the yard.

Yes, please. Come closer.

He removed the knife from the sheathe and left his hiding place, following the shadows toward the unknowing woman. This was too easy. It was as if she'd ventured outside as a willing sacrifice.

Closer now. She stood ten steps away with jittery eyes fixed on the night. She sensed him.

His hand curled around the hilt. The woman shifted so her back was to him. She'd never see him coming.

A deer bounded out of the brush and startled the woman. Jeremy ducked behind a hemlock tree when she whipped around. The blood thrummed in his ears until he only heard his own breathing. The animal disappeared up the ridge line and angled toward the state park.

Before he lunged, the spooked woman backed away and rushed inside the house. He cursed beneath his breath.

No matter. He'd come back for her.

9

He'd made a mistake coming home to Wolf Lake. Thomas wore a painted-on smile as he passed Maggie's desk and wished her a good morning. Sheriff Gray was waiting for Thomas inside his office.

He hadn't slept. Thomas figured Chelsey moved to the other side of the world and settled down with a nice guy, someone who cared about her. Seeing her with Ray Welch sucked the life out of him. He grabbed a coffee out of the break room. Sheriff Gray sipped from a mug when Thomas knocked on the door.

"Bright and early on your first day," Gray said, gesturing at the chair across from his desk. "That's what I like to see."

"I wake up two hours before work and exercise."

"Great. Time to hit the ground running. You'll work with Deputy Aguilar this morning. You'll like her. Veronica joined the department three years ago, and she's our best resource on Harmon gang activity." As Thomas nodded, Gray opened a drawer and slapped a folder on the desk. "Speaking of Harmon, a woman went missing over the weekend."

Gray opened the folder. The first picture was a school photograph of a young teenage girl, her tawny hair tied into a ponytail, eyes hopeful. The second photograph appeared taken from the window of a police or sheriff cruiser, the subject blurry and looking away from the camera. It was the same woman, now three to five years older. From the fishnet stockings and heels, Thomas surmised the girl worked the streets.

Gray tapped a finger on the second photograph.

"Girl's name is Erika Windrow, eighteen-years-old. Grew up in a suburb outside of Syracuse. She ran away from home at fifteen and ended up walking the streets in Harmon. The 315 Royals run the prostitution ring, and the Harmon Kings are at war with the Royals."

"You think gang activity played a role in her disappearance?"

"It's no secret the Kings want in on the competition's prostitution empire. If the Kings wanted to send a message, knocking off a rival's hooker would do the job. Bet you thought you were finished with this gang crap when you left LA."

"It was a matter of time before it arrived in Nightshade." Thomas turned the picture of a younger Erika Windrow toward him. She was the all-American girl next door. What drove her to prostitution? "Who reported the girl missing?"

Gray sat back and exhaled.

"The mother. Tessa Windrow keeps tabs on her daughter and claims she tried to talk her into returning home. According to Tessa, Erika agreed to meet her mother for coffee Saturday morning. The girl never showed, and the mother suspected the worst. Deputy Aguilar interviewed the girls who work Erika's corner. Most of them wouldn't talk, but one confirmed the 315 Royals are searching for her."

"She could have run off. Maybe she wanted to get away from the Royals and start a new life."

"That's the best-case scenario. For now, we're treating this as a missing person case. Bottom line, Tessa Windrow is a nuisance, and I want her out of my hair. She came in screaming an hour ago and threatened to turn the case over to a private investigator. It's a free country, but I don't want some local P.I. firm butting its nose into our investigation."

Wolf Lake had a private investigation firm in town? That was news to him.

After Gray finished, Maggie confirmed his bank account information and asked him to sign another document. Deputy Aguilar waited for Thomas in the break room. The woman stood five feet tall in her shoes. What she lacked in height, she made up for in muscles. The woman's biceps bulged against her sleeves, and her short-cut black hair framed an angular nose and square chin. Aguilar struck Thomas as someone he'd want by his side when all hell broke loose.

"You're the local boy," Aguilar said, giving Thomas a firm handshake.

"I grew up here, yes."

"I looked into your background, Deputy Shepherd." He cringed as Aguilar spoke. Too many officers treated Asperger's like a disability. "LAPD. You played in the big leagues."

"It's not so different from Wolf Lake. Problems are the same everywhere."

"Yeah, but Los Angeles has four million people. Nightshade County tops out at ninety thousand. More people, more problems. I understand you ran point on gang activity in South LA."

"For four years and two months."

"Then you'll be an invaluable asset to the department." Aguilar cracked her knuckles and worked a kink out of her neck. "We'll cruise Harmon and speak to Erika Windrow's known contacts."

"What about the 315 Royals? Will they talk to us?"

"The head a-hole is a scumbag by the name of Troy Dean. He runs the prostitution ring. If our timing is right, we might catch him with the girls. Otherwise, the guy is a ghost. He doesn't stay in one spot long."

"What can you tell me about this LeVar Hopkins I keep hearing about?"

"Bad news personified. He's the enforcer for the Harmon Kings. If someone owes the Kings money, they meet LeVar and usually regret it. What do you know about LeVar?"

"My neighbor is the ranger for the state park. According to him, LeVar canvassed Wolf Lake."

"You're referring to Darren Holt."

"You've met Holt?"

"Nope, but I came through the Syracuse PD academy. They all knew Holt and called him one of Syracuse's finest. Not sure why he traded the force to scoop bear shit off the trails. To each their own."

Aguilar grabbed a protein bar for the road. The clock read nine when they set off for Harmon.

10

Raven Hopkins detested cases like this. Her long braids draped over the seat as she sank low in her black Nissan Rogue and watched the two-story motel across the road. Sitting on the edge of the village, the Wolf Lake Inn had lost its moniker as a family friendly destination. Now it catered to call girls, the drug game, and anyone who desired a clandestine rendezvous over lunch. The letters on the sign out front flickered as she pressed the binoculars to her eyes. The curtains stood closed on room eighteen.

A week ago, Hugh Fitzgerald staggered into the office with the reddened eyes of a hangover. Raven had been alone in the office. Hugh wanted proof Phoebe, his wife of twenty years, was sleeping with her supervisor, a ginger-haired beanpole named Norris Loxley. Hugh's words, not hers. Wanting no part of another infidelity investigation, her boss handed Raven the case with a good-luck wink. For the last seven days and nights, Raven had followed Phoebe from her home to her office job on the village's east end, then tracked the two-timer on lunch dates with Norris.

At age twenty-five, Raven craved a career change. The long

hours in the Rogue locked up her back and gave her legs pins-and-needles, and she felt like a gossipy middle schooler when she caught people cheating on their spouses. But money was money, and Hugh paid handsomely for dirt on his wife. The camera on the passenger seat, affixed with a telephoto lens, held enough pictures to implicate Phoebe. Over the last seven days, Raven had photographed Phoebe and Norris holding hands on a park bench, both wearing black sunglasses as if playing roles in a tacky spy movie. She caught Phoebe kissing Norris behind an Italian restaurant and logged two pages of notes depicting the times and locations of various indiscretions.

This was the coup de grâce. Phoebe and Norris had entered the seedy motel room an hour ago and pulled the curtains. Raven photographed them entering the room. Now she just needed to snap their pictures on the way out, log the time, and hand Hugh a thumb drive of evidence.

Norris's green VW bug sat on the street beside an expired parking meter. A car buzzed past Raven's Rogue, fast enough to shake the SUV and give her a sense of vertigo. The curtains rustled as someone peeked out. Finally, some action inside the room. Raven edged up in the seat and scanned the silhouetted figure with the binoculars. Phoebe. Cursing herself for not photographing the woman's paranoid glance, Raven snatched the camera and placed the binoculars beneath the seat.

Her phone hummed. It was Chelsey.

"Not now," she muttered, recognizing her boss's name on the screen.

The door to room eighteen opened a crack. A man with a ski slope nose, glasses, and a goatee stuck his head out and scanned the parking lot. Then a woman's hand touched his arm, and the door swung shut again. Had Raven spooked them, or was Phoebe hungry for another romp? A snicker escaped Raven's lips before her phone rattled again. She'd better take the call.

"Yeah?"

"Where are you?"

"Outside the Wolf Lake Inn, catching Phoebe Fitzgerald and her boy toy in the act, like you asked."

Chelsey sighed. Raven loved her boss and cherished their friendship, but Chelsey always stuck Raven with these infidelity investigations.

"We have a problem."

"Uh-oh," Raven said, watching the door through the camera lens.

"Hugh called the office and sounded like he'd been drinking."

Raven felt the investigation spinning out of control.

"Yeah?"

"He found out where Phoebe and Norris are shacking up."

"Shit. Tell me he isn't on his way." Tires squealed around the corner before Raven's boss answered. "He's here. I've gotta go."

Raven tossed the phone in the glove compartment and holstered her gun. As the door to room eighteen opened, Hugh's massive Dodge Ram 1500 fishtailed around the corner. Norris pulled Phoebe inside the room, but kept the door open as the truck sped down the thoroughfare with ill intentions. Raven shot out of the Rogue, expecting to intercept Hugh before he got hold of Norris and did something stupid.

The truck kept coming. Raven lunged back from the street as the Ram changed directions and veered toward the curb. Christ. Hugh set his sights on Norris's VW.

The truck pancaked the VW from the side and drove it against the mailbox. Tires and metal shrieked. Envelopes rocketed into the air. The Ram smashed the VW over the curb where it toppled and spun on its top like a cartoon turtle. A hissing sound filled the air as someone screamed. Windows slid open, and looky-loos ventured outside to check on the clamor.

Hugh's Ram lay disabled. The front end perched upon the mailbox, the wheels spinning with unspent momentum. Raven dragged herself off the sidewalk and dusted the grit off her hands. Her body trembled with shock.

Norris staggered into the parking lot with his hands pressing against his cheeks and his chin hanging to his chest. The driver's side door opened on the Ram, and Hugh stumbled out of the vehicle and landed on his ass. He winced and sat there a moment. There was something in his hand. A gun? Raven sprinted toward Hugh as Phoebe stood frozen in the lot with a disbelieving hand over her mouth. The reality registered on Phoebe's face, and she broke away from Norris and marched toward her husband. Right into the line of fire.

"Are you insane?" Phoebe stomped her feet. "What the hell are you doing?"

Norris tried to hold her back as Hugh rose to his feet. The gun dangled off the husband's fingers. No time to think, Raven leaped the wreckage and drove her shoulder into Hugh, blindsiding the larger man. The gun clinked against the ground. Good lord, it wasn't a real gun. Hugh came armed with a child's toy.

Raven struggled with Hugh until she wrestled his arms behind his back. She held him flat and reached for the zip tie in her back pocket. A moment later, she secured Hugh by the wrists as a siren approached.

"You cheated on me, you lying bitch!"

Spittle flew from Hugh's lips. At least he didn't fight Raven. He didn't even pay attention to her.

"Look at what you did," Phoebe said, motioning wide-eyed at the crumpled VW. "You could have killed somebody."

"What do you see in this guy? You slept with him? He's a pencil neck geek."

"Hey!" Norris said, fixing his crooked glasses.

"Hold still," Raven said. "The sheriff's department is on the way. This will go better for you if you relax and cooperate."

Phoebe swiped a tear off her eye.

"Well, at least he pays attention to me. I lost two dress sizes over the last three months, and you didn't even notice."

"I work long hours," Hugh said. "Someone has to put food on the table."

"I work too, you fat jackass."

"Yeah, for the guy you're sleeping with."

Phoebe dropped to her knees in front of Hugh. Raven eyed the woman with consternation. If Phoebe or Norris attacked Hugh, Raven would lose control of the situation.

"Why did you do it, baby?" Hugh said, crooning. "Twenty years together, and you don't love me anymore."

"Oh, you big fool. I love you. All I wanted was someone to treat me like a woman for once. You think I care about this loser?"

"Whoa," Norris said, lifting his palms. "I'm right here."

"Shut up, Norris."

"Don't tell me to shut up. You know what? You can have your asshole husband. Pick up your belongings and don't come back to the office. You're fired."

Hugh thrashed beneath Raven.

"You can't talk to my girl like that. We'll sue you for sexual harassment. Yeah, sleeping with your employee and firing her after she dumps you. That has to break like five or six constitutional amendments. Take the tie off my hands. I'm gonna punch his lights out."

Phoebe dropped a hand on Hugh's shoulder. Her presence tamed the unruly beast. Nonplussed, Raven observed the interchange as Norris marched back and forth between his shattered car and the sidewalk. The sheriff's department cruiser buzzed around the corner with flashing lights.

"You'd stand up for me and save my job?" Phoebe asked with misty eyes.

"You're my girl, baby cakes. It's you and me forever." He craned his neck to stare back at Raven. "This is all a big misunderstanding. Let me go. I promise I'll pay for the damage."

Raven sighed.

"That's between you and the deputies, Hugh."

"Ah, shit."

The cruiser stopped at the curb as Raven pinned him to the sidewalk. First thing tomorrow, she was asking for a raise.

11

A second cruiser pulled behind Thomas and Aguilar as they stepped from the vehicle. Aguilar let him take the lead, and she wore a wry grin, anxious to watch Thomas work through the logistics of this mess. He looked over his shoulder as Sheriff Gray crawled out of his cruiser and hobbled to the curb on old knees.

A scene from *The Far Side* played out in front of Thomas. A skinny man with a bad goatee and crooked glasses pulled his hair as he gazed at a crumpled VW. The car lay belly up. Steam poured from the hood. On the sidewalk, a rotund man wearing a tee-shirt soaked with sweat stains had his wrists bound behind his back. A woman, ostensibly the man's wife or girlfriend, knelt beside him and stroked his greasy hair. Then there was the Dodge Ram wedged upon a mailbox with half the village's mail blowing back and forth on the sidewalk.

The woman holding the man flat pulled his attention. He recognized her from Hattie's. This was Chelsey's friend, the woman who rolled her eyes at Ray Welch. What was she doing here?

"You know her?" Thomas asked Aguilar.

"Not by name. She works for Wolf Lake Consulting. That's the P.I. firm Erika Windrow's mother hired."

"What the hell happened here?" Gray asked, removing his hat and wiping his head.

"What do you think, Mr. LAPD detective?" Aguilar asked, snickering. "Sort this mother out for us."

Thomas listened as the private investigator detailed the events. Raven seemed an appropriate name for the investigator. Her eyes pierced through Thomas when she spoke, and her physique rivaled Aguilar's, though this woman stood several inches taller and possessed a lean strength that nobody in their right mind would tangle with.

"Now I've seen it all," Gray said after Raven finished.

The skinny guy with the goatee was Norris Loxley, Phoebe's boss. He kept screaming he'd sue Hugh Fitzgerald, and Phoebe better not show her face at the office. Aguilar read Hugh his rights. He didn't hear a word, he was so focused on Phoebe's doe eyes.

"We'll need a tow truck for this mess," Gray said.

Aguilar spoke into her shoulder radio.

"Good thing he didn't strike the hotel," Aguilar added after she confirmed tow trucks were on the way. "I can't believe the VW is the only damaged vehicle."

"Damaged?" Norris said with incredulous eyes. "That bastard destroyed my car. What if I'd been inside when he crashed into it? He would have killed me."

"Can it, Mr. Loxley."

Norris opened his mouth to argue and clamped it shut as Aguilar fixed him with an icy stare. The female deputy tossed the cruiser's keys to Thomas and hauled Hugh to his feet.

"You're in charge of taking statements, rookie," Aguilar called over her shoulder as she marched Hugh to Gray's cruiser. "Meet you back at the office."

The paperwork for this case would keep Thomas busy for the next week. His fellow officers detested paperwork. Thomas found working in silence soothing.

"Where are you taking my husband?" Phoebe yelled. "He said he was sorry."

Raven stood and brushed her clothes off. She shared a grin with Thomas as Phoebe protested her husband's arrest.

"Don't I know you from somewhere?" Raven asked as Gray's cruiser drove off.

Phoebe and Norris awaited questioning, avoiding each other in the parking lot.

"I don't think we've met," said Thomas, hoping she didn't recognize him from Hattie's.

Eventually, Chelsey would learn Thomas was in Wolf Lake. He was delaying the inevitable. After introductions, Raven gave Thomas the rundown and recounted Hugh's onslaught after he caught Phoebe cheating on him. Raven lived a mile from Thomas, which meant Chelsey might pass his place on her way to Raven's house. When the private investigator left, Thomas watched her black Nissan Rogue round the corner.

He took statements from Phoebe and Norris while two trucks towed away the damaged vehicles. He radioed back to the office after he finished. It was almost lunchtime, and his stomach grumbled. A familiar scent reached his nose. Fresh donuts. On the next block, he recognized the sign for the Broken Yolk. Ruth Sims had owned the shop since he was a kid, and she'd always served the best coffee and glazed donuts in the village.

He moved the cruiser to the municipal lot and circled back to the sidewalk. When he turned the corner, a black Chrysler Limited passed the inn. Hip hop blasted from the speakers, the bass so heavy Thomas felt it in his bones. Thomas watched as the vehicle slowed in front of the wreckage. A black male with dreadlocks and tattooed arms leaned out the window as he cruised past. LeVar Hopkins. He seemed to be looking for someone.

Thomas's heart raced and his hands tingled. He couldn't shake the image of the rival gang pulling up during the raid. Then shouts from a DEA agent to get down before the shooting started. Thomas threw himself at another agent, who reacted too slowly. The bullet struck him from behind and drove the air from his lungs. It felt as if his back caught fire as he fell on his hands and knees.

As the Chrysler crawled down the thoroughfare, Thomas snapped photographs with his phone. LeVar's head turned toward the deputy, and for a second, their eyes met. When LeVar didn't find his target, he kicked the accelerator, pulling the vehicle down the road.

Thomas followed LeVar with his eyes until he turned toward the north end of the village. If LeVar didn't veer off course, he'd drive past the A-frame and the state park. Thomas swiped the phone to his messages and sent a text to Darren. The ranger requested Thomas alert him if he spotted LeVar near the lake. Did LeVar and the Harmon Kings have something to do with Erika Windrow's disappearance? He pocketed his phone and radioed Aguilar that LeVar was in the village again. Then his stomach reminded him why he'd walked down this block.

A bell rang when he stepped inside the Broken Yolk. The sweet warmth of freshly baked donuts made his mouth water. He ran his eyes over the chalkboard menu affixed to the wall behind the register. Ruth had added healthy options since he moved away—egg white sandwiches, smoothies, and Acai bowls. But it was too late to change his mind. He could taste the glaze melting in his mouth as he glared at the donuts behind the glass.

A portly woman in her early sixties stepped out of the back

room and wiped her hands on an apron. Tied in a ponytail, her ash brown hair held more salt than pepper these days. He recognized Ruth as she waddled to the counter. Her eyes widened.

"Thomas Shepherd, I heard you were back in town." she said, circling the counter. Ruth pulled him into a hug. Then she straightened his shirt and brushed confectionery sugar off his arm. "The uniform looks snazzy on you. Your folks must be so proud."

"It's good to see you, Ruth."

He was glad Ruth didn't press him about his parents.

"Come in and sit," she said, gesturing him toward three open tables along the window.

"I can't. I'm on shift and need to get back to the station. But not before I grab a coffee and—"

"Glazed donut to go." She gave his shoulder a playful tap. "I remember your favorites."

Ruth made small talk as she poured coffee and bagged the donut. She wanted to give him lunch on the house. He insisted on paying. Still, he caught her sneaking a second glazed donut into the bag. He kept his mouth shut, not wanting to offend her. When he returned to the office, he'd give the donut to Gray. No chance Aguilar would go for the unhealthy treat. He'd only known his fellow deputy for a few hours, and he already pictured her blending a protein shake in the break room.

After he convinced Ruth to take his money, her eyes moved to the storefront window.

"Wolf Lake isn't the same, Thomas."

"It still has its heart," he said, lifting the bag.

She gave the compliment a wan smile.

"It's not safe here anymore. We thought Harmon's problems wouldn't bleed into our village, but we were fools."

12

His featureless face left a hole in your memory. As Jeremy stood at the corner, watching the whores wear a groove in the sidewalk in front of the adult video store, he pulled the ski hat down to his brow and buttoned the jean jacket. He was a chameleon, able to blend in with any crowd, or avoid attention when he wished to be alone.

A grin curled his lips. He'd taken one of their own, and they didn't know his name. For weeks he'd stood at this corner, eyes locked on Erika. Now and then, the girl would stop and stare in his direction after he ducked around the corner or merged into the crowd, as if she sensed a dark presence. Many times he considered propositioning the woman, taking her to his apartment, and spilling her lifeblood over the shag carpet. But eyes followed any man who approached the street walkers. He worried Troy Dean, the leader of the Royals, would recognize him. It had been two years since the man met Troy. But Jeremy wasn't the type to stick in someone's memory. So he'd played it cool. Waited until Erika slid into the backseat of an Uber and followed the girl into Wolf Lake. He grinned when she disappeared inside the hotel. All Jeremy needed to do was wait for the girl to emerge from the room. She'd order a ride back to Harmon or call Troy to pick her up, and he'd be there waiting. It wouldn't take long to swipe the blade across her throat. But she made it easy on him when she strolled down the night-shrouded sidewalk, desperate for a ride. Had the john ripped her off?

Now the orange-haired woman on the corner, legs that stretched into the heavens, strong ankles sturdy on spiked heels, bent forward and whispered into a client's ear. The guy wore a gray sweatshirt with the hood pulled tight around his face. It was difficult to gauge the john's age, except for the gray beard bristling out of the hood.

Stepping off the curb for a better look, Jeremy stood in silence after a taxi honked an angry horn. He felt the breeze of the passing vehicle against his face, smelled the greasy exhaust as the endless winter curled around him. He could take the whore any time he wished. But the woman didn't appeal to him. He needed a girl like Erika.

EVERY KID on the bus stared.

The wheelchair lift jammed and caused the bus driver to grumble to himself as he unstrapped Scout's wheelchair. Air too cold for mid-April blew inside the bus and searched for exposed skin. The boy in the next seat chattered his teeth, while the girl beside him rubbed her arms and squirmed. This was taking too long. Scout sensed the resentment building. Impatient eyes watched and whispered comments flew around the bus.

At the curb, her mother drove her hands into her pockets and marched in place to stay warm. She did her best to appear casual. The chairlift made a metallic clunk as it came to life. To Scout's ears, it sounded like something broke. She eyed the lift warily as the driver wheeled her forward. If the lift snapped and she crashed against the road, would her classmates laugh or feel bad for complaining?

A beeping sound pierced her ears as the lift descended. She white-knuckled the chair arms, certain the lift was about to fail. When she touched down, she breathed a sigh of relief. Mom wheeled her along the curb to the driveway. On the bus, someone shouted, "Finally!" Laughter followed.

"Don't listen to them," Mom said, pushing her up the driveway and past the wheelchair accessible front porch. "They don't understand."

"Where are we going?"

"I painted over the chips on the front door and need to let it dry. We'll use the patio door."

The patio had a small ramp, but it was the yard that worried Scout. Last night she awoke to rain pattering the window after midnight. The old saying claimed April showers brought May flowers. But in her experience, April showers brought another week of slop.

The wheels jounced over a rock as the driveway ended and the grass began. Five steps from the patio, the wheels sank into the muck. Scout tried to warn her, but Mom shoved the wheelchair and drove the wheels another two inches into the ground. Now she couldn't budge the chair. Mom lowered her shoulder and grunted after the chair dropped lower. Was this grass and dirt, or quicksand?

"We're making it worse," Scout said, glancing around the yard for a way out of this mess.

"I have an idea. Hang on for a minute."

"Uh, I'm not going anywhere."

Scout shivered in the backyard as the wind crept inside her jacket. Her hair blew into her eyes. She stuck her hands inside her pockets and searched for the neighbor. They needed Deputy Shepherd's muscle now. Past the deputy's guest house, the lake crashed against the shore, driven by northerly winds. A broken boat oar and a plastic cup had washed ashore, and the water extended ten feet up the hill separating his backyard from the lake.

The garage door opened in front of the house, and ten seconds later Mom returned with a plank under her arm. After Mom wedged the board under the left wheel, the wheelchair inched forward.

"You almost got it," Scout said, glancing down at the wheels.

Mom knelt and adjusted the board before circling behind the chair again.

"When I push, try to wheel yourself forward."

"I'll do my best."

Mom panted and drove with her legs. Her sneakers slipped on the wet lawn, and she splattered knee first against the ground. Scout strained to look behind. She wanted to tell her mother they should have gone through the front door and risked smearing the paint. But Mom had her hands full, and playing Devil's Advocate wouldn't help.

Another shove, and the wheelchair lurched forward. Scout almost toppled out of the chair before she clutched the wheels and kept the momentum going. At last, the wheelchair dislodged from the wet ground. As Mom directed Scout up the ramp and onto the patio, she wheezed and coughed. Exhausted, she leaned against the house and set her hands on her knees. Scout could take it from here. Sliding the glass door open, she pushed the wheelchair over a smaller ramp and coasted into the kitchen.

Ah, it was wonderful to escape the wind. The kitchen held heat from the oven, and she smelled the cherry pie before she spotted it cooling on the stove top. Mom closed the door and prevented the cold from entering.

"The weatherman says it's supposed to hit sixty next weekend," said Mom as she tore a sheet of aluminum foil and fitted it over the pie. "I've had enough winter."

The warmth thawed Scout's hands, but the chair left muddy streaks on the floor. She wished she could clean up after herself. More work for her mother to do. It wasn't fair. She was sick of making everybody's lives difficult.

"We should take Deputy Shepherd up on his offer to pave a path in the backyard."

Mom opened her mouth to offer a contrary opinion and stopped. Instead, she sorted through the mail on the granite counter and feigned interest in bills and coupons.

"Well, that was fun," Scout sighed. "I better start on my homework before dinner."

As she swiveled the chair toward the hallway, Mom leaned her arms on the granite.

"Scout, did you hear anyone on the lake last night?"

Scout recalled the rain hitting the windows. A distant splash had woken her up at ten o'clock.

"I think so."

Mom glanced out the kitchen window toward the trees. The lake churned beyond the property, hidden behind a row of hemlocks.

"Nobody's supposed to be on the lake after dark."

13

It was after six when Thomas drove into his driveway. Light faded from the turbulent gray sky, and he didn't relish cooking after a long day. The paperwork from the fiasco outside the Wolf Lake Inn took him all afternoon. He never realized he'd worked ninety minutes past his shift until Tristan Lambert, the tall deputy with the military haircut, told him to go home.

Lowering his head against the breeze, he climbed onto the front deck and pulled on the storm door. Naomi had taped a note inside. He kicked a glass container set at his feet as he scanned the note. Naomi left him butternut squash and a slice of cherry pie. They'd wanted him over for dinner, but he'd worked late. That was nice of them, he thought while he fit the key into the lock. Thomas glanced toward their house and didn't see anyone at the window. He waved in case Naomi or Scout was looking, then brought dinner inside and set it on the counter.

His mouth watered at the savory scents. Even with lids on the containers, the dinner made his downstairs smell like Thanksgiving. He called Naomi to thank her for her generosity.

But the call went to voice mail, so he left a message instead and promised to wash and return the containers after he ate.

He dug into dinner, sitting on his back deck with a view of the lake. Breakers frothed and slammed the shore, and a cold mist wet the guest house. A broken oar and miscellaneous pieces of trash littered his shore. Anything lost to the lake over the last decade would wash up on the southern shore if this wind continued. He braved the cold for five minutes before the wind chased him indoors.

His phone rang when he opened the sliding glass door. With his dinner plate balanced on one hand, he hustled to the granite and snatched his phone before the caller gave up. It was probably Naomi returning his call. He answered without looking at the screen.

"So, Thomas. When were you planning to tell us you returned?"

He stumbled and almost dropped the plate.

"Hello, Mother."

"Really, when the rumor you came back to Wolf Lake reached me, I figured it was a brief visit. But you're working for the county sheriff, and you bought my brother's house without consulting either of us."

The whip to his mother's voice made him flinch. Thomas slid into a chair and shoved the food away, his appetite disappearing. He'd meant to call his parents and head off an argument.

"Sorry. I got caught up with a repair project and forgot to contact you. That was immature of me."

"It's like you're avoiding us." She laughed without humor. "You can't move to Wolf Lake without the Shepherd family knowing. You're lucky I found out first. Had it been your father—"

"I apologized. Let's not argue over this. I meant to call once I settled in."

She sniffed.

"I have no intention of fighting with my only child. I'm just hurt you didn't inform us of your plans before you left California."

He rose from the chair and crossed the kitchen as she talked. A pull on the refrigerator door informed him he'd put off too many chores and focused on minor repairs. He appreciated the free dinner even more as he sifted through a mostly empty refrigerator for something to drink.

"I don't mean to be rude, but I should run to the store for groceries before it gets late. My shift starts at eight o'clock tomorrow morning."

"Cutting me off so soon?"

"It's not like that at all. I'm happy to hear your voice."

She grunted, unconvinced.

"Save your grocery money, Thomas. You'll need it with the pittance the county pays its employees. Your father and I will see you tomorrow after your shift ends."

She choked on *shift*.

"Are you inviting me to the estate?"

"Don't refer to it as an estate, Thomas. I won't be rich-shamed by my blood, and frankly, it's beneath you. You will join us for dinner."

Thomas switched the phone from one ear to the other and closed the refrigerator. Nobody told Lindsey Shepherd *no*.

"I'm working a missing persons case, so I'll let you know if I'm running late."

"Not a minute after five. That should give you enough time to clean up after work and drive across the village. And, Thomas?"

"Yes, Mother?"

"Wear appropriate clothing and don't fight with your father."

"I wouldn't dream of it."

"Five o'clock," she repeated, as if he was in grade school.

"I'll see you then."

The call ended. No *I love you*, or *it's wonderful to have you back in town*. Tomorrow, maybe he'd make amends with his parents and they'd forge a relationship together. A lifetime of disappointment taught him otherwise.

14

"All I'm saying is you need to be careful."

Chelsey Byrd clamped the phone between her shoulder and cheek. On tiptoe, she reached for a box of brown rice and tossed it into the shopping cart. An instrumental jazz version of a Foo Fighters song played over the supermarket speakers.

"He's my brother," Raven said. Chelsey pictured Raven pinching the bridge of her nose as she did when stressed. "I can't turn my back on him."

Chelsey pressed her lips together and wheeled the cart around a woman who'd stopped in the pasta and rice aisle. Raven was the best investigator Chelsey had hired at Wolf Lake Consulting. Strong and brave, Raven possessed a sixth sense for danger and an uncanny ability to see through a lie. These qualities abandoned Raven when judging LeVar. Raven's brother wasn't just a member of the Harmon Kings gang. He was their enforcer, the last guy you wanted to run into if you had a beef with the Kings.

Since the weekend, Chelsey had hidden the LeVar investigation from Raven. She didn't know how her partner would react if she found out. Saturday night, Tessa Windrow called Chelsey at home and pleaded with her to take the case. Her daughter, Erika, a prostitute working for the 315 Royals, had vanished without a trace, and Tessa suspected the rival Kings played a part. Though Chelsey withheld her theories from Tessa, she didn't believe Erika Windrow was alive. When an eighteen-year-old prostitute vanished in Harmon, you didn't expect a happy ending. If the Kings abducted Erika and murdered the teenager, LeVar was involved. He might be the killer.

"If the sheriff's department finds out you're hiding LeVar—"

"I'm not hiding anyone," Raven snapped, causing Chelsey to flinch. "Look, I can't prove he's been to my house."

"But you suspect he has. You said your dinner leftovers disappeared from the refrigerator. Food doesn't walk away on its own."

Chelsey winced. That sounded like something her mother said when she was a kid. Remembering her teenage years creased her eyes, and she shoved the cart past a middle-age man stocking shelves. Major depression. That's what her psychiatrist called it. To Chelsey, it was hell. She once had a bright future with a full scholarship to SUNY Cortland. Besides constant thoughts of suicide, she developed severe social anxiety. She needed to force herself to vomit before she left the house. Otherwise, she risked becoming sick in front of others.

And she'd thrown away the only relationship worth remembering. Chelsey wondered what became of Thomas Shepherd. The newspaper said he made detective in Los Angeles and took a bullet during a raid. He'd overcome so much to become a police officer. She wanted to track down his number and call. Ensure he was okay. Mostly she'd wanted to hear his voice again. But that was ridiculous. She couldn't live in the past, and she'd made the right decision to cut ties and put Wolf Lake behind her.

After bouncing around the central plains and northeast for a decade, working dead-end jobs and suffering through one failed relationship after another, she answered a help wanted ad for a private investigation firm in Philadelphia. The job's daily independence drew her. She could do this. Driven for the first time since high school, she enrolled at a small university outside Philadelphia and attained a criminal justice bachelor's degree in three years. Armed with a P.I. license, she returned to New York and established Wolf Lake Consulting.

Hiding the LeVar investigation from Raven sickened Chelsey. A gang banger with suspected ties to multiple murders didn't belong on the streets, but she understood Raven's point of view. LeVar was her only family. There was a mother in Harmon that Raven never mentioned—Serena Hopkins was an unemployed junkie living on Harmon's south side.

"It shouldn't be difficult to prove LeVar broke into your house," Chelsey said. "You have tools at your disposal. Set up a camera and catch him in the act. If he breaks in, press charges."

Raven blew out a defeated breath.

"Would you if it was your brother?"

Good question.

"Don't let him ruin your life, Raven. Listen, I should finish shopping before they close the store. See you tomorrow morning?"

"I'll be there."

"Hey, Raven. You did great on the Fitzgerald case. Don't let the LeVar situation get you down. I'm here if you want to talk."

"Thanks, babe."

Chelsey put her phone away. It was almost nine o'clock, and the store cleared to a few last second shoppers rushing toward the checkout line. She bagged as much produce as she could grab in a frantic minute before turning the cart around. Oh, she forgot cat food. She raced across the store and snatched the last organic bag off the shelves. She'd found Tigger, an orange tabby kitten, shivering in the cold and pawing around her garbage last month. Since Chelsey took Tigger in, the skin-and-bones kitten had filled out and no longer lingered on death's edge. And she loved the tiny squirt.

Night blackened the storefront windows. An overweight teenage checkout boy threw his hands up as shoppers lined up. He requested someone named Kathy to open her lane, but nobody came. The boy raced against time to bag groceries. Chelsey made it through the line in ten minutes, the lights shutting off as she pushed the shopping cart through the automatic doors.

She pressed the key fob on her green Honda Civic. A man in the neighboring parking spot loaded grocery bags into a silver Ford pickup. He wore a baseball cap over his brow, his back to her as he hefted the bags into the cab. When he turned around, her heart skipped a beat. Thomas Shepherd. She clutched her shopping bag against her thighs before she dropped it. His mouth hung open.

"Thomas? What are you doing in Wolf Lake?"

He spoke, but nothing came out. Shuffling his feet, he said, "I might ask you the same question."

So there it was. She hadn't seen him since the breakup, never explained why she tossed him out of her life, and she only asked why he was here.

"I heard about the shooting," she said, cringing when her voice cracked. "Are you okay?"

He touched his nose and glanced around the lot, as though searching for an escape route.

"Rehabilitation worked. I have my strength back."

"But are you *okay*?"

He raised his eyes to Chelsey, understanding the meaning.

"It's a process. I'm giving myself as much time as it takes to make peace with what happened."

"That's good." Another uncomfortable bout of silence passed between them. She stopped her toe from nervously tapping against the blacktop. "So, are you back from California, visiting your family?"

"No...I live in Wolf Lake now."

Chelsey didn't know how to respond. Thomas Shepherd lived in the same town? And why did her chest flutter when he looked at her? He still had those sea blue eyes, inquisitive and deep enough to drown in.

"I should go," she said, suddenly sick to her stomach.

"Chelsey, we never talked after—"

"Sorry, Thomas. I'm not feeling well. It was good to see you again."

She piled into her car. Dammit, she was a heel for cutting him off. After this much time, he deserved an explanation. But if she went forward with this conversation, nothing good would come of it.

The engine turned over. As she threw the Civic into reverse and backed out of the parking space, he turned his back and stacked the last shopping bag into his truck.

15

Moonlight drew long, sinuous shadows over the cabin walls. A noise jolted Darren Holt out of a deep sleep, and the state park ranger rested with his elbows propping up his head and chest. Strange shapes played over the burgundy area rug between the wall and the foot of his bed as a stiff wind rustled the trees outside the window. The curtains stood open, inviting the night into the cabin.

He pressed the heels of his palms against his eyes and cut a glance at the clock. One in the morning. Hands behind his head, he stared at the exposed beams overhead. The ceiling stared back at him. A light affixed to the wall angled over the headboard. In the dark, it looked like a monstrous spider leg. The odds on Darren falling back to sleep lengthened with each second he lay awake. It would be a long night. Fortunately, nobody camped in the park tonight and he kept his own hours. Whether he awakened at the break of dawn or slept past noon, it wouldn't matter.

Right now he needed a glass of water. He swung his legs off the bed and waited for his body to catch up to his sleepless mind. Wind moaned around the cabin, and a branch snapped inside the woods and crashed to the forest floor.

Darren drank a full glass of water at the sink, then poured himself a second. He shuffled to the foot of the bed, stepped out of his pajama bottoms, and slid his bluejeans over his hips. Cold seeped beneath the door and bled across the room. In upstate New York, winter refused to obey the calendar. Last April, a freak storm dropped six inches of snow on the forest and brought down two spruce trees. He hoped spring arrived by the weekend. After donning his shoes, Darren pulled his jacket off the hanger and buttoned it. He patted the pocket and confirmed his keys lay inside.

When he touched the doorknob, a scream brought his back erect. Darren spun and grabbed the Glock firearm he'd carried as a Syracuse police officer. He kept a flashlight beside the door. Grabbing the light, he threw the door open and clutched his coat as a blast of polar air struck his face. The scream sounded as if it had come from below the ridge line, but he couldn't be certain in the rising gale. He swept the beam across the trail. The neighboring cabins watched him with black, lifeless eyes.

Two decades ago, he rented an apartment bordering a wildlife reserve. One night, he swore he heard a child crying in the woods. The sound came from a bobcat. Was that what he'd heard tonight? Bobcats ventured out of the hill country and into the state park every few years.

Another scream pulled his head around. That wasn't a bobcat. He sprinted down the trail, blocking tree limbs with his forearm. As he reached the bottom and crossed from the park onto private land, he pulled up. This was Thomas Shepherd's property. Cutting between the trees, he almost ran into the deputy. Thomas carried his own Glock. The deputy's flashlight blinded Darren's eyes.

"It's Darren," he said, concerned the deputy wouldn't recognize him in his confused state. The same live wire tension coursing through Darren's body revealed itself in the former LAPD detective's eyes.

"The scream came from that way," Thomas said over the wind. He pointed past his neighbor's house toward the lake.

Whitecap waves threw themselves against the shore. Lights flickered on inside the Mourning home while Darren followed the deputy's lead through the backyards. Darren didn't know where Thomas was taking him until he spotted a woman pointing toward the shoreline.

A gray mass bobbed against the rocks. Even from a distance, Darren knew it was a body.

"Keep the woman back," Thomas told him as he pressed his phone to his ear.

The distraught woman fell to her knees and covered her mouth with both hands. Darren recognized her. She and her husband owned the pale blue boathouse beside the Mournings' property.

"Mrs. Kimble, did you see anyone else on the water?"

She leaned over and regurgitated into the grass. The cold numbed Darren's fingers. At the shore, Thomas used a branch to direct the corpse toward the rocks before the waves stole it. Christ, the head was missing. Blocking the macabre scene with his frame, he set a hand on Kimble's shoulder. She wiped a forearm across her mouth and coughed.

"I couldn't sleep on account of the wind. A shutter kept knocking against the house, so I came outside to lock it down."

"Where's your husband, ma'am?"

Kimble shook her head.

"He works overnights this week. Oh, God. Who would do such a thing?"

Darren sent the distraught woman inside and told her to stay in the house until the sheriff arrived. After Kimble turned away,

Darren descended the slope and helped Thomas drag the remains onto the rocks. The deputy stood knee-deep in the water, his shirt soaked through by the waves. Without a jacket, Thomas must have been freezing.

Darren could see the indecision etched into the deputy's face. Touching the corpse tainted the evidence. But if he left the body alone, the lake might swallow it and drag the corpse under. The man's lips took on an unhealthy pallor.

"Give me your hand," Darren said after the deputy nudged the body past the reach of the waves.

Thomas stared with his teeth chattering. The water, which had stayed frozen until March, still held winter's touch. Darren worried about hypothermia. He edged closer to the water, careful not to disturb the headless corpse. Extending an arm over the water, he waited until Thomas clutched his hand. Darren hauled the deputy out of the lake. Thomas dropped into a crouch and rubbed his arms. He needed dry clothes and a blanket.

"The sheriff is on the way," Thomas said, his words clipped. He winced when the wind gusted. "Something tells me we found our missing person."

The bloated body appeared as if it had been in the water for twenty-four hours or longer. Skin peeled away along the torso, and something had nibbled a chunk of flesh from the leg. It was a woman. No way he could identify the victim. A black crown on the dead woman's forearm pulled his gaze as sirens approached from the village center.

"That's a gang tattoo," Darren said, pointing at the crown. "She belonged to the Royals."

Thomas met his eyes. This was Erika Windrow.

16

Thomas didn't want to accept the blanket, but Sheriff Gray insisted. What he needed was a hot shower and dry clothes. He wouldn't leave the scene until they were certain Erika Windrow's missing head wasn't bobbing in the lake, waiting to wash up on someone's property.

"I've got a diving team on the way from Harmon," Gray said, surveying the lake with consternation creasing his brow. "You're certain you didn't see anyone else on the lake after Kimble screamed?"

Thomas glanced at Darren, who shook his head. The ranger gave Gray and the investigation team room, but the former Syracuse police officer champed at the bit to help.

"Well, someone must have dumped this woman in the lake," Gray continued, frustrated. "It's this damn wind. Everything in that lake will end up on the south shore by the time it lets up. Bang on every door along the lake shore. If anyone was on the water after dark over the last twenty-four hours, I want to know about it."

Two crime scene techs in jumpsuits set down markers and picked over the corpse. They wore face masks. Booties covered their shoes. The first tech, a fifty-something woman with hard eyes and a firm set to her jaw, tried to erect a tent. The wind kept knocking it over. Over Thomas's shoulder, Naomi and Scout watched from the patio, the girl smothered in a bulky winter coat as her mother stood behind the wheelchair.

"Give me a second," Thomas said, tilting his head toward the Mourning family.

Gray grunted and mingled with the female technician. The woman urged the sheriff to stay back as he clamored for answers she couldn't give him. Thomas pushed through a tangle of brush beneath the hemlock trees. Naomi raised a hesitant hand as he approached.

"Is it true? Mrs. Kimble found a dead body in the water?"

Thomas looked back at the investigation team. No point lying to Naomi and Scout. The news would hit the internet within the hour.

"We haven't identified the woman."

"Tell me she drowned and washed ashore."

"I can't speculate."

Naomi glared at Thomas. She knew he was holding back. Naomi's hand slid from the chair arm to Scout's shoulder.

"My daughter wants to tell you something."

Thomas looked between Naomi and Scout, then knelt before the teenager. The girl's eyes darted up to her mother in question. Naomi nodded.

"Last night, someone went out on the lake."

Thomas fished inside his pocket for a pen and notepad before he remembered he'd thrown on street clothes after Kimble woke him up.

"What time?"

"A few minutes after ten o'clock."

"Tell me what happened."

"There was a loud splash, like something heavy fell into the water."

"I heard it too," Naomi said in confirmation. "As Scout said, it was a few minutes after ten."

A soaked strand of hair dropped across his eye. Thomas brushed it away.

"Did either of you see a boater on the water?"

"Neither bedroom faces the lake. I got up and looked out the kitchen window. There's no lake view from our yard. But there's something else that might be important."

"Go on."

"Sunday night around the same time, somebody came through our yards. It sounded like he hiked down from the state park. I figured it was the ranger. But I didn't see a reason he'd cross through our properties."

"It couldn't have been Ranger Holt. We drove to Hattie's Sunday evening and didn't return until eleven. You're certain someone was behind our houses?"

Naomi rubbed her arms and looked away.

"I'm not sure what to believe. A buck crashed through the bushes and startled me, so I ran inside. I tried to convince myself that's what I'd heard before, but I'm not so sure. You know that sensation you get when someone's watching you? I'm certain someone was behind your house, hiding near the trees."

Thomas's jaw worked back and forth.

"I should get back to the investigation. If you remember anything else, call me. And if you catch anyone in the yards again—"

"You don't have to ask. I'm scared enough as it is."

He gave Naomi and Scout a reassuring smile and walked back to the lake. The blanket flapped behind him like a cape, but Thomas didn't feel like a superhero. Someone dumped a murdered woman in the lake under his nose. Had the same person stalked through his backyard and frightened Naomi? Unease crept through his bones.

When he arrived at the shore, the medical examiner joined the crime scene technicians. The wind tossed the man's gray hair around. He stooped over the victim's remains, snapping photographs as he pointed at the tattoo.

"Did your neighbors have anything to say?" Gray asked, lifting his chin at Naomi and Scout.

Thomas could still see them past the tree line.

"That's Naomi and Scout Mourning. The girl claims someone was on the lake last night after ten o'clock, and the mother confirmed the story."

Gray tugged at his mustache.

"Nobody's allowed on the lake after dark. Village ordinance."

"The mother also claims someone watched her Sunday night from my yard."

"Your yard?"

"I don't understand it, either. But I suggest we bring flashlights and check the path from my house to the state park. Mrs. Mourning thinks the person came down the ridge."

"All right. After the ME takes the body, we'll check it out. And Thomas?"

"Yes, Sheriff?"

"Your house is a two-minute walk. Go home and change into dry clothes. I can't lose my newest deputy to pneumonia."

Thomas didn't want to leave the scene, but Gray was right. He trudged back to the house, his sneakers making squishing noises that wrangled his nerves as he angled around the guest house. After he removed his shoes at the back door, he peeled the sodden clothes off in the kitchen and walked naked to the staircase. It occurred to him Uncle Truman's house had too many windows, and he wrapped a towel around his waist before he climbed the stairs. In the bathroom, he tossed the clothes into the hamper, made certain it was completely closed, and stepped into the shower. He moaned when the warm spray massaged the chill off his flesh.

After, Thomas flicked the light switch inside the kitchen. Two floodlights lit the back deck like a landing strip. He grabbed his flashlight and slipped into a coat. Gray and a bleary-eyed Deputy Lambert waited for him when Thomas stepped outside. The deputy's shift had ended at midnight. He suspected Gray's call woke Lambert up an hour after he'd fallen asleep.

Thomas joined Gray and Lambert in the backyard. Naomi and Scout had retreated into their house, and the lights were off. Darren stood with his arms folded, hoping someone would request his assistance.

"The more the merrier," Gray said, waving Darren forward. "You got your flashlight, Ranger?"

"I do."

"Start searching. The night isn't getting younger. Shit, I have to be up in five hours."

"What are we looking for?" Lambert asked, sweeping the light from the deck to the tree line.

"Footprints. Anything that confirms someone was in Shepherd's yard Sunday night."

Even if they found a footprint, it would be difficult to separate it from their own footprints. How many times had Thomas walked through the yard since he moved in? Too many to count.

"I didn't want to say this while the women were outside," Gray said, glancing at the Mournings' home. "But this might be a wild goose chase. The woman th*ought* someone was watching her? That's not a lot to go on."

"She's not alone," Darren said, pulling Gray's attention. "Last week, I tracked somebody moving down the trail toward the water after dark."

"Hmm. Probably a camper."

"We haven't rented a cabin since the end of March. Given winter's refusal to pack up and head north, I don't blame anyone for avoiding the park."

Lambert moved toward the guest house. He ran the light over a series of impressions leading back to the house.

"This you?" Lambert asked Thomas.

"Yes. I'm fixing up the guest house."

"Let me know when you finish. I'll move in. This place is sweet."

Darren worked toward the ridge while Thomas concentrated his search near the trees. As Thomas bent to examine a muddy impression, Darren called out from the shore. Gray led the deputies to the ranger's position. Between the grass and water, brush hunched over as though someone had stomped through. Two streaks cut into the mud.

"Someone dragged a skiff through here," Darren said, pointing at the markings. "You have a boat, Deputy Shepherd?"

"A kayak, but I haven't taken it onto the water yet."

Had the killer entered the lake from Thomas's yard?

17

Thomas arrived at the station Tuesday morning, sporting a headache. A half-hour later he returned to the lake. While Gray and Aguilar drove to the county morgue, Thomas directed his cruiser to the state park. He sipped from his coffee, the caffeine cutting through the haze. If he'd slept more than an hour last night, he couldn't recall. Every time sleep dragged him under, his eyes snapped open to a noise outside—branches rustling, banging shutters. He needed eight hours per night to think clearly, four to function.

Darren waited for Thomas at the park entrance. The ranger appeared as tired as Thomas while he leaned in the doorway.

"Are you up for an early morning hike, Deputy?"

"I can't wait," Thomas said, rubbing his eyes.

Sunlight waged war with the persistent clouds. Orange shafts penetrated the gray canopy and painted a checkerboard across the distant hills. Frost melted off the flora, and dew wet their pant cuffs as he pushed through the grass.

"Two trails run through Wolf Lake State Park," Darren said, pointing at a large map encased behind glass. "We'll take the ridge trail down to the lake trail. That's where I heard activity last week. It seems like a lot of work for your killer to canvass the lake. Keep in mind the lake is 320 feet deep at the center. It's a great place to dump a body."

Thomas nodded.

"You still think LeVar Hopkins came down these trails?"

"Can't prove anything. As I told you, I spotted his Chrysler Limited cruising your end of the lake. No reason for a Harmon gangster to be here unless he's running drugs."

"Why murder an eighteen-year-old girl?"

"Simple. She belongs to the Royals, and LeVar's gang wants to destroy their prostitution ring."

They pushed past a tree limb growing over the trail. The sun broke through the canopy, and for the first time since Thomas returned home, spring seemed near.

"Here we go," Darren said, pulling up.

Footprints trailed down a steep incline. Someone had come through in recent days, and the muddy grounds held the evidence.

"You're sure those aren't from your shoes?"

Darren placed his shoe beside the print.

"Not even close. This guy is two or more shoe sizes larger." He pulled back on another branch and opened a view to the water. "That's where he boarded the skiff."

Thomas cupped a hand over his eye to block the glare. Darren was correct. Someone moved along this trail and boarded a skiff he'd dragged to the shoreline. Thomas's property gave the killer direct access. Grass and weeds grew thick south of the lake. If the killer backed a truck to the shore, he'd find tire tracks.

"He must have carried the watercraft."

"Either he owns a lightweight skiff, or we're looking for a powerful guy."

"Considering he carried a dead woman to the water, I'd lean

toward the latter. Next question. What was he doing on the trail? Seems counterproductive. Why drag the skiff to the lake, dump the body, then move up the trail?"

"If LeVar was heading toward the school—"

"The school is east of the lake. This guy went due north and doubled back. What's at the north end of this trail?"

"Just the cabins."

Thomas fixed Darren with a glare.

"*Your* cabin."

The implication was clear. What if the killer stalked Darren and watched him inside the cabin? Getting rid of the ranger would make it easier to dump a body unnoticed.

"I'll keep my eyes open."

"Do you have a security system?"

"It's a log cabin in the middle of a state park. Not a hot spot for criminal activity."

"Or so you figured."

A vein pulsed in Darren's neck. He raised binoculars to his eyes, scanned the shore, then handed them to Thomas.

"He must have spent a long time on the water. Remember how strong the winds were over the weekend?"

"Straight out of the north."

"Right. So he sets the woman inside the skiff and rows toward the deep waters. Trouble is, the waves fight him and drag the boat toward the shore. No way he rowed out of the shallows in a few minutes."

"Someone might have seen him."

"He dumped the girl under the cover of night. Nobody would have seen a light. Not on a small skiff."

Thomas raised the binoculars and followed the matted bramble along the shore. Across the water, a dilapidated boathouse sat on the west side of the lake. Smoke curled from a vent. The scent of a wood stove rode the air.

"Who lives in the boathouse across the way? Maybe the owner saw something."

Darren led Thomas to the parking lot and climbed into the passenger seat of the deputy's cruiser. They followed the road past the A-frame and the Mournings' residence. One eye on the road, Thomas couldn't look away from the Kimble residence. What was more horrifying than finding a headless woman floating in the water outside your home?

A dirt driveway curled down a hill to the broken down boathouse. The cruiser's tires slipped in the mud before Thomas shifted the vehicle into sport mode. A rusty pickup truck stood beside the house. A skull and crossbones bumper sticker adorned the back of the truck, and a confederate flag waved in the breeze behind the cab. Darren raised an eyebrow.

Thomas banged on the door. A dog the size of a grizzly barked inside. Cursing followed as a man told Buster to shut the hell up. The man who opened the door had a scruffy red beard. His belly hung over his jeans, and a cap with a bald eagle topped his head. He stood a hair taller than Thomas and Darren.

"What the hell do you want?"

The man blocked the entryway with his body to keep the dog back. Thomas sensed the man was more interested in keeping them out.

"Are you the home owner, sir?"

"Yeah, my name is Buck Benson. If you'd taken five seconds to look at the mailbox, you coulda figured that out for yourself. Why are you on my property? I paid my taxes."

"Mr. Benson, I'm Deputy Shepherd with the Nightshade County Sheriff's Department, and this is Darren Holt, the ranger at Wolf Lake State Park. I'm investigating a murder."

"I heard your emergency vehicles. You kept me up half the night with your damn lights and sirens."

"Did you see anyone on the lake Sunday night around ten o'clock?"

Benson rubbed his beard and narrowed his eyes.

"It's too dark over the water that time of night. But I saw a guy hanging around the shore."

Thomas perked up.

"Can you describe the man?"

"Sure as hell can. Black as the ace of spades, if you know what I mean. He wears them damn curls down his shoulders."

"Curls?"

"You know. Like those druggie reggae types."

"Dreadlocks."

"I don't know what the hell they're called. All I can say is we don't have nobody like that in my neighborhood."

"What else can you tell me about this man?"

Benson shrugged. The dog lunged at the door, and he kicked it back. The dog retreated with a yelp.

"Big guy, lots of muscles. Probably did prison time."

"Why do you say that?"

"Because of the tats up and down his arms. Plus, you don't have time to build muscle like that unless you're in prison. Then you have all the time in the world, and hardworking folks like me pay for your room and board."

Thomas shared a glance with Darren. He doubted Buck Benson had a bone in his body that wasn't tainted with racism. But the man had described LeVar Hopkins.

"Ever see this guy before?"

"I seen him around. Scumbag drives a big black car. Always moving slow, like he's scoping for a place to rob. Figure he's from Harmon. That's where all the welfare degenerates come from." He tilted his head toward a gray one-story with blue shutters up the road. "We got another *blacky* over there. A woman. Bet they're friends."

"What was this guy doing Sunday night?"

"Standing along the shore a quarter-mile up the road. Up to no good, I can tell you that. I would have called you guys, but he disappeared after I grabbed my shotgun." Benson glared at Thomas in challenge. "I got a permit, not that I should need one in a free country."

Thomas dug into his wallet and handed Benson a card.

"If you see him again, or you think of anything else, I want you to call the number on the card."

Benson raised the card to his eyes and squinted.

"Yeah, I'll do that. But if he shows his face on my property, I'll deal with him my way."

"Just call the department, Mr. Benson."

Benson grinned before he slammed the door in their faces.

18

After Thomas dropped Darren at the ranger's cabin, he circled past his house and grabbed a coffee from the Broken Yolk. His radio buzzed with activity when he climbed into the cruiser. Something about a video of Erika Windrow's murder posted to the internet.

He pressed the gas and raced back to the department. When he arrived, Aguilar sat before a computer with a hand over her mouth. Gray stood behind, ashen-faced.

"You have to watch this," Aguilar said, looking back at Thomas.

He took a knee beside the female deputy and peered at the screen while she moved the time marker back to the beginning. The video, titled *A Death in Wolf Lake*, appeared shot from a camera set on a dashboard. Darkness cloaked the vehicle's interior, and the focus kept pulsing in and out as the camera struggled to find a subject. Enough grainy light existed for Thomas to see a woman on the passenger side of the vehicle. Two hands curled around her neck, the killer's body off camera. Her bare feet kicked up and pressed against the dashboard for purchase. She pushed off, but he was too strong. For three excruciating minutes, he strangled the woman until her struggles slowed and became lethargic. Now and then, the automatic exposure increased, adding noise to the picture as it drew out her features. She was young. A teenager. The picture was too distorted to identify the woman, but this had to be Erika Windrow. They needed to send this video to a lab. A technician would clean up the video and help them identify the victim, possibly pick out a key piece of evidence inside the vehicle.

"Copy the video before it disappears," Thomas said. "Murders captured on camera vanish quickly on the internet."

"Wait," Aguilar said. "There's more to the footage."

She glared at Thomas as if to ask him if he was ready. His stomach curled in on itself. Could the video become more disturbing?

The woman went slack in the seat. She appeared dead, but it took several minutes to murder someone by strangulation. More likely she was unconscious and hanging on by a thread. The killer's hands disappeared from the frame. When one hand returned, it held a serrated knife.

"Jesus," Gray said, turning away.

Willing the woman to wake up and escape, Thomas stared at the screen as the knife swept across her throat. Black blood spilled from the gash as the murderer sawed through her neck.

"He's beheading her on camera," Aguilar said. "What kind of sicko would murder a woman and upload the evidence?"

Thomas narrowed his eyes and studied the shadowed body leaning into the frame. The man faced away from the camera, his body a black silhouette that blotted out two-thirds of the picture. His body pulsed with energy, muscles rippling his shoulders and neck. This guy was strong. It explained how he carried the skiff to the shore and rowed into the lake against a stiff current.

The woman's head lolled to one side before the video cut off.

A dead silence fell over the room. Maggie broke the quiet and strolled down the hall with a folder in her hand. Thomas blocked her from approaching.

"I'll take that," he said, giving her a meaningful glare.

"What's wrong?"

"You don't want to know, Maggie. Please return to your desk."

She craned her head to see past him. Aguilar and Gray stood in front of the screen until the secretary retreated to her desk. Thank God Maggie hadn't seen.

"Shut that door," Gray said, pointing at the door dividing the hallway.

Thomas removed the stopper and let the door swing shut. After a glance from the sheriff, he twisted the lock so Maggie couldn't barge in on their conversation. The sheriff removed his hat and scrubbed a hand through his hair.

"This guy is taunting us. He murders a prostitute and uploads the video so everyone can see. How do we catch this guy? Talk."

Aguilar glanced at Thomas.

"The first thing we should do is send the video to a lab," Thomas said, folding his arms as he leaned against the wall. "Harmon PD has one, but the lab in Syracuse is state-of-the art. I'll call Darren Holt. He may know someone at Syracuse who can expedite the process."

"Good. What else?"

Aguilar narrowed her eyes at the video.

"For one thing, we're looking for a vehicle with a bloody passenger seat. This guy isn't very subtle. What about bringing in the FBI?"

"I doubt they'll come for one murder, but it never hurts to check."

"Okay, let's rattle the bushes in Harmon. Either the Harmon

Kings picked off a prostitute to hurt the 315 Royals, or the Royals had this girl murdered. Maybe Erika Windrow ratted out one of their members or threatened to take incriminating evidence to the police."

Gray tugged at his mustache.

"The guy who uploaded the video goes by the name Max Cady. Is that a legitimate name?"

Thomas shook his head.

"Max Cady is a character from *Cape Fear*. In the movie, Cady stalked the family of a lawyer who wronged him. This guy is a fan of thrillers and horror movies."

"Not much to go on, is it?"

"No, but we can search for internet posters using the same name. That's one way to track him. What if he screwed up along the way and left a breadcrumb?"

"We need to follow every lead. Aguilar, take Shepherd to Harmon. Someone has to know why this guy murdered Erika Windrow. Shepherd, before you leave, get that video to the Syracuse lab."

"I'll copy the video and send it over now."

19

The school day lasted forever for Scout.

She never fell back to sleep after the body washed up on shore a few hundred feet from her house. Mom encouraged her to take the day off and rest. But Scout needed to be around people, even though she drifted without notice like a ghost at school. During lunch, while she sat alone at a corner table in the cafeteria, a ruckus broke out among the popular kids. They passed phones around as Scout listened and picked at a ham sandwich with disinterest.

The killer had uploaded murder footage to the internet. YouTube and Vimeo removed the videos after they became viral. Less popular hosting sites cast a blind eye, greedy for the traffic. News of the murder reached the major media sites. The sleepy village of Wolf Lake was a household name in places like New York City, Chicago, and Los Angeles.

Scout confirmed the stories on her phone. Her next stop was Virtual Searchers, the amateur teen sleuthing forum she frequented. She located the threads as soon as she logged in. The trouble was the media-heavy site bogged down under the slow Wi-Fi. Scout would need to wait until she returned home.

Her body buzzed with excitement. Paying attention during Spanish class proved challenging. She couldn't take her mind off the murder and the viral video. Between classes, as she wheeled down the gloomy hallways, her neck hairs prickled. What if the killer targeted her neighbors? Or her mother?

After the bus dropped her off in front of her house, Scout lied to her mother about the ton of homework she needed to complete before dinner. Then she pushed herself into her bedroom and closed the door. The dark computer screen stared back at her. She hadn't watched the video yet. Maybe she shouldn't.

Entering her password, Scout tapped her fingers beside the mouse as Windows loaded. She opened the browser and clicked on the Virtual Searchers link. Over the three hours since lunch, the number of posts had tripled. The forum buzzed over the news, but she couldn't read any of it until she entered her user name and password.

She typed in *Rokdablz*, and a picture of a young LL Cool J appeared as her profile picture. Like most of the forum members, she used an anonymous name and picture. No one needed to know who she was or whether she was male or female. Besides, she loved hip-hop and rap, especially the old stuff. A private message waited. She clicked on the envelope icon with a red exclamation point drawn through the center. Scout's friend, Harpy, had written her. Harpy's profile picture was a fantasy creature with a woman's body and bird's wings. Though Scout didn't reveal her name to Harpy, she entrusted the girl with her location.

Harpy: I can't believe it. The murder happened in your village! You must be freaking out.

Scout typed: *I know, right? The sheriff's department pulled the body from the lake last night. It's hard to believe something like that happened here.*

Before Scout opened the forum thread about the murder, a reply popped up from Harpy. The girl was online.

Harpy: Wait, did you see the body? How close to the lake do you live?

Scout hesitated. She'd already told the girl she lived in Wolf Lake. Harpy had helped solve two crimes already. She had a talent for ferreting out information. No sense hiding the truth when Harpy would figure it out.

Scout: Like right on the lake.

Harpy: Jeezus. Don't tell me you saw the dead woman.

Scout: No way. Nothing like that. Besides, my mom was with me when the sheriff's department arrived.

Harpy: Wow. So you live in the village. Who did this? You must have a suspect or two.

A moment passed before Scout replied.

Harpy: You still there?

Scout: Yeah. I don't know who would do something like this. I need to play the video first.

Harpy: Oh. You haven't played it yet? OMG it's disgusting. It will literally give you nightmares. Go watch the video and tell me what you think. There has to be a clue that we can use to catch him.

Scout: Checking it out now. Talk to you soon. Bye!

Harpy: Hugs.

Scout clicked on the thread and bit her lip. This was crazy. She was about to watch a woman die, the same woman who washed up on the Kimble's shore. What was poor Mrs. Kimble going through? The killer cut the victim's head off, and Kimble found the remains.

After a quick scan of the messages, Scout found the video link. She moved the mouse over the link and hesitated. By now, the hosting site must have removed the footage. A part of her prayed the video had disappeared. But it was still there.

She clicked the link and turned her head away. Her eyes

drifted to the screen. What she saw would give her nightmares for the rest of her life. When the psychopath finished strangling the woman, he put a knife to her throat. When the blade swept from left to right, Scout turned the monitor off and breathed. Her heart thumped, and her stomach flopped. The speakers remained on. The horrible death sounds continued, her imagination filling in the blanks.

When the video ended, she turned the monitor on and stared at her trembling hands. Perhaps it was smarter to let Harpy and the others solve this crime.

Except the killer dumped the body on her doorstep. Until the authorities caught the madman, Scout and her mother would be in danger. Her father once told her, the best defense is a good offense. He'd been talking about sports, but it seemed à propos. She needed to go after this guy and catch him before he hurt someone else.

Copying the killer's profile name, she wrote Max Cady on her notebook. The name didn't mean anything to her. She moved the video to the beginning and clicked the playback icon. This time she concentrated on the surroundings. It was a good excuse not to glare at the horror unfolding. They were inside a vehicle. The windows were rolled up, and the engine was off. She increased the volume. Gagging sounds filled the bedroom. Pausing the video, Scout switched to headphones so Mom wouldn't overhear. She willed herself to block out the death noises and concentrated on the ambient sounds.

Spring had been too cold for the crickets to emerge. Dead silence wrapped around the vehicle as though it conspired with the madman. Scout stopped the video and narrowed her eyes. Though the killer aimed the camera at the passenger seat, the picture passed over the dashboard, which had an unusual wavy shape. Not much to go on, but it was a start.

Scout captured an image and saved it to a private folder.

Then she opened the picture in Photoshop, boosted the exposure, and cleaned up the noise. Now she could see rear seating. She searched for an item strewn on the seat, anything that might help her identify who this guy was. A knock on the door stopped her.

Scout minimized the browser and removed her headphones. She had just enough time to open her Spanish textbook before Mom walked in.

"Everything all right? I thought I heard you gagging."

Scout copied a verb conjugation into her notebook.

"Sorry, I coughed."

The corners of Mom's eyes creased with worry.

"You aren't sick, are you? We were up so late last night."

"I'm okay. Just swallowed down the wrong pipe."

"All right, if you're sure you're okay. Dinner's on the table."

The door closed, and Mom padded to the kitchen. When she was certain Mom wasn't coming back, Scout opened the browser and clicked out of the video. Then she shut the computer down and pushed herself back from the monitor.

As she turned toward the door, a motor rattled her window. Scout pulled the curtain back as a black Chrysler Limited slowed to a crawl outside her house. Her skin prickled.

Murderers returned to the scenes of their crimes.

20

Thomas parked his truck along the curb and shut off the engine. Through the passenger window, he stared at the contemporary four-bedroom home he'd grown up in. Poplar Hill Estates catered to the wealthy. A gate barred entry, and a security guard forced visitors to display identification before entering. The engine ticked. He lowered the visor as sunlight blasted through the windshield.

Two minutes until five. If he showed up a minute later, his parents would give him the death stare over dinner. After work, he rushed home and threw on khakis after showering. The navy blue polo would have to do. He wasn't willing to indulge them with a button down and tie.

Thomas checked his hair in the mirror and brushed a lazy strand off his forehead. It hadn't gone well at work. Nobody in Harmon spoke to Thomas and Aguilar. He often marveled at opposing gangs protecting each other, as though street rules took precedent over their war. He caught his fingers digging into his thighs. Was he anxious because he couldn't track down LeVar Hopkins for questioning, despite the gang leader cruising through Wolf Lake like he owned the village? Or did he dread the forthcoming dinner?

He stepped from the truck and followed the concrete walkway toward the steps, counting each stride. It took fourteen strides to reach the stairs when he was a child, ten as a teenager. It took nine this time. He paused, shifted a few inches backward, and held his breath until he completed his tenth step.

The landscapers must have worked overtime. Deep green poured out of the lawn in July colors, and they'd trimmed the hedges to razor sharp perfection. He wiped his shoes on the mat, though they were clean. Old habits died hard. When he pressed the doorbell, chimes rang through the house like echoes through a canyon.

His mother opened the door. She wore a cashmere sweater, slacks, and heels that cost more than Thomas's entire wardrobe. A pearl necklace draped to her chest.

"Thomas," she said, eyeing the grandfather clock in the entryway. She shot him a frosty look. "You're late."

He wasn't. His watch read five o'clock, but it wasn't worth arguing.

"Good to see you again, Mother."

Lindsey Shepherd ushered him inside. Her quick glare at his shoes confirmed she worried he'd track dirt into the home. He wasn't ten-years-old and hadn't spent the afternoon playing in the mud—another thought he kept to himself. He followed her down a long corridor to the dining room. His father sat at the far end of the table. Thomas swallowed. Mason Shepherd appeared twenty years older than when Thomas had last seen his father. Gray hair receded from his forehead and matching creases ran down each cheek. In Thomas's mind, Mason stood half a foot taller. Maybe it was because his father slumped in a chair with financial statements spread across the table. He hadn't noticed Thomas enter.

"Put the statements away, Mason," Lindsey said, lifting her chin. "Our son is here."

His father cleared his throat and glanced up. He clicked the papers together and slipped them into a leather portfolio, but he didn't rise.

"Sit," his father said, gesturing at the open chair kitty-corner to his. "You remember your old place at the table, I trust."

"Yes, I remember. It hasn't been that long."

"How was the flight from California? Pleasant, I hope."

"I drove my truck. A 2017 Ford F-150."

Lindsey put a hand to her chest, and Mason shook his head.

"Whatever for? The trip must have taken you five days."

"Seven, actually. I took it slow and did a little sightseeing."

Mason harrumphed.

"Nothing between California and New York except wasteland and manure." Lindsey shot Mason a glare, and he changed the subject. "I understand you purchased Truman's old home. Quaint little place. Personally, I wouldn't pay a penny were it not for the lake frontage. Would you consider building a new home on the property? I know a builder who'd give you a deal."

"I'm happy with Uncle Truman's house. Remember I watched him build it from the ground up."

"I don't recall." That was a lie. "The important thing is you're back in Wolf Lake, Thomas. Family should stay together, don't you agree?"

"Always."

Lindsey moved between the kitchen and dining room as Mason expounded on the tremendous quarter for Shepherd Systems. His father owned a project management, accounting, and collaboration software firm. As Mason loved to explain, he created the concept while studying business and marketing at Union. The personal computer was novel to most homes then, and no one had conceived of the internet. But Mason Shepherd envisioned a future where the largest companies in the world used his software to improve performance and drive profits.

When Lindsey set the filet mignon on the table, Thomas wrinkled his nose. His mother knew her way around the kitchen, but he couldn't recall the last time she cooked. Trina took care of the meals. Thomas wondered where the cook was today.

His mouth watered at the first bite. Lindsey hadn't lost her touch. But each clink of fork on plate grated on Thomas as he waited for the inevitable. They hadn't brought him here to welcome their only child back to Wolf Lake. An ulterior motive always existed.

He sipped from a Finger Lakes Chardonnay and enjoyed the silence. As a rule, his parents didn't speak during meals. Crème brûlée followed the main course. If Lindsey and Mason intended to butter Thomas up before they cornered him, they were doing a helluva job. Afterward, Thomas stood.

"Let me do the dishes, Mother."

"Nonsense. Sit with your father. You have so much to catch up on."

Mason blanched. It seemed his father was just as uncomfortable speaking with Thomas.

"So, Thomas." Mason's fingers laced together. "Did you sign a contract with the county?"

"A contract, sir?"

"How long are you tied into the deputy position? Send me a copy of the agreement, and I'll have the lawyers look it over."

"I don't understand."

Mason set his elbows on the table.

"You don't mean to work as a county deputy for the rest of your life, do you?"

"I filled out an application and interviewed. This job is important to me."

"Thomas." Mason closed his eyes for a composing moment. "You're a smart boy. Apply your talents toward worthy endeavors. Challenge yourself."

"My degree is in criminology. I'm doing exactly what I prepared myself for."

Mason pulled the portfolio from beside his chair and opened it. He removed four sheets of paper, one with a colorful bar graph depicting rising profits over a five-year period, the other three comprising balance sheets, a cash flow analysis, and growth prospects for the next ten years.

"Shepherd Systems completed its strongest fiscal year last quarter," Mason said as Thomas flipped from one page to the next. Was he gloating, or shaming Thomas for settling for less? "And the next decade will make last year look like a drop in the pond."

"It seems you have the company firing on all cylinders, Father. Congratulations."

He passed the papers to Mason. Mason blocked his hand and pushed the papers back.

"Those are for you."

"I've already memorized the figures. I don't need to keep—"

"Thomas, I won't beat around the bush. Tomorrow, you'll announce your retirement and tell Sheriff Gray you made a mistake."

"That's preposterous. Why would I do such a thing?"

"Let me finish," Mason said, raising a hand. "I'm bringing you aboard at Shepherd Systems."

Thomas wrapped his feet around the chair legs to keep still. He ran a hand through his hair and glared at the documents. So this was the reason his parents invited him to dinner. To insult his career choice and strong-arm him into joining the family business.

" This isn't my area of expertise. I didn't study business and marketing."

"You should have. You have a mind for it, and you're a Shepherd. I can't think of one good reason you refused to attend Union like your mother and me. You settled, Thomas, and as your father, I can no longer sit by while you compromise. Time is running out."

Lindsey emerged from the kitchen, her hands wringing at her hips.

"You shouldn't have asked me to dinner." Thomas pushed his chair back. "Must you always have an angle?"

"Sit down."

"No, thank you."

"This isn't an entry level position. You'd come on as Chief Operations Officer, starting salary a quarter of a million dollars."

Thomas wavered on his feet. This was insane.

"I'm not qualified to be your COO. Find a worthy candidate."

Mason threw his chair back and slapped the table.

"No! It must be you."

Thomas glanced between Lindsey and Mason. His mother raised a hand to her mouth. Her eyes glistened.

"Thomas, please listen to your father," Lindsey said, swiping at a tear.

Sinking into his chair, Thomas felt the stately home shrink. The vaulted ceiling lowered, and the faraway walls surrounding the open floor design converged.

"I'm dying, Thomas."

21

The sun's dying embers burned on the horizon as twilight pushed across the sky. Thomas pulled the pickup into his driveway and sat with the engine off and his hands gripping the steering wheel.

Dying.

His father had lung cancer, which seemed inexplicable. He never smoked a day in his life and avoided smokers as though they spread the black plague. Now he understood his father's offer. The COO position would be temporary. Thomas would take over the company after Mason passed, and the Shepherd empire would be his.

He removed his hands from the wheel and covered his face. This wasn't real. He'd wake up from the nightmare and go about his day. The truck made an electronic whir when the battery shut down. Taking that as his cue to leave, he climbed down from the truck and crossed the lawn toward the front deck. Scout sat on her front lawn. He hadn't noticed the girl when he drove in, too consumed with the news.

She raised a hesitant hand, and he waved back.

"Good evening, Deputy Shepherd."

Thomas swallowed the lump in his throat.

"Hello, Scout. Aren't you cold sitting out here by yourself?"

The temperature had dropped ten degrees in the last hour. A thick frost would cover the lawn by morning.

"May I talk to you?"

He leaned closer.

"Is everything okay? Your mom all right?"

"Yes, sir."

Thomas strode to Scout. The girl wore the same bulky winter jacket he'd seen her in when Mrs. Kimble discovered Erika Windrow's remains. He assumed it was Erika Windrow. The ME hadn't got back to Sheriff Gray yet.

"Would you like to take a walk?" he suggested.

Scout nodded.

He pushed the wheelchair through the grass until they reached the shoulder. The soggy April fed the lawn and encouraged the grass to grow past his shins. This weekend he'd mow the Mournings' yard. This was too much for Naomi to handle, considering she had her hands full with Scout.

The windless night seemed secretive. Stars burned through the building twilight, and the night held the crispness of midwinter. He shivered as they walked, but Scout seemed warm enough dressed in thick layers.

"Scout, if you want to talk about last night, I'm here for you. It's all right to be scared. But it's important you understand I live next door, I'm monitoring the house, and I won't let anything happen to you or your mother."

Water sloshed against the southern shore of Wolf Lake in hushed whispers. Full dark loomed on the horizon, but they had enough light to move down the lake road. Scout remained quiet. She held something back. Thomas could see it in her tight grimace.

"Deputy Shepherd, is it true criminals return to crime

scenes? Or is that just a cliché from movies and television programs?"

He tilted his head in thought. Scout wouldn't ask unless she believed the killer would come back.

"That's an unexpected question. Why do you ask?"

"Just curious. If I tell you something, will you promise not to laugh?"

"I would never laugh at you."

And he wouldn't. He recalled his anger and frustration when classmates laughed at him.

She paused in consideration. Her hands tightened on the chair arms.

"I'm an amateur sleuth."

Thomas stroked his chin. He'd read about amateurs solving crimes on the internet, but never took the concept seriously. After a story surfaced about online amateur detectives uncovering evidence which led to a serial killer's capture last year, his interest grew. Still, he had a hard time accepting amateur sleuthing as serious crime solving.

"So you look into cold cases and ongoing investigations, and send your theories to the police."

Her hands fell into her lap and she glanced down.

"I never found evidence worth sending to the police, but my friends have."

"What does this have to do with what happened last night?" A cold thought occurred to Thomas. "Scout, you didn't download the video, did you?"

Her silence spoke volumes. A shiver rolled down her neck.

"It's all over the internet."

"You shouldn't watch it. Does your mother know you saw the murder?"

"No. And please don't tell her."

"I realize I just met you and your mother. But I'm obligated to tell her if I'm worried about you. And I am."

"I looked away during the bad parts. And anyway, this isn't about the video. Someone drove down the road earlier, and he slowed when he passed our houses."

" A good detective doesn't jump to conclusions. What makes you think it was the man who threw the body into the lake? Yes, it's true some killers return to crime scenes. But the murder didn't occur at the lake."

She sighed and wrung her hands.

"Maybe you're right. But the person who drove past scared me."

"Did you recognize the car?"

"It wasn't anybody who lives around here. I can't get around much, so I spend too much time watching people drive past. I've probably memorized every vehicle on this road."

What if Scout saw LeVar Hopkins? Darren Holt claimed Hopkins canvassed this road multiple times in recent days.

"If I showed you a picture of the vehicle, would you recognize it?"

"Yes."

Thomas dug his phone out of his pocket. He called up the photograph of LeVar Hopkins driving past the Wolf Lake Inn. Then he reconsidered. If Scout was picking faces out of a book of convicted criminals, he'd display several photographs and force her to choose the correct picture. He opened a browser and searched for black sedans. A myriad of choices filled his screen.

"Is this the car?" he asked, showing her a black Lincoln.

She raised the phone to her face and shook her head.

"Not that one."

He swiped to a different car, and she gave him the same

answer. After he showed her five different vehicles, he found a black Chrysler Limited on a used car site.

"All right. How about this one?"

Her eyes lit.

"That looks like the car. But there's something different about it."

Could be LeVar drove an older model. He showed her the photograph of LeVar's Limited.

"That's it. That's the one!"

22

Jeremy Hyde sat inside the Chevrolet Trax and watched the deputy push the disabled girl down the shoulder. With night thickening by the minute, he harbored no fear they'd see him. The SUV slumbered below the shoulder amid the forest, the grill angled toward the road. When they crossed in front of him, goosebumps spread over his body. If he twisted the ignition and punched the accelerator, he'd crush the deputy and girl and leave them to die. They wouldn't have time to escape.

The little bitch wanted to catch him. How amusing.

Jeremy had taken an interest in the mother. Her name was Naomi Mourning, and she lived alone with the girl. The information proved simple to find on the internet. Watching her from the trees Sunday night increased his hunger to kill again. But his focus shifted to the girl now. He frequented the same teen investigation forum. He found it easy to hide behind an anonymous user name and profile picture. He hid among them. An insurgent. A wolf in sheep's clothing.

The wonderful thing about teens was they couldn't keep their mouths shut. It wasn't a surprise the girl in the wheelchair gave herself away. Though she hid her name online, she revealed she lived in Wolf Lake and had seen the body on the shore. What was that saying about loose lips and sinking ships?

His hand moved to the serrated survival knife on his hip. He stroked the hilt. A part of him wanted to slip out of the vehicle and follow them down the road. The dark would hide him until it was too late. He'd drag the blade across the cop's throat first and let him bleed out on the shoulder. Did she believe a false hero would save her?

Jeremy pulled a camera off the seat and zoomed in on the girl. *Click-click*. Then he focused on the deputy and snapped another picture.

You could find anything on the internet these days. Not only had he learned the deputy's back story with the LAPD, he'd discovered the daughter of his red-hot neighbor was the same girl tracking him on the forum. This was perfect. Three birds, one stone.

They were easy to track and kill because they were so predictable. The only surprise was how much these people cared about the teenage whore. Since when did society give a damn when a worthless hooker died? His body quivered with amusement. The deputy, the media, the so-called amateur sleuths all wondered what he'd done with the head. In two days, the world would learn.

Now the deputy pushed the girl too far down the road for him to see. The windows misted over. A heavy fog would form overnight, allowing him to creep unseen to both of their doorsteps and kill them all. Would tonight be the night, or would Jeremy toy with his prey?

He started the engine and crawled out of hiding. Instead of following the deputy and girl through the darkness, he turned right and headed for Naomi Mourning's house.

Play time was over.

23

The fog didn't burn off until ten o'clock Wednesday morning. Puffy clouds against a sea-blue backdrop hinted at afternoon storms as Thomas rode shotgun in the cruiser. Tristam Lambert, working a quick turnaround—an evening shift followed by a day shift—navigated the cruiser out of Wolf Lake and toward Harmon.

"Does Harmon PD realize we're searching for LeVar Hopkins?" Thomas asked, clamping a travel mug of coffee between his thighs.

The tall deputy scratched behind his ear.

"Yep. They have two patrol units keeping an eye out for LeVar. Someone will see him."

The properties became stunted and rundown as they approached Harmon. Then they merged onto the highway, and the buildings rose before them like alien giants. Traffic choked the roads, reminding Thomas of Los Angeles. He didn't miss sitting in traffic for hours just to drive ten miles.

"The Royals run this section of the city," Lambert said, pointing toward a row of abandoned buildings covered by graffiti. "The Harmon Kings are moving in on their territory, taking one bloody piece at a time."

Harmon had gang issues when Thomas grew up in Wolf Lake, but nothing like this.

"I checked the statistics. There were seven homicides linked to Harmon gang activity last year, up from five the year before. That's a forty percent increase."

"Harmon rivals the big northeast cities for gang-related murders. It gets worse every year." Lambert drove with one hand on the wheel and ate a roast beef sandwich with the other. "Which is why I live in Wolf Lake. How's the village treating you since you returned?"

Besides a grisly murder and the news his father was dying from lung cancer?

"Every village has its issues, but I'll like it better than Los Angeles. Deputy Aguilar tells me you grew up in Minnesota."

He nodded.

"Another small town, minus the lake and wealth."

"Did you always want to be a police officer?"

A memory pulled a grin out of Lambert.

"Nah. I had it in my head that I'd play professional football. I was pretty good in high school. Then I hit college, and I wasn't the biggest and strongest guy on the team anymore. That was my wake up call. I quit school my sophomore year and joined the army, did a few tours overseas, and pursued a law enforcement career after I got out."

"How did you end up in Wolf Lake?"

The deputy shrugged.

"A buddy from my army days sent me the job listing. He lives on the north end of the county and has a wife and three kids." Lambert fiddled with the radio. "Luck brought me to Wolf Lake, but the village grew on me. I prefer living where neighbors know each other."

"The village has a lot of history and tradition."

Lambert swallowed the last of his sandwich and gave Thomas a playful slap on the shoulder.

"Speaking of tradition, are you going to the Magnolia Dance Friday night?"

A flood of memories rushed at Thomas. Every April, the village closed off three blocks in the center of town. Local musicians played on a stage, and everyone came out to dance. The locals considered the Magnolia Dance more romantic than Valentine's Day. It marked the beginning of true spring in Wolf Lake and began the march toward summer. He hadn't attended the dance since high school when Thomas took Chelsey. His throat constricted when he pictured her, a pink magnolia tucked behind her ear. His father drove them to the dance.

"I forgot about the celebration."

"Yeah, right. You should go. That's your best chance to meet someone."

Thomas set his elbow on the sill and rested his chin on his palm.

"The Magnolia Dance isn't for me. Besides, I've only been back a week, and I can't go alone. I don't know anyone my age outside the office."

"Take Aguilar."

Thomas felt a jolt run through him. He tried to picture the muscle-bound deputy in a dress and failed miserably.

"I don't believe Deputy Aguilar would attend a dance with me."

"Why not? She went stag last April and giggled at the drunk people. Said it was the best time she had all year."

"I don't know."

"Think about it. Who else could you take and have no pressure? It's not like she's interested in hooking up. So you go together, nobody feels awkward, and you search the faces for someone you want to meet. You never can predict when lightning will strike."

Scratching his chin, Thomas glanced at Lambert.

"What about you? Who are you going with?"

"I'll be on shift."

"How convenient."

"Gray has me working the dance, so I'll keep an eye on the two of you. Don't get out of line, and there won't be any trouble."

Thomas tapped his feet.

"You're not taking no for an answer, are you?"

"Hell, no."

"All right. I'll ask Deputy Aguilar."

How the heck would he approach Aguilar? He imagined the conversation.

"Hey, we just met a few days ago. But how about you and I make a date for the most romantic celebration of the year?"

Yeah, it sounded ridiculous.

Lambert glanced across the seats.

"I have to say, before Gray told us, I'd never have guessed you had..." Lambert coughed into his hand as Thomas stared straight ahead. "That didn't sound as bad inside my head."

"You don't need to apologize. I've lived with Asperger's my entire life. It's a mild case."

"How do you want to handle this?" Lambert asked, desperate to change the subject. He took the exit ramp into the heart of the city. "If we find LeVar Hopkins, he won't sit down and have a peaceful conversation with us."

"I'd like LeVar to tell us why he spends so much time in Wolf Lake."

"Was there another sighting?"

Thomas bit a thumbnail.

"My neighbor's daughter, the teenager in the wheelchair I

told you about, saw a black Chrysler Limited crawl past her house yesterday."

"Crawled past her house, or past *yours*?"

"That's a good point."

"Could be he's scoping out the new deputy in town, wondering if you'll get in his way."

"This rumor that the Kings traffic drugs across the lake seems far-fetched. There has to be another reason he hangs around the shore."

"Yeah, so he can dump bodies after dark."

The cruiser stopped at a traffic light. A bearded homeless man in a drab sports coat and high-top sneakers staggered to the passenger door with an open hand. Thomas dug into his wallet.

"I wouldn't do that," Lambert said. "He'll just take it to buy booze. And don't make eye contact."

"It's no problem." Thomas unrolled the window and handed the man a ten-dollar bill. "Buy yourself something with nutritious value."

"I will, sir...officer. And God bless you."

The light changed, and Lambert directed the cruiser down a side street lined with vape shops and adult magazine stores. When they passed an alleyway with a rusty green garbage container, the deputy turned his head and slammed the brakes. Thomas braced his arms against the dash, then reached for his gun.

"What happened?"

"It's him. LeVar took off down the alley."

Thomas glanced past Lambert as a black teenager with dreadlocks shot down the alleyway and took a sharp right. He opened the door and hopped out.

"I'll go after LeVar. Circle around and cut off his escape route."

Tires squealed. Thomas crossed behind the cruiser and held

up a hand as a sports car skidded to a halt. He squeezed between two parked sedans, hopped the curb, and sprinted down the alley. A rotten meat scent spilled out of the garbage container. Rats picked at chicken bones on the broken macadam.

His arms and legs pumped. Thomas knew Lambert had the best chance of catching LeVar. Though he kept in shape, Thomas couldn't outrun an eighteen-year-old with a sprinter physique. But as he followed the gang member's route, Thomas was shocked to see LeVar two hundred feet ahead. He'd gained on the boy. A surge of adrenaline shot through his body. LeVar looked over his shoulder, spotted Thomas, and ran faster. At the end of another alleyway, the teen stopped when the cruiser screeched to a halt, blocking his escape route. The boy turned on a dime and cut past a row of brownstone apartments. Thomas pointed in the direction LeVar ran, and Lambert threw the cruiser into reverse.

Chain-link fences guarded the apartments. An elderly white woman with a cigarette dangling between her lips eyed him from the steps. When Thomas asked which direction LeVar ran, the woman turned her head and took a long drag on the cigarette. The clamor of a metal trash can toppling caught Thomas's attention. He raced toward the noise as LeVar, who'd fallen, dragged himself up and limped toward an abandoned warehouse. Boards covered half the windows. The open windows were soulless eyes peering out at the city. When LeVar kicked through a doorway, Thomas raised the radio to his lips.

"Lambert, he's inside a warehouse on the corner of Greenbriar and State."

"Roger that. Backup is on the way."

Sirens howled inside the city. His chest heaving, Thomas drew his weapon and plunged inside the warehouse. Dust motes swam through shafts of light. Vermin droppings covered the floor, and the warehouse smelled like urine and vomit. Two doorways stood closed to his left and right. Another door hung open straight ahead. It led down a dark hallway. His heart pounded as he listened.

Footfalls thumped at the end of the hall before another door slammed. Thomas radioed to Lambert again and hurried toward the hallway. Insulation and spiderwebs hung from the ceiling, and missing ceiling tiles revealed rusted pipes and frayed wires. His shoe crunched on a piece of glass. Two hypodermic needles lay amid the trash. Another door opened and closed inside the warehouse. The sirens drew closer, though it was impossible to gauge their distance inside the rundown labyrinth.

Thomas crossed a storage room littered with decaying cardboard boxes. Reams of paper drifted like phantoms as the wind crawled through the building. He'd lost LeVar. Lambert and local backup might catch the teenager if they blocked the exits. But that wouldn't stop LeVar from leaping out a broken window and sprinting down another alley.

A noise on the other side of a closed door brought Thomas to a stop. He placed his back against the wall and waited, one hand edging toward the cobweb-covered doorknob. A floorboard squealed from the next room.

Drawing a breath, Thomas reached for the door and spun through the entryway with the Glock raised.

The gun barrel pushed against his back. His vision clouded as the phantom of a gunshot wound from six months ago clawed at his insides. He heard the blast of the gun, then frantic yells as the task force hit the ground.

"Freeze!"

A woman's voice. Thomas lowered his weapon and glanced over his shoulder.

Chelsey Byrd fixed her gun on him.

24

"Shit!"

Chelsey stuffed the pistol into her holster.

"Chelsey? What are you doing here?"

"I should ask you the same question."

Chelsey wore a black leather jacket, blue jeans, and running sneakers. She was better dressed to chase a fleeing suspect than Thomas. At the far end of the building, a window shattered.

"Dammit," Chelsey said, pacing the room. "I lost him."

"Why are you chasing LeVar Hopkins?"

"That's none of your business."

"This badge says it *is* my business. LeVar Hopkins is a suspect in the Wolf Lake murder. You shouldn't be here, and it's illegal to interfere in a county investigation."

She sniffed.

"Back for one week, and you already run the place."

"What's your stake in this, Chelsey? You realize how dangerous this part of Harmon is."

"I can take care of myself."

"Are you certain? What if I was LeVar, or a member of the Kings?"

"Then I would have squeezed the trigger. Don't act like I can't take care of myself, Thomas. I got the jump on you."

He opened his mouth to argue and bit his lip. She was right.

"Let's start over. My partner and I spotted LeVar a few blocks east of the warehouse, and I chased him inside. Why are you after LeVar?"

Chelsey set a hand on her hip and stared at the open ceiling tiles in frustration. She fished inside her leather jacket, removed a white card, and handed it to Thomas. He turned the card over in his hand and stared.

Chelsey Byrd
Private Investigator
Wolf Lake Consulting

"You're a private investigator?"

She squared her shoulders.

"Is that a problem?"

"Wolf Lake Consulting. Wait, I just met someone from Wolf Lake Consulting. Raven?"

Chelsey took the card back and stuffed it inside her wallet.

"She's my partner, yes. How do you know Raven?"

Thomas took a step backward. Chelsey Byrd ran a private investigation firm in Wolf Lake? His head swam.

"I arrested a man outside the Wolf Lake Inn after he rammed some guy's VW with a truck."

"The Hugh Fitzgerald case," Chelsey said with an eye roll. "That turned out to be one big cluster. Raven handled the mess, but I never should have accepted the case. The guy is out of his mind."

"And now someone hired you to investigate LeVar Hopkins."

"That's between me and my client."

Thomas swiped a cobweb off his sleeve.

"Wait, you're the private investigator Tessa Windrow hired."

Chelsey pantomimed zipping her lips shut.

"I never imagined you'd become a private investigator," Thomas said.

She watched him from the corner of her eye.

"Surprised?"

"A little. Okay, a lot. Still, you have the mind for the work."

"Thanks, but I don't need you to justify my career path."

"I didn't mean it that way." After years of wondering what had become of Chelsey, they ended up tracking the same criminal. "Off the record, multiple eyewitnesses spotted LeVar canvassing the area between the lake and state park. Then Sunday night, someone dumped a body in the water."

Her eyes swung to his.

"Was it Erika?"

Thomas stuffed his hands into his pockets.

"I can't tell you that."

"Now who's being uncooperative?"

"The truth is, I'm waiting on a definitive answer from the medical examiner's office."

"Thomas, I saw the video."

"Yeah, you and the rest of the world. Every time a site bans the video, another posts it." He leaned against the wall and closed his eyes. "I can't definitively say the woman in the video is Erika Windrow. The picture is too dark and grainy."

"But you're sure it's her. Who else could it be?"

The old building stood in quiet solitude as grit rained through holes in the ceiling. Upstairs, rats skittered and clawed across the floor. A vein pulsed inside his neck. He had so many questions for Chelsey, and none of them seemed appropriate for the current situation. But he couldn't avoid her forever. They lived in the same village, and now that he knew Chelsey was a private investigator, they'd cross paths until one of them moved on.

"Chelsey, what's done is done. But I wish you'd spoken to me when—"

"I don't want to talk about it, Thomas. That was a long time ago, and we moved on."

More unasked questions lingered. Why was it important to him? His time with Chelsey occurred a lifetime ago.

"Look," she said, releasing a breath. "We have to coexist. This isn't the last time we'll run into each other on a case. The past is the past, and we're adults now."

"For what it's worth, I think it's great you became a P.I. I have no problem working with you."

She glanced at him in suspicion.

"I'm a different person now."

"That's obvious."

She let out a breath and folded her arms.

"Now I have to tell my client I lost LeVar again. Second time this week." Second time? Chelsey had a better bead on LeVar Hopkins than the Nightshade County Sheriff's Department. "Anyway, it's futile. You don't find LeVar Hopkins. LeVar Hopkins finds you."

His radio squawked. A Harmon PD cruiser spotted LeVar a quarter mile from the warehouse as he cut between two apartment complexes in the center of the city. They'd lost him. Thomas sighed.

"Let's get out of this place before it grows on us."

"Good idea," she said, swiping insulation off her shoulder.

An uncomfortable moment followed when they moved toward the door at the same time. Thomas solved the issue by pulling the door open for Chelsey. She pressed her lips together and hurried past. Before they reached the corridor, he moved in front of her.

"You don't have to protect me, you know?" she said from behind. The smell of her perfume made his chest thump. "My gun is bigger than yours." He snorted and ignored the double entendre. "I should have asked. How are your parents?"

He stumbled and regained his footing.

"They're the same," he said. This wasn't the time to tell Chelsey about his father's diagnosis. "They're still unhappy I went into law enforcement. Remember Uncle Truman?"

"Sure do. I heard he passed a while back. I'm sorry." She remembered. He chewed on the inside of his cheek. "Do you recall what you told me after we started dating?"

He sifted through a catalog of memories as he led her through the crumbling warehouse, one eye on the sagging ceiling. The building wanted to collapse and smother them, claiming Thomas and Chelsey as its final victims.

"I don't remember. Like you said, that was a long time ago."

"You told me you'd buy Truman's house one day."

Thomas cleared the frog from his throat.

"Well, I made true on my promise."

She grabbed his arm and pulled him around. Chelsey's eyes lit with excitement and a touch of wonder.

"Seriously? The place on the lake? You really did it. Congratulations."

Thomas shrugged and continued toward the exit. Where was it? He'd taken the wrong hallway and gotten them lost.

"The house needs work, but it's coming along."

He wanted to invite her over. Then he remembered Ray Welch. If Chelsey had her life together, what was she doing with a creep like Ray?

A floorboard creaked at the end of the hall. They both reached for their weapons before the door swung open. Deputy Lambert raised his head in alarm.

"Everything all right here?" Lambert asked, eyeing Chelsey with suspicion.

"We're searching for a way out of the warehouse."

Thomas made introductions as they walked. Lambert ushered them out of the building. The cruiser waited at the curb.

"Do you need a ride back to your car?" Thomas asked, hoping Chelsey would say yes.

"I'm right around the corner. See you soon."

Then she disappeared around the warehouse.

25

He'd been inside her house again.

Raven Hopkins scanned the downstairs of her one-story house two hundred yards east of the lake. A couch cushion jutted forth like a protruding tongue, and the blanket draped over the end appeared rumpled. She'd folded it better than that. LeVar had been inside the house and slept on the couch while she was at work. She moved to the kitchen and peered inside the refrigerator. One can of Coke missing, along with a few slices of ham. If she checked the bread, she'd find two slices gone.

She collapsed on a chair at the kitchen table and rubbed her eyes. There was no point in calling her brother. He'd deny coming to the house, as always. LeVar didn't have a key. Raven got the distinct impression locks didn't stop her brother. Was he in trouble and hiding from somebody? LeVar never should have joined the Kings. Guilt chewed a hole through Raven's stomach. After her mother threw her out of the house at seventeen, she vowed she'd never set foot in her home again. Already addicted to drugs, Serena gave birth to Raven at sixteen. She wasn't prepared to raise a child. Now Serena didn't make it through a day without a heroin fix, and she hadn't held a job in two years. LeVar covered the rent. The Harmon Kings paid well, but membership came at a price.

Through the window, Raven watched Buck Benson's truck motor up his driveway. The confederate flag rippled with pride. Raven's great aunt flew a confederate flag in front of her South Carolina home. It seemed odd—a black woman displaying the confederate flag. But Aunt Martha grew up in the south and considered the flag a symbol of southern pride. Buck Benson was a lifelong resident of Nightshade County. There was only one reason he flew that flag. She caught his beady eyes glaring with disdain toward her property. Benson gunned the engine and rocketed down the lake road, leaving a trail of exhaust smoke.

Her phone rang. Chelsey.

"Where are you?" Raven asked, moving to the counter. As she theorized, she'd misplaced two slices of wheat bread.

"I'm coming out of Harmon and driving back to the office."

"Harmon? What are you doing there?"

Chelsey paused.

"Just checking on a new client." A horn beeped in the background. "Hey, when is the last time you heard from your brother?"

"A few weeks ago. Why?"

"My client owns a business in Harmon. Someone robbed the place, and he thinks the Harmon Kings might be responsible."

Raven always knew when Chelsey twisted the truth. The waver in the woman's voice gave her away.

"LeVar is a lot of things, but he's not a thief."

"I'm not accusing him, just wondering if he knows who hit the place up. Could you tell him to call me?"

Raven tapped her nails against the kitchen table.

"I'll give him your number."

No way LeVar would call Chelsey. He could smell a setup.

The realization slapped Raven across the face. Chelsey was investigating LeVar.

"Thanks, Raven. Look, I have two more stops to make, then I'll swing by the office, if you want to meet me there. We need to complete the paperwork on the Fitzgerald case."

Raven glanced at the time. If she hurried, she'd beat Chelsey to the office and snoop around before her boss arrived.

"That works for me. I'll meet you in half an hour."

After Chelsey hung up, Raven surveyed the windows and doors and ensured she'd locked the house tight. Between her brother breaking in and a redneck psycho living down the road, she wasn't taking chances. She pointed the key fob at her black Nissan Rogue and hopped in. Ten minutes later, she drove into the small lot behind Wolf Lake Consulting. The office was a converted two-bedroom, single-story house three miles from the lake. She slipped the key into the door and searched the street for Chelsey's vehicle. Then she stepped inside and locked the door behind her.

A greeting desk stood beyond the entryway, but the firm didn't employ a secretary. They didn't attract enough clients to justify the cost. On the right side of the hallway, a kitchen painted in powder-blues held a refrigerator. A kettle sat on the gas stove, and two boxes of tea and an economy size can of coffee rested on the counter. The converted master bedroom served as the office's focal area. Chelsey's desk sat near a window overlooking the village shopping district, and Raven's table offered a stream view. She set her bag down on the table and hurried to Chelsey's computer. Damn. Chelsey had shut the PC down before she left, and the ancient computer took a lifetime to reboot.

While the system loaded, Raven pulled the drawers open on

Chelsey's desk. She felt sleazy searching through her boss's files. Chelsey was her friend, and Raven trusted her. But family came first. Besides, she wasn't tampering with Chelsey's investigation, just checking what the woman had on LeVar. She found the Fitzgerald file, and below that, a folder holding the Merriam case from last month. Nothing else.

She whipped open another drawer and found a set of keys and wasp spray. They'd battled a wasp nest last autumn. Outside, a motor rumbled as footsteps shuffled up the walkway. Raven threw the drawer shut and backed away from the desk. Moving along the wall, she returned to the entryway and peeked through the window. False alarm. The sound she'd heard was a woman power walking past the office. She checked for Chelsey's car again and hurried back to the computer. The PC took forever to load, and now it asked her to install an update.

She clicked out of the message and scanned the hard drive. Where would Chelsey hide information about LeVar? None of the folder names caught her eye. But she knew her way around a computer. Clicking on the sorting tool, she displayed the folders by date. Someone had modified a folder named TW this morning.

A noise inside the house brought her head up. The old place always popped and groaned when the temperature changed. Her senses on high alert, she skimmed the file contents and opened a sub-folder of pictures. The photographs depicted a teenage girl with light-brown hair pulled into a ponytail. She recognized the girl from the newspaper. Erika Windrow, the teenager who disappeared from Harmon. The second photograph of Erika appeared recent. Gone was the hopeful smile from the first picture. This version of Erika was sullen. She wore fishnet stockings and heels with a purse slung over her shoulder. Two fingers clamped on a cigarette as the girl stood across the street from an adult toy store.

TW. Wasn't the girl's mother Tessa Windrow? Yes, Raven remembered the woman's name from the newspaper article. Which meant Tessa Windrow, not some nameless store owner in Harmon, was Chelsey's secret client.

In the third picture, someone had cropped the previous photograph and zoomed in on Erika's tattoo. The poor girl belonged to the 315 Royals.

A fourth photograph caught LeVar crossing a busy city road. Raven recognized the Harmon backdrop.

Before she could dig through the other photographs, a key turned in the lock. Raven began clicking out of the photographs, but she'd opened too many. As she raced to close the images, the front door swung open, and village sounds filtered through the converted home.

"Raven? You here?"

Raven's hands trembled while the mouse flew around the screen. Three more pictures to close. The floorboards groaned outside the threshold. The last image closed when Chelsey turned the corner. Raven sat on the edge of the desk and opened a blank document.

"Hey, I got here a few seconds ago," Raven said, fighting to keep her voice steady. "I'm starting a new document so we can close out the Fitzgerald case."

Chelsey set her keys on the desk and studied Raven. She knew something was up.

"You want coffee?"

"Please," Raven said, pinching the bridge of her nose. "I've been battling a headache since this morning."

"I'll start a fresh pot and grab you the ibuprofen bottle."

"Appreciate it."

She waited until Chelsey reached the kitchen before exhaling. Her eyes moved back to the screen. She'd forgotten the tattoo photograph. It displayed beneath the blank document. Praying Chelsey hadn't noticed, she closed the picture.

Was LeVar a suspect in Erika Windrow's death?

26

Jenson Hodges shoved the rolling mail cart out of the elevator and followed the long, gloomy hallway inside the *Bluewater Tribune* headquarters. He hated the mundane work. But the Wolf Lake High careers program earned him a free pass from study hall and home economics. An aspiring journalist, Jenson dreamed of a full ride at Syracuse University's Newhouse School of Communications. He needed work experience to beef up his application.

Not that he learned a damn thing working at the Tribune. While the reporters researched stories and raced against deadlines upstairs, Jenson brewed coffee, ensured the kitchen stayed clean, and every weekday at eleven o'clock, he gathered the mail. The postman delivered to the first floor and set envelopes and packages on a counter inside the receiving room. It was Jenson's job to sort through the deliveries, categorize the mail, and make certain the mail reached the appropriate personnel.

Thursdays dragged longer than other weekdays. The proximity to the weekend, so close he could almost touch it, made Thursday worse than Monday. Tomorrow night was the Magnolia Dance. Until he put twenty pounds on his waif-like frame and cleared up the acne, he wouldn't win a girlfriend. Still, attending the dance was fun, and his friends would be there. He nudged his glasses up his nose and wondered if contacts would help his chances.

Except for the administrative assistant on the first floor, nobody worked on this level. Occasionally Jenson passed the janitor mopping the floors, and the reporters bustled through at lunchtime. He passed time listening to music and podcasts. Today, he caught up on sports scores.

He stopped at the receiving counter and sneezed. This room was dusty as hell. Green tiles peeled off the floor, and mouse droppings littered the corner. He couldn't see past the filthy window. Shadows strolled past as people moved through the village, and a hint of dingy yellow on the glass told him the sun was out. He grabbed two fistfuls of envelopes and placed them on the cart for sorting. The square cardboard box caught his attention. No return address listed. The sender addressed the box to the *Bluewater Tribune* editorial staff.

Jenson eyed the box with suspicion. There were a lot of crazy people in the world, and lunatics with agendas sent bombs when they disagreed with opinionated articles. The box was about the right size for a bomb. Or was it? He'd never seen a bomb. All he had to go on were the black oval bombs from Saturday morning cartoons, the ones with long fuses that sparked and whirred. He nudged the box with his toe and something shifted inside. Next, he lifted it from the sides and tested the weight. The size looked appropriate for a bowling ball, but this box was too light. Plastic crinkled inside.

The smell hit him. Jenson recoiled and placed a hand to his mouth. Sometimes readers sent food to the newspaper, and this genius didn't realize perishable food spoiled. He wanted to toss the box into the trash. Better not. If the package turned out to be important, he'd catch hell from the editor.

The stench grew as Jenson hovered over the container and considered what to do. He didn't want to get close to the package. Maybe he should call upstairs and ask the editor. Not a good idea. Nobody took Jenson seriously, and at this rate, he'd never convince the reporters to let him coauthor an article.

He bent at the knees, held his breath, and hefted the cardboard box. The bottom tore. As he fought to gather the contents before it smashed against the tile, the severed head broke through the cardboard and splattered on the floor.

Jenson leaned over the garbage can and vomited.

THOMAS STOOD over the woman's head. Virgil Harbough, the Nightshade County medical examiner, knelt and clicked a photograph. Behind them, Sheriff Gray ordered Aguilar and Lambert to keep the reporters from reaching the scene. The irony wasn't lost on Thomas. The deputies prevented photographers and reporters from covering a story inside their own building.

"I take it this is Erika Windrow's missing head," Harbough said, rubbing his mustache.

The ME had determined the butchered body belonged to Erika Windrow.

"It's hard to tell, but the facial features appear consistent with a female teenager," Thomas said.

The ME wore ashen slacks and a blue button-down. In the autopsy room, he'd wear scrubs. His striped tie dangled over the head, and Thomas worried the tip would drape against Erika Windrow's bloated lips. Harbough tucked the tie inside his shirt and wiped beneath his nose. Gray pushed the entry door open and let the CSI team inside.

"Is that the kid who discovered the head?" Harbough asked, tilting his chin at a scrawny teenage boy in the corner.

"Jenson Hodges," Thomas said.

"He doesn't look old enough to work at the *Tribune*."

Thomas explained Jenson was a high school student. The boy clutched his arms together, unable to stay warm, though the crowded room felt stifling. Thomas and Harbough cleared out when a female CSI technician from the county lab approached.

"Did either of you touch the remains?" she asked. Thomas shook his head. "What about the kid?"

Thomas moved his gaze to Jenson, who answered Aguilar's questions while Lambert kept the reporters at bay.

"He claims he didn't. The box broke when he lifted it, and the kid says he jumped back. Sounds like a natural reaction. But I won't be surprised if he touched the head."

Harbough nursed an achy back as Gray joined Thomas.

"I'll have an answer for you tomorrow morning," the ME said.

"Thanks, Virgil," Gray said. The sheriff turned to Thomas while the medical examiner took a phone call. Gray nodded at the torn cardboard box, marked by a yellow evidence card. "We can figure out who sent the box, right?"

"The barcode will tell us where the package originated from. Chances are our killer paid cash and lied about his name. If we're lucky, the post office cameras caught this guy."

Gray puffed out his mustache.

"The forensics team needs to process the evidence before we take the box."

"We don't need the box," Thomas said, removing his phone.

He swiped to the camera app and photographed the code.

"Will that work?"

"It should. Let's take this to the nearest post office and figure out who sent the box."

27

The woman behind the counter at the Wolf Lake post office scanned the barcode while Thomas and Gray waited. The female postmaster told them the package came from Harmon. Gray wasn't surprised. Everything bad came from Harmon.

Thomas rode shotgun in Gray's cruiser. The sheriff weaved through rush hour traffic, flashing his lights to bypass a glut. Thomas sensed the sheriff's desperation to get answers.

"I can't wrap my head around it," Gray said, searching for an opening as two delivery trucks blocked a busy intersection. He laid on the horn. "What kind of sicko dumps a body in a lake, knowing it will wash ashore, then sends body parts to the newspaper?"

Peering through the passenger window, his eyes scanning the sidewalk for LeVar Hopkins, Thomas said, "The killer wants attention. It's a game to him."

"The idiot psycho will get himself caught. You'd assume he'd bury the body where nobody would find it."

Thomas grunted. During his decade with the LAPD, he worked alongside homicide detectives. Most killers functioned as Gray theorized—they buried the evidence. On rare occasions, homicide encountered a lunatic who flaunted his murders. Thomas rubbed his chin. Why would LeVar Hopkins or the Harmon Kings advertise a murder? Gangs didn't relish police attention and preferred to rule over their fiefdoms without interference.

As if Gray read Thomas's thoughts, he said, "We need hard evidence on LeVar Hopkins. I'm tired of conjecture and rumors. This scumbag spends more time on the lake than I do, and nobody can find him. We still haven't linked him to a single gang-related homicide."

Gray turned the cruiser into the parking lot and angled the vehicle between two postal trucks. The Harmon post office nestled between a hardware store and a Chinese restaurant on the east side of the city. The beige brick building was a squat rectangle with a handicap accessible ramp in front. Three blue mailboxes lined the concrete sidewalk leading to the ramp, and a food donation box stood beside the entry doors. Inside, their footsteps squeaked and echoed on the polished floor. A heavy warehouse, cardboard scent pervaded the building.

The sheriff led Thomas to the counter and waved down a bearded man behind the desk. Pete Bottoman, the Harmon postmaster, called an employee from the back to man his place at the counter. Bottoman met Gray and Thomas at the end.

"I need a barcode scanned," Gray said, motioning for Thomas to hand him his phone.

Thomas loaded the picture and placed the phone on the counter. Bottoman donned reading glasses and examined the photograph.

"This should do," the postmaster said. He scanned the image and waited until his computer beeped. "All right, Sheriff. The package in question originated at this post office at eleven o'clock yesterday. Sender listed as Henry Washington."

"Generic name. Did he show identification?"

The postmaster shrugged.

"Even if he did, he could have used a fake."

"Eleven yesterday." Gray set his arms on the counter. "Any chance you have surveillance cameras?"

"We do," Bottoman said, nodding at a camera pointing down from the ceilings.

"I need the footage from yesterday morning."

Bottoman cocked an eyebrow, but he didn't question why.

"Give me ten minutes to make the transfer."

After the postmaster disappeared, Thomas questioned the two employees working the counter. Neither remembered the box. The Harmon post office was the county's busiest, and it was impossible to remember everybody who came through.

"Sorry about the delay, Sheriff," Bottoman said, handing the sheriff the USB thumb drive. "Our computer systems are running like molasses today."

Thomas slid into the passenger seat and pocketed the thumb drive. Gray slammed the door. Frustration tightened the sheriff's hands. When was the last time Nightshade County dealt with a high-profile murder? Thomas couldn't recall anything like this during his childhood.

A long sedan pulled beside the cruiser at the red light. Music poured through the windows, and a mix of white and black teenagers, some wearing bandannas, glared at Thomas through the windows. His spine clenched. The kid in the passenger seat reminded Thomas of a gang member at the house the LAPD and DEA raided. Hidden in his lap, his hands twisted into fists until the light turned green and the sedan drove off.

"I want you to sift through the footage when we get back to the station," Gray said, not picking up on Thomas's anxiety.

"I'm familiar with process."

How long would his PTSD last?

"Lambert is on his way to Harmon to question the prostitutes again. Not that it will do a damn bit of good." He shook his head. "One of their own died, and they refuse to talk. You'd think they'd cooperate so we can catch the bastard. If LeVar Hopkins is killing prostitutes, any of them could be next."

Thomas shifted in his seat. He wanted to argue they lacked evidence linking LeVar to Erika Windrow's murder. But he wasn't an LAPD detective anymore, just a county deputy. Sheriff Gray had run this county for nineteen years and served the department twice as long. If there was one thing Thomas knew about Gray, when the sheriff got an idea in his head, you couldn't dislodge it with a pry bar. He'd blame Father Josiah Fowler for Lana's death forever, though he couldn't prove Fowler crossed the centerline and forced Lana off the road. Still, Gray was a good man and right more than he was wrong. Gray believed LeVar killed Erika. Thomas needed evidence LeVar was innocent before he crossed the sheriff.

The cruiser hit the interstate when Gray's phone rang. The sheriff dropped the phone and cursed.

"I can't figure out this Bluetooth nonsense," he said.

Thomas picked the phone off the floor. Aguilar was calling.

"It's Deputy Aguilar," said Thomas. "You want me to answer?"

"Might as well. I can't talk to her unless I stop."

Aguilar sounded surprised when Thomas answered.

"The forensics team found a handwritten link inside the box," Aguilar said.

"A link to a website?"

"It looks that way. I'm back at the office now and typing the URL into the computer."

Gray glanced at Thomas.

"What's happening?"

Thomas lowered the phone.

"Something about a website link written on the box."

Fiddling with the console, Thomas reset the Bluetooth settings and pushed the call through the stereo speakers. Aguilar drew a sharp breath.

"It's another video."

Gray stepped on the gas and passed an eighteen-wheeler.

"What do you mean, another video?" Gray asked, his voice tinged with irritation and panic.

Aguilar's voice cracked.

"The killer. He has Erika Windrow's head."

28

Raven slapped the steering wheel. She'd forgotten her lunch for the second time this week. As she motored home along the lake, she glanced over the water, where a sailboat cruised with the wind. Winter had given up, sun glistened off the water, and there wasn't a cloud in the sky. She could think of a million things she'd rather be doing besides filing paperwork at the office. And since Chelsey was at the office, Raven couldn't hack through her computer files.

She parked the Rogue in front of the garage and stepped into the driveway. The temperature hovered in the sixties, and she stretched her arms toward the sky, relishing the heat. Maybe she'd call Chelsey and take the afternoon off. Her boss wouldn't appreciate the short notice, and they still needed to finish the Hugh Fitzgerald paperwork. But Chelsey owed Raven three days of vacation time before June.

She rounded the vehicle and snatched her purse off the passenger seat. A glint of metal caught her eye as her gaze wandered to the lake road. Beyond the bend, a black Chrysler Limited motored closer. LeVar.

Thinking on her feet, Raven jumped into the car and backed

up the driveway. A stand of pine trees shielded her SUV from the road. She nestled the Rogue behind the trees, worried the tires would stick in the muddy terrain. Then she sat and waited.

A minute later, LeVar's Chrysler stopped in front of the garage. Her brother hopped out of the car while she watched him through the trees. He wouldn't notice the Rogue unless he circled the house. But LeVar sensed something was wrong. He jiggled the keys in his hands and moved his eyes across the windows. For a moment, Raven thought LeVar would climb into his car and drive away. After a second of consideration, he strode to the door and climbed the steps. His eyes swept left and right. From his pocket, he removed a lock pick set. Son-of-a-bitch. If he'd asked Raven for a key, she would have given him one. This violated her trust.

The door swung open. He stood on the threshold, listening, still sensing eyes on him. Then he stepped inside.

Raven slipped out of the Rogue and edged the door closed. She crept past the pines, thankful for the soft bed of needles concealing her movement. The woman moved to the outer wall and stood with her back against the house. A window inside the kitchen stood open a crack. Inside, dishes clinked as LeVar fished inside the cupboards. With her brother occupied, Raven jogged to the driveway and waited on the top step. She could be quiet when she needed to be. A quick turn of the lock, and she'd take LeVar by surprise.

Her hands went cold and tingled. LeVar was the Harmon Kings' enforcer. No matter how much she loved her brother, she feared him. LeVar didn't go anywhere without a weapon. What if he turned on her?

With one trembling hand, she inserted the key and twisted. Raven gritted her teeth when the locking mechanism clicked.

She darted from the entryway to the hallway and waited. The refrigerator opened as he rustled inside the drawers. When plastic crinkled, Raven swung around the wall and moved on cat's paws into the living room. Her back against the dividing wall, she stood ten feet from the most feared gang member in Harmon.

He's my brother, she told herself. LeVar won't hurt me.

When footsteps moved across the kitchen, Raven held her breath and spun around the wall. He pulled up in shock and nearly dropped the sandwich. Dreadlocks spilling down his shoulders, he glared at her with his chin hanging to his chest. Blue jeans hung low on his hips, and a muscle shirt displayed chiseled, tattooed arms. Her eyes fixed on the Taurus 9mm poking out from his waistband.

He glared at her, at a loss for words. After he set his sandwich on the counter, he folded his arms over his chest.

"What up, Raven?"

"You break inside my house and ask me what the hell's up?"

"No need for that noise. I'm just grabbing a little food for the road."

"That's not your food, LeVar. Last I checked, you don't buy the groceries around here."

He puffed his chest out and pushed past her. As she stood frozen to the floor, he opened the pantry and pawed inside.

"Yeah, well, you don't buy Mom's groceries, neither. That's all me. And the rent. So don't come at me with no bullshit 'cause I made a sandwich." He grunted. "Don't you got protein bars or something? What's this granola shit? You a squirrel?"

Raven pulled his hand away and closed the pantry door.

"You can't come here unannounced like you own the place."

"I'm getting a drink of water, then I'll get out of your hair."

She swerved to block his access to the sink. He tilted his head and narrowed his eyes. She responded by folding her arms over her chest.

"Stubborn bitch."

"Something is going on with you, LeVar. I don't hear from you for months, and now you're stealing my food and sleeping on the couch when I'm not home." He blinked in surprise. "Oh, you think I didn't notice? I work for a private investigator. Nobody breaks inside my place without me finding out."

"Ain't like I'm stealing. Now move out of the way and let me get a drink."

She sighed and moved away. He opened the tap and placed his lips under the stream before she yanked him back.

"What are you, an animal? I'll get you a glass."

LeVar's lips pulled tight. Raven stood on tiptoe and removed a glass from the top shelf. She set it down hard in front of him. Not removing his eyes from hers, LeVar filled the glass and drank half the contents before coming up for air. Something was up with her brother. His feet shifted.

"I need to ask you something," she said, fixing him with a hard glare.

"Ask away, Sis. I got nothing to hide."

Yeah, right.

"Did you kill that girl?"

"What girl? I ain't killed nobody."

"The girl on the television, LeVar. Don't play stupid with me. She whored for the Royals."

"Dammit, Sis. You trying to say I had some bitch killed because the Royals owned her? You're crazy."

"The cops say you did it."

"The cops don't know shit."

"You better watch yourself, LeVar. People are looking for you right now." Should she tell him about Chelsey? How would LeVar react to Raven's boss investigating him? "If you're innocent, come forward and clear your name."

He snickered.

"Listen to you. Are you from Wolf Lake or Harmon? Since

when do cops give a shit about guilt and innocence in the hood? Fuck that. They want me, they can come looking."

"Don't talk like that."

"Why not? I'm a cold-blooded killer. Ain't that what everyone says?" He set the glass down with a thunk. "I'm using the bathroom, then I'm out of here."

Exasperated, she collapsed into a chair and ran a hand through her hair. Down the hall, he relieved himself with the door wide open. He flushed and ran the water. At least he washed his hands afterward.

"You're not a cold-blooded killer," she said, scrubbing a hand across her face.

"What?"

"I said you're not a—"

A car motored down her driveway. One eye on the hallway as she fretted over LeVar, Raven rushed to the living room window and peered between the curtains. A green Honda Civic stopped halfway up the incline. Shit. Chelsey was here. Had her boss followed Raven? Outside, Chelsey climbed from her car and removed the gun from her holster.

"LeVar," she whispered.

No answer.

The faucet shut off inside the bathroom. Raven ran to the hallway and bent her neck around the wall.

"LeVar, my boss is here."

Would he recognize the danger? LeVar had no idea Wolf Lake Consulting pursued him. A knock brought Raven's head around. Chelsey looked like a phantom through the translucent curtain. Excuses flew through Raven's head. She couldn't hide LeVar's presence. His Chrysler sat in clear view.

"Raven? Are you okay?"

Christ.

Chelsey considered LeVar a threat. If she broke inside and

drew her gun, the encounter would end with somebody dead. As Raven contemplated opening the door, the bathroom window slid open. She wasted ten seconds, giving LeVar time to squeeze through the window while Chelsey jiggled the doorknob.

Raven pulled the door open and feigned indifference.

"What's wrong, Chelsey?"

Chelsey barged inside and swept her gaze across the room.

"Where is he?"

"Where's who?"

"Don't start. Your brother's car is in the driveway."

When Chelsey moved toward the hallway, Raven slid in front of her.

"Yeah? So what?" The challenge on Raven's face dared Chelsey to admit she was investigating LeVar. "He's my brother, and he's welcome in my house anytime."

"So why did he climb out the bathroom window?"

How did she—

Before Raven could react, Chelsey whipped around. Outside, the Chrysler roared to life. Chelsey stumbled onto the front steps as LeVar's vehicle spit gravel and carved two divots through the grass. The car burst up the driveway and squealed when the tires met the lake road. Chelsey stuffed the gun into her holster.

"God dammit!"

"You want to tell me what that was about?"

Chelsey swirled to Raven.

"How many times has LeVar been to your house? You shouldn't hide these things from me."

"You're acting crazy, Chelsey." Chelsey opened her mouth and stopped. Raven set her hands on her hips. "No more bull-shit. Why are you after my brother?"

Chelsey dropped her arms to her sides and paced.

"I didn't want to tell you. Erika Windrow's mother hired me to investigate the murder, and LeVar is my top suspect."

"That's ridiculous. LeVar didn't kill that girl."

"No? Then why did he run?"

"Probably because you broke into my house with a gun. Where we're from, someone comes into your home with a gun and starts yelling nonsense, you don't stick around to ask what the issue is. When were you gonna tell me?"

Chelsey chewed on her response.

"You saw the files on my computer," Chelsey said. "The modified date changed on the folder."

Now it was Raven's turn to go silent.

"I didn't touch your files."

"No, but you created the Hugh Fitzgerald document. By default, you saved it to the last folder you opened."

"Shit."

"Trust me, Raven."

"Trust is a two-way street. You're here because of LeVar, and you didn't tell me anything about the case."

"Because you're biased. You never would have let me investigate LeVar."

"It's not bias. I know my brother better than you or the sheriff. He's not a killer."

"LeVar runs with the most dangerous gang in the county."

"Doesn't mean he killed anyone."

Chelsey pulled the keys from her pocket.

"I should get back to the office. We'll discuss this later." As Chelsey turned to leave, she glared over her shoulder. "If your brother makes contact, you better tell me, Raven."

29

The video spread like wildfire across the internet while Thomas reviewed the footage. The killer stood off camera. He zoomed in on Erika Windrow's face, the head surrounded by burning candles, part of some sick ritual.

"She's the first, but she won't be the last," the disembodied voice boasted.

The killer disguised his speech with a voice changer, deepening the voice so it sounded like something out of a spy movie.

"Can we determine who uploaded the video?" Gray asked behind Thomas.

"He used the name Max Cady as before."

"What the hell is it with the internet? You can upload anything without revealing your name. I don't understand how any of this is legal."

Thomas exhaled.

"They embed EXIF data in images and videos. The data tells us when the user created the image, and often where he captured the footage."

"So if he recorded this footage in Wolf Lake, we can prove it."

"Theoretically."

"Get that information. Then go over the post office footage. If the camera caught LeVar Hopkins shipping the package, we'll nail him to the wall."

Thomas downloaded the video and interrogated the file. According to the EXIF data, the killer created the footage two days ago, and the video originated from Harmon. Still, he couldn't prove the date and origin. If the killer brought the footage into editing software and compiled the recording, the data would refer to when he edited the video.

On a memo pad, he jotted the information down and left it on Gray's desk. Then he inserted the USB drive into the computer and downloaded the recording. While he waited for the copying process to finish, his phone rang.

"Hey, Thomas. This is Darren at the state park."

Thomas switched the phone to his other ear and picked up a pen.

"Hi, Darren. Sorry I haven't gotten in touch with you. We're up against it at the office with this murder case."

"Are the internet rumors true? The killer sent Erika Windrow's head to the *Bluewater Tribune*?"

"We're waiting on the ME for verification. But we have every reason to believe it's her."

"Any way to trace the sender?"

"I'm working on that right now. We have video footage from the Harmon Post Office. Is there a reason you called?"

"I spotted LeVar Hopkins down your way today."

Thomas tore another sheet from his memo pad.

"When?"

"About twenty minutes ago."

"Curious. I can't track him down in Harmon, and he keeps showing up near my house. What was he doing?"

"He pulled into a driveway on the opposite end of the lake. I did a little snooping, and the house belongs to Raven Hopkins,

LeVar's sister."

Chelsey's partner?

"Any chance this Raven Hopkins works for Wolf Lake Consulting?"

"That's her."

Thomas rubbed the back of his skull where a headache lingered.

"You there, Thomas?"

"I'm here. Just trying to process a series of coincidences. I need to go, Darren. Thank you for the information."

"Sure thing. I'll call you if LeVar shows his face again."

The internet gave Thomas the phone number for Wolf Lake Consulting. The last person he wanted to call was Chelsey Byrd. But if anyone could give him insight on Raven and LeVar, it was Chelsey. He stared at the number and concocted excuses not to call. Chelsey was Raven's boss, not her keeper, and she wasn't obligated to tell Thomas about Raven and LeVar. Still, Chelsey tried to capture LeVar yesterday. She also wanted to question the Harmon Kings member.

Before he decided, the copying process ended. Calling up the recording, Thomas scanned the video at high speed until the time code on the top right approached eleven o'clock. A flurry of activity kept the workers behind the counter busy. The line stretched out the door. Two minutes before eleven o'clock, a black youth in low hanging jeans and a t-shirt entered the picture at the back of the line. He held a square cardboard box in front of him. Thomas froze the image and enlarged the frame. Doing so blurred the picture and added noisy artifacts. But he saw the emblem on the youth's right arm. HK—Harmon Kings.

The youth wore a baseball cap, pulled low over his brow to conceal his face. This wasn't LeVar Hopkins. The kid wore his hair short, and he appeared small compared to the people waiting in line. Thomas captured the image and saved it to the disk drive. Maybe the lab could enhance the gangster's face.

The gang member moved two steps closer to the counter. A woman in heels and a long coat eyed him with trepidation. When the postal worker called the youth forward, the boy glanced at the camera. A quick swivel of the head. But it was enough for Thomas to freeze the video and capture a better photo. Now he saw facial features, including a crooked nose and a face splattered with freckles. So young. This kid wasn't older than fourteen, and Thomas doubted his name was Henry Washington. Why was he in the Harmon Kings? The idea this kid hacked Erika Windrow to pieces, filmed the remains, then mailed the head to the newspaper didn't sit right with Thomas. The kid on the security footage wasn't a hardened criminal or murderer.

Perhaps Gray was right about LeVar. The faux Henry Washington might have delivered the box under LeVar's orders. Whoever the boy was, Thomas needed his name.

He picked up the phone and dialed Wolf Lake Consulting before he talked himself out of it. Chelsey answered on the second ring. She sounded out of breath, as if she ran into the office moments ago.

"Chelsey, it's Thomas."

A quiet moment.

"What can I do for you?"

"You didn't tell me LeVar Hopkins's sister works for Wolf Lake Consulting."

"Is it important?"

Thomas waited until Maggie walked past.

"We're after the same perpetrator. Help me out, Chelsey. I haven't lived on the lake in over ten years. Now I discover Raven Hopkins lives a mile from my house, and the top suspect in Erika Windrow's murder is Raven's brother. You realize how many LeVar sightings I've fielded in the last week?"

Over the phone, he heard Chelsey tap her nails on the desk.

"Raven doesn't believe her brother murdered Erika Windrow."

Thomas glanced over his shoulder. Gray sat in his office, and Aguilar ran the blender inside the kitchen.

"The sheriff believes the Harmon Kings are involved."

"How did he determine that?"

Should he tell her about the post office footage?

"Eyewitness at the Harmon Post Office. Someone with an HK tattoo mailed that package to the Bluewater Tribune. There's a new video, Chelsey."

"Oh, no. Did he kill again?"

"Not yet. He posed her head among candles and uploaded the video."

"That's disgusting. Why?"

"Probably to gloat. We can't catch him, and he's toying with us."

"Send me the link."

"I'll send it through your contact form. Is that okay?"

He didn't want to ask Chelsey for her cell number.

"Yeah, that's probably the best way."

Did he hear disappointment in her voice?

"I need to speak with Raven."

"She won't talk about LeVar, Thomas."

Gray sauntered past. Thomas waited until the sheriff rounded the corner and lowered his voice.

"If she believes her brother is innocent, she needs to tell me what she knows and how I can get a hold of LeVar."

"Don't hold your breath. LeVar is a hard guy to find, and he likes it that way. I'll pass along the message. But I suggest you drive to her house. She'll avoid you, otherwise."

"Okay, that's what I'll do. Shall we keep the lines of communication open on LeVar Hopkins?"

"Only if you share information with me."

"You have my word, Chelsey."

"Promise me."

"I promise."

"Then we have an agreement."

"Thank you."

His insides buzzed when he hung up the phone. Three times he'd spoken with Chelsey since he returned to his hometown, and he couldn't get her out of his head.

Yet he sensed evasiveness. Did Chelsey intend to catch LeVar on her own?

30

Two days of sunshine had allowed the ground to dry. After a long day at the office, Thomas rented a sod cutter and grabbed supplies at the hardware store. When he arrived at Naomi's house, he unloaded 2x6 boards behind the house and built a pile. Removing the grass would have taken hours with a spade. The sod cutter proved its worth as he cut a long path from the backyard toward the lake and a bisecting walkway into his yard.

The sod cutter rumbled like a motorcycle, and the noise brought Naomi into the yard to observe. She demanded to pay for the supplies. Thomas declined since it had been his idea.

After he carved a shallow path, he laid the boards and framed the future walkway. As he set the frame in place, the deck door slid open, and Scout lifted herself over the lip and coasted down the ramp. Naomi followed with two glasses of iced tea. Thomas cut the motor and wiped his forehead on his t-shirt.

"Beautiful day," Naomi said, setting the drinks on a picnic table. "Except you won't take my money, and I feel guilty you're doing the work for free."

"It's no trouble. The ground finally dried, so I wanted to finish the project while the weather cooperated."

Naomi's eyes kept shifting to her daughter, as though she wanted to speak to Thomas without Scout present.

"Good afternoon, Scout," Thomas said, smoothing the soil. "The backyard seems in better shape. Why don't you check out my guest house? I unlocked the door."

The girl glanced at her mother for approval. Naomi nodded.

Scout pushed across the yard. When she was far enough away, Naomi turned to Thomas.

"I'm worried about Scout."

Thomas sipped his iced tea.

"Why are you worried?"

"It's this amateur investigation hobby. At first, I considered it a positive. Scout doesn't have friends at school, and I worry she's observing life rather than participating. Solving crimes, making friends on these forums, it seemed like a good thing for Scout. But now I'm worried. She won't admit it. But I'm positive she's trying to catch the crazy person who dumped the body in the lake. She's secretive, and she hides her computer screen when I come into her room. I'm worried she'll see something on the internet and it will affect her forever. She's only fourteen."

Thomas set his ankle on his opposite knee.

"You're right to be concerned. The horrors that make it onto the internet turn my stomach, and I've worked too many murder scenes to count."

She bit her lip and swiped the hair off her brow.

"Thomas, I saw the video."

"Erika Windrow's murder?"

"Yes. A friend sent me the link, and for reasons I can't explain...I made a mistake. I turned the video off after ten seconds. That was long enough. I haven't slept a wink since. Do you think Scout saw the video?"

Thomas thought back to his conversation with Scout yesterday. He didn't want to betray the girl's trust. But he felt obligated to protect Scout.

"She did."

Naomi covered her mouth.

"What? She told you?"

"Yesterday, while we walked. She didn't want you to find out. But I wouldn't promise to keep her secret. I should have told you sooner."

Naomi swallowed.

"That's not your duty. You're not her father. But I appreciate you looking out for her. How did she seem to you? Was she upset?"

"She has it in her head that the killer will revisit the scene."

"Is that a legitimate concern?"

Thomas lifted a shoulder.

"It's unlikely. But I live next door, and I'm friends with the state park ranger. He lives up the ridge and monitors the lake." Thomas glanced toward the guest house. The door stood open, and Scout's shadow wheeled past the window. "Would you like me to speak to Scout about what she saw?"

"That would mean a lot to me. I just don't want her getting in too deep. She can't trust everyone she meets online, and some of these crime scene photographs..."

Naomi's fingernails dug into her jeans.

"I'll speak with Scout when she returns."

"You're a good man, Thomas. One week next door, and you treat us like family."

Her words unearthed unwanted memories. He'd followed his own path and fought to please his parents, and they'd labeled him a failure. Now he was an adult, and a chance to make amends stood before him. Yet fate had snatched the opportunity away. His father was dying, and the family business would follow him to the grave, if Thomas didn't come up with a solution. He finished his drink and cleared his throat. Scout exited the guest house with a wide grin. After she closed the door, she wheeled back to them.

Naomi patted Thomas on the shoulder and took his drink.

"I'll get you a refill. Be right back."

Scout reached the picnic table at the same time Naomi closed the deck door.

"What did you think of the guest house?"

The girl's eyes lit.

"That was beyond cool. It's like an entire house, but miniaturized. Do you ever spend the night?"

"I did many times when I was your age."

"I sat at the window while the sailboats moved across the lake."

"Beautiful, isn't it?"

"The best."

"When it's finished, maybe you and your mom can camp out and spend the night."

"Are you serious?"

Thomas smiled and looked toward the structure, memories of his aunt and uncle leaving warmth inside his chest.

"The guest house is for family and friends, and anyone who needs a place to stay. You can stay on one condition."

She swiveled to face him.

"What's that?"

"You don't watch murder videos on the internet."

Scout lowered her head.

"Does Mom know?"

"She worries about you. Those videos are too much for me, and I'm a sworn deputy to Nightshade County."

She fidgeted in her chair.

"But I can catch him."

"That's my job, not yours."

"We know what we're doing. You should join the sleuthing forum. There are a lot of smart people on the site."

"That's another thing. Your mother wants you to cut back on the investigating. Stick to less intense crimes."

"She's treating me like a baby."

Thomas leveled his eyes with Scout's.

"No, she's keeping you safe. You're not an adult. Slow down."

She moved her gaze to the lake road. Her hands gripped the chair arms.

"Is there something you need to tell me, Scout? If you're still worried about the killer returning, I promise I won't let anyone hurt you or your mother."

Her eyes glistened as she took a deep, shuddering breath.

"Don't most serial killers begin by killing animals?"

The question stunned Thomas.

"Not always. Why do you ask?"

"There's a girl I correspond with. She goes under Harpy, but I don't know her actual name. Harpy investigated a creepy guy who posted videos over the last year. He killed animals."

"Why do you believe it's the same person?"

"Because the man was from around here. Seems like an awful big coincidence—two creepers in the same county uploading sick videos to the internet."

"Can you send me the video links?"

She nodded. The door slid open, and Naomi returned with a drink refill.

"Let me message Harpy. I'll send the links to you tomorrow."

"Scout, if you notice anyone canvassing the lake road, tell me."

31

Night slid down the windowpane as Scout shifted the wheelchair in front of the computer. In sharp silver and green tones, the Virtual Searchers website loaded in her browser. She typed queries for animal torture and murder into the search box. A confusing array of results filled her screen. A few months ago, the videos caused a stir on the forum.

As she altered her search terms, a chat window popped up in the lower right corner of her screen. Harpy was online.

Harpy: Hey there.

Scout: Glad you signed on. I'm having a hard time locating an old investigation.

Harpy: I'm just the girl for the job. What are you looking for?

Scout: Remember the sicko killing animals and uploading videos?

Harpy: Yeah, we never caught the creep. Don't tell me he's back.

Scout: Not that I've heard. Didn't we determine he lived near Wolf Lake?

An hour glass displayed while Harpy typed.

Harpy: Maybe. Been a long time since I saw the videos.

Scout: That's the problem. I can't locate the threads.

Harpy: Yeah. The Virtual Searchers search algorithm is jacked up. You can't find anything older than three months without Google. Give me a sec.

Scout grabbed her caffeine-free soda off the desk and drank. She eyed the clock. Almost nine. She'd stayed up late before to research crimes on school nights. But she had an exam tomorrow morning, and she hadn't studied yet.

Harpy: K. Didn't find the thread. But I found the videos. You want them?

Scout: You're a lifesaver. Send the links.

Harpy: They're on a dark website. Don't recommend downloading from the site unless you want your PC hacked. I have a safe method for downloading. Will send them to you.

Scout: Wow. That's just what I needed.

A minute later, an icon displayed beside Scout's profile. Her files had arrived. Sickness gurgled in her stomach. She'd avoided the videos last winter when they surfaced. Scout couldn't watch animals die. But she'd taken part in the hunt. Someone needed to catch the monster and lock him up before he hurt another animal. Now she'd have to watch the videos. What choice did she have? She couldn't prove this guy was the Wolf Lake murderer. But the coincidence ate at her.

Harpy: Did you get the files?

Scout: You bet. Thanks again.

Harpy: Cool. Hope this helps. I have to run. Paper due tomorrow. Gotta start before my parents lose their minds.

Scout: Ha ha. Same here. Talk to you tomorrow.

After Scout logged out of the chat, she downloaded the files. Harpy had combined the videos into a zip file to reduce the size. Though she trusted Harpy's judgment, Scout ran a virus check before she unzipped the videos. Everything checked out. She created a folder called *Sicko Videos* and saved the files.

For five minutes, her hand held the mouse without clicking.

Once she saw the videos, there would be no going back. Her heart pounded in her chest. In the living room, a sitcom with a laugh track played. The television was too loud for Mom to overhear.

Scout opened the first video.

Grainy footage displayed a guinea pig inside an aquarium. The pet crunched on kibble, then the guinea pig padded to the glass, stood on its hind legs, and clawed against the enclosure. The video continued like this for a full minute. Scout was about to skip ahead when a black sack filled the upper right corner of the screen. Her hands turned clammy. She didn't see the man, only the sack as it unfurled. Scout's breath caught in her throat when the boa constrictor, thick as her arm, dropped into the enclosure. The snake's tongue flicked. Panicked, the guinea pig scurried to the far corner and froze. Too late. The snake struck.

Scout turned away. Awful sounds played through the speakers—the desperate squeal, crunching bones.

Her hands clasped to her face. She peeked between two fingers. The snake coiled around the guinea pig until she stopped the movie.

She clicked out of the window and sobbed. Her stomach lurched, and she leaned her head back and breathed until the nausea passed. After she gathered herself, she stared at the filenames. The madman labeled the videos with chilling descriptions:

Guinea pig and snake
Puppy suffocation
Kitten and scorpions

Right-clicking on the files revealed the EXIF data. The killer recorded the videos in Harmon, NY, last December. Now she had evidence linking the animal torture to the Erika Windrow murder. The events took place in the same city, separated by four months. She read articles on murderer profiling. Many serial killers murdered animals before graduating to humans. She would tell Thomas tomorrow.

Armed with new information, she queried the website again. By changing the terms and including the EXIF data, she located the message threads. She skimmed the forum. Most members displayed outrage. They wanted frontier justice. How could this guy murder innocent animals on camera and get away with it? Why weren't the police investigating? Other members remained calm and listed the facts. Scout's eyebrows shot up. When the videos first appeared, the psycho used the name Max Cady. The name came from the movie *Cape Fear*. After she researched the false name online, Scout had forced her mother to rent the movie from Amazon. Though it was more thriller than horror, *Cape Fear* frightened Scout. She didn't sleep for a week. Why hadn't she remembered the killer's name?

Now she raced through the internet at lightning speed. Searching for the Erika Windrow murder video, she slapped a frustrated hand against the desk. The websites had removed the copies. No question she'd find the files on the dark web. But her mother forbade Scout from venturing down those paths, and she didn't relish losing her computer to a virus or hacker.

The television turned off in the living room. Mom's footsteps passed Scout's room and stopped. She lingered outside the door, listening. The lights inside Scout's bedroom poured beneath the threshold.

Scout closed the browser and shut the computer down. Then she pushed the wheelchair to her bed, struggled onto the mattress, and flicked the light off. Full dark enveloped the bedroom. Every shadow looked like a killer with a knife. On the lake road, a car crawled past.

How would she find Max Cady?

32

The Friday morning editions of the *Bluewater Tribune* lay stacked on the sidewalk when Violet Kain unlocked the door to South Street News. The stale interior carried tobacco and parchment scents, and a yellow trail beside the counter told Violet the mousetrap had failed again. She blew out a breath and set the keys on the counter, flicked on the lights, and flipped the sign over to *Yes, We're Open!*

No sooner did she wipe the mess with a paper towel than the bell rang. She didn't lift her head until the size eleven black boots stepped into her personal space. Whoever this creep was, he almost crushed her fingers.

"Could you give me a second? I just turned the damn sign over."

"*Bluewater Tribune*. Now."

"You'll need to wait until I cut the bundle."

"I did it for you."

The knife he produced had deep, jagged teeth. Like the maw of a werewolf. And there was something caught between the serrated points. It almost looked like hair. She caught her breath, heart slamming as she carefully rose.

The man stood a foot taller than Violet, his razor-buzzed hair color a purgatory between blonde and brunette. Deep-set eyes as black as coals. Face red and irritated. Not acne. More like an allergic reaction.

He slapped the newspaper down. She couldn't take her eyes off the knife as she rounded the counter, hands trembling as she opened the cash register.

While he waited on the other side of the counter, nothing to stop the man from blocking her exit and jamming the blade into her belly, he unfurled the paper and grinned at the headline. Someone had mailed a severed head to the newspaper. Was the man laughing?

Attached to the wall at shin level, a red button jutted forth like a miniature clown nose. All she needed to do was touch the button with the toe of her sneaker, and the police would come. South Street News had seen its share of robberies over the last decade, and though the man hadn't demanded money, she wasn't chancing fate.

"I wouldn't do that if I were you."

Her eyes shot up. Somehow, he knew. The man tossed four quarters onto the counter. One rolled off and clanged against the floor. As she knelt to retrieve the coin, she thought about the alarm again. And the gun. Herb Ryerson kept a pistol in the back room, locked inside a safe. Little good the gun did her now.

When Violet stood, the door swung shut, no sign of the man.

FROM THE SAFETY of his tiny apartment high above the city, Jeremy Hyde snapped the newspaper open. He couldn't have hoped for a stronger response from the *Bluewater Tribune*. His delivery headlined the small town newspaper, and the city toddled on the edge of full-scale panic. All because of him.

The writer named him Vlad, after the infamous Transylvania impaler known for beheading his enemies. But Jeremy didn't aspire to military conquest.

He couldn't explain what drew him to Erika Windrow. From the first time he saw the girl working her corner, Jeremy craved to slit her throat and watch the beautiful crimson spill out of her.

Below his window, cars raced through the intersection like worker ants, the drivers unaware he watched over them like a malevolent god. Turning his laptop toward him, he loaded the photograph of Naomi Mourning pushing Scout up the ramp in front of her house. He giggled. Now that he knew the girl's name and address, it would be a simple matter to murder Naomi and Scout. Then the hero deputy.

He couldn't wait to read those headlines.

Inspiration struck, tingling his skin with excitement. He needed to meet Deputy Shepherd, stand face-to-face with the man who vowed to catch him. Jeremy grabbed his keys and rushed down the stairs, too impatient to bother with the elevator. The clock read twenty minutes until eight as he drove the Trax out of Harmon. Twenty minutes until the hero deputy arrived for his shift at the Nightshade County Sheriff's Department. He'd followed Shepherd for days and knew when his workday started, where he shopped, who his friends were, and where he could find his family.

Jeremy pulled into the municipal parking lot two blocks from the sheriff's office. Before he climbed out of the Trax, he pulled the hood of his sweatshirt over his head and tugged the strings until only his eyes were visible. Keeping his head down, feigning a chill as his breath puffed condensation clouds, he walked faster. The hero deputy crossed the street at the same time Jeremy turned the corner.

A barreling freight train, Jeremy strode at the deputy. At the last moment, the startled deputy looked up before the collision. Jeremy's superior strength and size capsized the pathetic hero and knocked him to the sidewalk.

"Oh, I'm so sorry. I was in a rush and didn't see you."

He offered the deputy a hand, but the false hero brushed off his pants and glared at Jeremy.

"My fault," Deputy Shepherd said. "I wasn't watching where I was going."

"I contribute to police benevolent funds. You're the gatekeepers, Deputy. You stop the monsters from storming the village."

A muted laugh escaped Jeremy's lips, drawing scrutiny from the deputy as a train whistle sounded outside the village. He'd wanted to test the man's resolve. But the deputy was puny and weak. It almost disappointed him. Jeremy wanted to tell the deputy how he'd murder his beautiful neighbor and her nosy daughter. That he'd stand over Deputy Shepherd's crumpled body after he snapped his brittle neck. Instead, he snickered and showed plenty of teeth.

"Have a nice day, Deputy. And thank you for your service."

33

"Hey, Shepherd. I found the kid."

Aguilar's voice pulled Thomas to the deputy's desk. He'd stayed up late, following the Erika Windrow videos down internet wormholes. There had to be a way to catch the killer. This guy couldn't upload the video to dozens of websites without leaving a breadcrumb or two. Then he'd walked headfirst into a man on the sidewalk. He felt foolish. But there was something about the man in the hooded sweatshirt that set Thomas on edge.

Aguilar turned in her chair and pointed at the freeze frame on her computer.

"The teen's name is Anthony Fisher."

"You recognize him?"

"No, but I passed the image through Harmon PD, and a detective identified the kid. You're right. Fisher runs with the Harmon Kings."

Now they had proof a King's member dropped the package at the post office.

"Get me his address."

"Already found it," Aguilar said, waving a sheet of paper at

Thomas. "Give me a second to wrap up this paperwork, and we'll drive over to Harmon and pick the kid up."

Before Thomas set his keys down, Gray called him from the end of the hall. The sheriff scribbled a note as Thomas waited in the doorway. Gray glanced up and motioned at the chair across from his desk. When Thomas sat down, Gray's eyes softened. Elbows on the table, Gray formed a steeple with his fingers and pressed his lips against the peak.

"Thomas, I found out about your father. I can't express how sorry I am."

Thomas's gut clenched.

"Thank you. I just heard."

"Are things still bad between you and your folks?" Thomas's silence provided Gray with an answer. "Listen to me, son. I've watched too many family members go to the grave with unresolved conflicts. Nobody appreciates how important family is until it isn't there anymore. Work things out with your mother and father while you have time."

Running a hand across his forehead, Thomas leaned back in his chair.

"When I returned from California, I intended to make amends with my family. I'm trying. They're set in their ways."

"Stubborn."

"That's an accurate description."

"Look not beyond the mirror before acknowledging the reflection."

Thomas quirked an eyebrow. Did Gray just spout poetry?

"I'm unfamiliar with that passage."

"Something my father used to say. Don't know if it was a bible passage, or if he made it up. You have your own stubborn streak, Deputy Shepherd. Hell, I recognized it the minute you stepped inside my office as a wide-eyed teenager. You never would have convinced me to give you an internship, otherwise.

The Nightshade County Sheriff's Department doesn't need teenage volunteers. Doggedness got you where you are today. But it blinds you to your own faults. How long did you wait before you told your parents you moved home?"

Thomas shifted in his chair.

"That long?" Gray asked, his face masked in disappointment. "Why expect your folks to treat you with respect when you don't return the favor?"

"I wanted to call."

"No, you didn't. With family disputes, there is no *want*, only action."

"Now you're quoting Yoda."

The chair squealed when the big sheriff leaned back and clasped his fingers behind his head.

"Fix things with your parents, Thomas. You'll sleep better at night."

Gray's words drifted inside Thomas's head while Aguilar drove the cruiser toward Harmon. Reality lay heavy on his shoulders. How long did his father have? Six months? Three months? Less? For years he'd avoided his parents. Now Thomas imagined a world without his father in it, and he wasn't sure how to live in such a world. Despite the dangers of working law enforcement, his job shielded him from his troubles. He was the type to focus on the daily grind while pipes sprang leaks in the basement, and water seeped through the floor.

"You're quiet," Aguilar said, staring at him as she drove with one hand.

"Rough night."

"Too many drinks at Hattie's?"

He laughed.

"Nothing like that. Too many thoughts running through my mind."

She nodded in understanding. Aguilar didn't know

Thomas's family situation. But sleepless nights were part of the package when you signed up for law enforcement.

He remembered. Tonight was the Magnolia Dance, and he hadn't asked Aguilar.

He felt stupid. How did Lambert talk him into this? One glance at Aguilar, and Thomas chuckled. She glared at him from the driver's seat with an amused grin.

"Spit it out, Shepherd, or I'll beat it out of you."

Thomas drummed his knuckles against his thighs.

"Okay, if you insist. I've been meaning to ask you something."

"If you ask me for my training routine, I'll slap you."

"No, not that. Though I would like to know your biceps routine."

"You couldn't handle it, California boy."

"Probably not."

"What's got you giggling like a teenager?"

His keys dug into his thigh. Thomas removed them from his pocket and set them on the center console.

"It's the Magnolia Dance. Now that I'm back, I'm kinda obligated to go."

"If you're asking me to the dance, that's a pitiful proposal."

He rubbed his eyes with his thumb and forefinger.

"I'm not very good at this stuff. Would you like to go? To the dance, I mean."

She spit out a laugh.

"I didn't assume you wanted to go steady. We just met. And you couldn't handle it, honey."

"Come on, Deputy. Say yes."

She batted her eyelashes.

"What time are you picking me up, Romeo?"

"I arrive home fifteen minutes after four. I'll need time to cook and shower. How about seven o'clock?"

"That works. You renting a limo, or making me ride to the most romantic event of the year in a freaking pickup truck?"

He stammered. Should he call a limo? Could he even rent one on short notice?

"I'm kidding, Shepherd," she said, grinning.

"No obligations."

"Of course, not. We'll laugh at the locals and slam a drink or two. I went stag last year and had a great time. This will be twice as fun."

"Great. Seven o'clock, it is."

"And Thomas?"

"Yeah?"

"If you try to hold my hand, I'll bloody your lip."

Aguilar pulled the cruiser into a municipal lot across the street from a newsstand. City traffic buzzed past. A ten-story brownstone apartment building loomed across the street. According to county records, Anthony Fisher lived with his aunt on the fourth floor. They climbed the stairs. Televisions blared behind closed doors. When they reached the fourth floor, Aguilar rapped on the first door. Quiet emanated from the apartment. After ten seconds, she knocked again. Thomas peered down the empty hallway.

"You said Fisher lives with his aunt?"

"Perhaps she's at work."

"Nothing about this feels right."

"You don't believe the kid did it?"

Thomas leaned against the jamb.

"I don't. I observed Anthony Fisher's body language in the video footage. No anxiousness, no paranoia. I doubt he knew what was in the box. The boy isn't a serial killer."

"That won't convince Gray."

"You asked for my opinion."

She gave him a curious look.

"Tell you what. Let's grab coffee across the street and check back in half an hour."

They emerged into the harsh daylight. On the sidewalk, Thomas shielded his eyes and searched for Aguilar's coffee shop. His eyes stopped on a black Chrysler Limited parked at the end of the block. Aguilar nudged his arm.

"Isn't that LeVar Hopkins's car?" Aguilar set her hands on her hips. "I'll be damned. Should I call it in?"

Thomas chewed his lip.

"We have nothing on Hopkins."

"Except he ran from you."

"Running isn't proof of guilt."

"So what do you want to do?"

"Talk."

Thomas started down the sidewalk.

"Talk?" Aguilar said, rushing to catch up. "You don't just talk to LeVar Hopkins."

"Everyone talks. The human species would cease to exist without communication."

The Chrysler Limited sat vacant at the curb. A cross hung from a chain strewn over the rear-view mirror. He shot his eyes to the passenger seat. It wasn't soaked with blood. But LeVar might have reupholstered the seat, or murdered Erika Windrow in another vehicle. Thomas searched the street for LeVar.

"Now what?"

"We'll wait until he returns," Thomas said, leaning against the hood.

Aguilar cocked an eyebrow.

"You'll get your ass shot, cowboy."

"He'll come for his car. The police will ticket him if he parks for two hours."

They didn't wait long. The door opened on a twenty-four-hour diner with a bright blue awning. Two black males pushed through the exit and squinted into the sun. Thomas recognized LeVar. The other man stood two inches shorter than LeVar. But the bald male carried himself a foot larger. Prison tattoos marked his arms. He pulled up and swatted LeVar, then cocked his chin toward Thomas and Aguilar.

"See the scumbag?" Aguilar asked. "That's Rev."

"Rev?"

"Yeah, Shepherd. He runs the Kings."

"I thought LeVar ran the gang."

"LeVar is the muscle. Rev controls this half of Harmon. I should call for backup."

"We're just having a conversation."

Rev and LeVar strode at Thomas. Outwardly, Thomas fixed the two gang members with a stare. Inside, his heart raced. The shooting rushed back to him, and in that moment, he smelled the grass as he lay face down, felt the burning agony in the small of his back. A whiff of sulfur caught his nose. He imagined the gunpowder scent. It seemed real.

"Someone cooking ham?" LeVar asked Rev.

The leader of the Kings didn't smirk or flinch. His hands twitched at his sides, and Thomas caught the bulge beneath Rev's sweatshirt. The man packed a gun. This situation could spin out of control at any second. LeVar glanced between Rev and the two deputies. He set a hand on the gang leader's chest.

"I'll catch you after. Let me handle the cops."

Rev shot him a hard look.

"You sure about this?"

"I got you covered. Chill." LeVar waited for Rev to saunter down the walkway. The leader of the Harmon Kings kept looking back at Thomas and Aguilar with ill intentions. "All right, let's talk. I got nothing to hide."

"Why did you run from me Wednesday?" Thomas asked.

"I didn't know you were a cop. All I saw was a big guy with a gun. That means trouble down this way."

Aguilar cleared her throat and said, "We're not after you. Not today."

"Then why y'all in my neighborhood?"

"We're searching for Anthony Fisher." LeVar's eyes flickered with surprise. "You happen to see him this morning?"

"Not your business if I did. What you want with Anthony?"

"We're investigating Erika Windrow's murder."

"You sayin' Anthony is a suspect? I ain't tryin' to hear that. He's just a kid."

Thomas raised an eyebrow.

"So he's innocent? Maybe you'll tell us who we should be after."

"What you got on Anthony?" LeVar folded his arms as Thomas told him about the security footage from the post office. "So my boy mailed a package. That's all you got on him."

"That's enough, considering what was inside."

"Okay, so what was in the box?"

"I'm sure Anthony knows. Where is he?"

"Yeah, well, I haven't seen Anthony in a minute. He's up north at his Mom's. Anthony only lives here with his aunt while Mom gets her shit together. Bitch can't keep a job."

Thomas handed LeVar his card.

"When you see Anthony, call me. It would be better if we found him first."

"That a threat?"

"If he's innocent, I'll fight on his behalf. But this looks bad for Anthony. He needs to explain why he mailed that box."

LeVar turned the card over in his hand. His eyes darted between Thomas and Aguilar, as though deciding which threat he wanted to take out first.

"Whatever you think Anthony did, he didn't do it. But I'll tell him you want to talk."

"While we're at it, where were you Sunday night? I have multiple eyewitnesses who placed you at Wolf Lake last week."

"You can stop right there, Deputy Dog. I didn't drop no bodies in the lake. And my business in the village ain't your concern."

Thomas questioned LeVar about Raven. But the teen threw his hands up and walked away,

"Come back when you got a warrant," he said, grinning pearly whites back at them.

"You're letting him go?" Aguilar asked, grabbing Thomas by the arm.

"I can't bring him in without evidence. But that story he told about Anthony moving north was a lie. He's around. Keep your eyes peeled."

34

LeVar rounded the corner. When he was certain the two deputies weren't following and Rev wasn't around, he sprinted past a row of apartments and cut through the alleyway. He needed to beat Rev to the red-light district and find Anthony before Rev did. This was Royals territory. He risked his life going after the kid. The youngster couldn't get enough of the girls. Troy Dean let Anthony hang around because he didn't consider the kid a threat. Were the shoe on the other foot, Rev would have gutted a Royals youngster for walking through Kings territory.

He pulled up out of breath after sprinting four blocks. The girls milled in front of the adult video store. They wore high heels, crotch-high miniskirts, and lots of leather. And they all smoked or chomped on fruity bubble gum. Just getting near the women turned LeVar's stomach. He couldn't imagine why anyone would pay for an hour alone with them.

The cold thought rolled around inside his head. His mother hooked when LeVar and Raven were children. She put money on the table, though she injected half the earnings into her arm. Now LeVar hadn't been home in three nights. When he was away for multiple days, he feared he'd come home and find his mother dead on the couch, the needle hanging out of her arm like a broken diving board, eyes vacant, spittle dried upon crusted lips. She refused to get help, though LeVar promised he'd pay for rehab, therapy, whatever she needed. Without Raven to help, their mother was his responsibility.

Traffic buzzed through the intersection. He waited for an opening, threw his hood over his head, and strolled across the road with his hands buried inside his pockets. He kept his head down, expecting a bullet when someone recognized him. As he hopped the curb, he caught sight of a black teenager strolling out of the video store with a brown paper bag tucked beneath his arm. The kid was a little pervert, but LeVar didn't care. He preferred Anthony watched movies and fantasized. At least the kid was smart enough not to proposition the older girls. For a second, a thought played around in LeVar's mind. Someone offed Erika. Anthony? No, he refused to accept the kid was a murderer. Damn kid was too chicken to fire a gun. Why the hell did Rev recruit Anthony into the Kings?

"Anthony," LeVar said, keeping his voice low. The kid bounced on the balls of his feet, nervous. "Hey, Anthony."

Two street walkers glanced his way, and a Puerto Rican woman in a leopard-skin skirt whirled and ran inside the shop. Shit. If Troy Dean was inside with half the Royals, LeVar had a minute to live. He snatched Anthony by the elbow and dragged him away from the storefront. The young teenager whirled his head around in surprise.

"What the hell, LeVar?" Then his head swiveled toward the video store. "You shouldn't be down here."

"No shit. Follow me."

LeVar walked with purpose, his elbow hooked to Anthony's until they reached the alleyway. Pulling the kid behind him, LeVar ran without stopping. When he stepped off enemy terrain, a weight fell off his shoulders. Still, he scanned behind him for pursuit before he let his guard down.

"From now on, stay on this side of Harmon."

Anthony shuffled his feet.

"Nobody bothers me or cares I'm there."

"Troy cares, believe me. He lets you slide 'cause you ain't worth dealing with." Hurt bled into Anthony's eyes. LeVar raised his chin. "You think it ain't true? Why the Royals gonna start a war over your sorry ass? You want your damn girly videos, I'll get them for you. No reason for you to risk your head."

"Sorry."

LeVar lowered his voice when a Harmon PD patrolman passed them on the sidewalk. The heavyset officer glared their way with his hand an inch from his weapon. He spoke into a radio on his shoulder and crossed the street.

"You fucked up, Anthony."

"No, I didn't."

"Two county cops came looking for you an hour ago."

"What the hell for?"

LeVar grabbed the kid by the shoulders and shoved him against a brick building. Anthony's eyes widened.

"They got you on video at the post office."

"Yeah, so?"

"So? You stupid shit. Don't you watch the news? That girl you had your eyes on...Erika. Someone sliced her up like a slab of meat and mailed body parts to the press. You wanna tell me something, Anthony?"

Fear and revulsion worked through the kid. Whatever concern LeVar had about Anthony butchering Erika Windrow vanished. This kid wouldn't swat a fly without crying.

"I don't know nothing about that."

"You mailed the box, you dumb shit. And now half the

county is hunting you. Tell me what happened. And if you lie, I swear I'll bleed you here and let the vultures take the rest."

Anthony swallowed and stared at his shoelaces.

"This guy. He handed me the box and a hundred-dollar bill. Told me the money was mine. All I had to do was mail it."

Fury tightened LeVar's muscles. He composed himself before he knocked the kid's lights out.

"Some random guy approached you on the street and paid you a hundred dollars to mail a package. And you don't find it suspicious?"

"It was a hundred dollars. Wouldn't you do the same?"

"The fuck you talking about? No, I wouldn't risk my ass for a hundred bucks. Dammit, Anthony. I bail you out, and you wade back in. Rev was there when the cops showed up, asking questions about you."

"Rev was there? Oh, man. What should I do?"

"Don't do nothing. Lie low until this blows over. I'll handle the cops when they come back."

"I screwed up this time, didn't I?"

LeVar blew out a frustrated breath and paced in a circle. This was bad business. He couldn't guarantee Rev wouldn't put the kid down for bringing unneeded heat on the Kings. The line he gave the county cops about Anthony having a mother upstate wasn't a lie. Should he put the kid on a bus and get him out of Harmon? Hell, he wanted to buy a ticket and ride with the kid. Disappear to someplace where no one knew him. When he joined the Kings, the gang was a brotherhood. Then Rev rose to power, and the psycho turned his brothers into killers. He couldn't abandon his mother or escape gang life. Nobody in the Kings left Harmon without Rev finding out.

"You're staying at our apartment for a few nights." When Anthony opened his mouth to protest, LeVar dropped a hand on the kid's shoulder. "I need someone to watch over my mother.

Consider it payback. If Rev asks where you're at, I'll cover for you."

"Okay, I'll do it. How do I get out of this mess?"

"Tell me everything about the guy. Who is he, and what does he look like?"

Anthony described the stranger. The guy seemed vaguely familiar. But he couldn't place where he'd seen him before.

"You ever notice him hanging around Harmon?"

"Never."

"Dammit, Anthony. You'll get both of us killed someday. All right. I'll put the word out. Shouldn't take too long to shake him out of hiding. Until then, keep your head low. Understand?"

35

Conversation whirred inside the bus as everyone looked forward to the spring gala. Scout sat away from the other students, the wheelchair strapped to the wall and her knapsack clutched against her lap. She'd almost convinced Mom to take her to the dance. But Mom didn't know anyone in Wolf Lake, except Deputy Shepherd. And she couldn't picture the deputy and her mother on a date.

Sunshine spread over the dusty bus windows and raised spirits. Even for the kids not attending the dance, it was Friday. The weekend had arrived, and the weather was beautiful. And what did Scout have planned? Nothing the other kids would find entertaining.

Yet her body thrummed with anticipation. She was close to catching a killer. Nobody on the Virtual Searchers forum connected the animal murders with the woman dropped in the lake. Not that she craved fame and attention. A psychopath hunted Wolf Lake, and it was her duty to keep her classmates safe, even though they didn't pay her attention.

Twice she'd phoned the sheriff's department from school and asked for Deputy Shepherd. Both times he was out of the office, and the secretary who recorded Scout's messages didn't take the girl seriously. She doubted the deputy received either message.

To make matters worse, she overheard two girls chatting during gym class. The killer was a black male from Harmon. A leaked rumor purported the sheriff had two suspects—both members of the Harmon Kings. The logic didn't compute. Why would gang members target teenage prostitutes?

Her pulse raced as the bus turned down the lake road. Now that she had proof the animal killer and murderer footage came from Harmon, the killings separated by only four months, she would tell Deputy Shepherd and turn the evidence over to the sheriff's department. He'd listen to her. He had to.

The brakes squealed as the bus stopped in front of the house. Her mother waited in her usual spot with a painted-on smile. Scout sensed her mother's pain and understood she'd become a burden to everybody. That point became obvious when the bus driver took forever to unstrap the wheelchair, and the typical muttering began again. It wasn't four o'clock yet, and she'd already ruined everyone's weekend. The metronome-like beeps served as strange background music while the lift lowered. Mom thanked the elderly driver who grumbled and limped up the bus steps.

"How was school?"

"Glad it's over."

"Did something happen?"

"No, I just don't enjoy being there."

Mom stopped the wheelchair on the sidewalk and knelt before Scout.

"That's not like you. You've always loved school."

"Mom, what if we tried homeschooling?"

Her mother stood and tugged at her shirt.

"That's not possible. I work days. Tell me what's wrong, and I'll speak with the principal."

Scout shook her head.

"It's nothing."

"It doesn't sound like nothing."

"Forget I asked."

Mom sighed and shoved Scout toward the ramp. Scout glanced over her shoulder. The deputy's driveway lay vacant. He'd be home from work soon.

"Hey, Mom. Is it okay if I sit in the backyard for a while?"

"Sure, if that will brighten your mood. Want me to bring you a snack?"

"Maybe in a bit. I'm not hungry."

Mom wheeled Scout to the unfinished path. The deputy hadn't poured concrete yet. He promised he'd complete the pathway during a warm stretch of weather next week. Guilt gnawed at her. Deputy Shepherd did so much for Scout and her mother. She wanted to help him solve this case.

A minute after Mom entered the house, the loud motor of the Ford F-150 pulled her attention to the deputy's driveway. Deputy Shepherd stopped the truck with a jerk and leaped from the cab in one motion. Scout turned the chair around and pushed across the property line, intent on intercepting him before he unlocked the door. The deputy didn't have a ramp on his deck, so she couldn't reach his doorbell.

"Deputy Shepherd," she said, calling over the wind.

He didn't notice Scout as he fumbled for the correct key. Why was he in such a hurry? She had to tell him what she'd learned last night. When she called again, his head shot up. He gave a curious wave, then hopped off the deck and ran to her when the wheelchair careened down a slight grade.

"Careful, Scout. Hold still. I'll come to you." He glanced at his phone when he reached her. She wondered if he expected an important message regarding the murder case. "Is everything okay? Your mom all right?"

"Yeah, everybody's doing fine."

"Good. You had me worried for a second. Listen, Scout. I'm in a bit of a rush and have to shower and change."

"Are you going to the village dance?"

His shoulders shook with laughter.

"Unfortunately, yes. I don't understand how I get myself into these things."

"Deputy Shepherd—"

"Please, we're neighbors now. Call me Thomas."

"Thomas." She swallowed the nervous knot in her throat. The more she pieced the puzzle together in her head, the stronger her conviction grew that the videos came from the same madman. "I know you told me to cut back on the investigation stuff..."

The smile vanished from his face.

"Your mother made it clear, Scout. This is a murder investigation."

"But I learned something important. Do you know what EXIF data is?"

"You're not listening to me. I promised your mother I'd speak to you about the amateur sleuthing. No more videos, no more filling your head with violence. Let me do my job."

"But—"

"No buts about it. I'm sorry, but I have a busy evening and need to hurry. Let me help you to your yard."

He wouldn't even listen. A hurt feeling crawled through her chest. She was the outcast again. The girl nobody spoke to at school, the person the kids on the bus hated for slowing them down every day. She whirled the wheelchair toward her house.

"I can get back on my own."

"Scout, I apologize. I didn't mean to be short with you."

"It doesn't matter. I have homework and so many fun things planned this weekend."

Tears blurred her eyes while she wheeled the chair into her backyard. She sensed his eyes following, heard the regret in his silence. What did it matter? Fate confined her to this chair for the rest of her life. No amount of coddling would alter her reality.

JEREMY HYDE WATCHED the crippled girl push across the lawn. Standing amid the trees on the other side of the road, he stroked the knife hilt, at one with the permanent darkness beneath the canopy. The girl knew too much. But the damn deputy was always around when he paid his neighbors a visit.

He chuckled inwardly at the conundrum. Flaunting the murders made him ripple with excitement. Throwing the videos into their faces allowed him to relive the murders. He relished the cops discovering the files.

But he couldn't kill again if they discovered his name and locked him in a cell. And he intended to kill for many years. He'd developed a taste for it.

The girl asked too many questions on the amateur sleuthing forum. Now she'd gathered everything she needed to bring him down.

Jeremy stepped toward the ditch and froze when the deputy's eyes swung across the road. Toward him. He paused and waited. No chance the deputy saw him inside the shadows. Jeremy had to hand it to the false hero—the deputy sensed what lay hidden.

He drew the knife from the sheathe and waded through the tall grass lining the lake road. Behind the weedy growth, he gazed up and down the blacktop. Doors stood closed on the neighboring houses. Nobody outside working in the yards. He could cross the road while the deputy held his back to him. Plunge the knife into his back, dig the tip through the bullet wound that should have ended his sorry existence. The girl would be easy to catch. He'd outrace her to the ramp. If the mother interfered, he'd leave three bodies for the coroner.

When the deputy left the girl's side and crossed the lawn, his head hanging with regret, Jeremy stepped onto the shoulder and closed the distance on his prey. Before he reached the centerline, a car rounded the bend and raced up the road.

He darted into the shadows before the driver identified him. Lucky cop. Tonight, he'd show the hero he wasn't safe. Locked doors didn't stop him. Nothing stopped him. Through the trees, he stared as the girl struggled up the ramp and swiped a tear from her eye.

Poor, poor girl.

He'd give both of them something to cry about.

36

Hot spray from the shower rinsed the sweat from his body.

Thomas set the washcloth on the hanger and rubbed the soap sting out of his eyes. Regret clenched his muscles. He thought he'd done the right thing by keeping his promise to Naomi. But the woman wouldn't want him to hurt her daughter's feelings, and he'd done just that. Nausea crept up on him when he pictured the girl alone inside her bedroom, the lights low, the computer displaying Erika Windrow's murder. If he knew a way to block access to every video sharing site on the internet, he'd do so for Naomi.

Scout wanted to tell him something about the EXIF data. Thomas already knew the killer had shot the murder video in Harmon. There was one explanation for Scout possessing the EXIF information. She downloaded the videos again.

He cut the water off and pulled the shower door aside. When he reached for the towel, a thump came from inside the house. Thomas stopped and listened. Through the open window, the lake foamed against the shore. Maybe the sound came from outside.

After he dried off, he hurried to the bedroom and searched the closet for something appropriate to wear. Everything in his wardrobe appeared too casual or too formal. The Magnolia Dance wasn't a casual get-together with friends, but it also wasn't a wedding or funeral. He swept the hangers aside and settled on navy blue slacks, an off-white short-sleeve button down, and a casual sports jacket that he'd leave open. Tie or no tie? He hung three candidates against his throat, compared the outfits in the mirror, and tossed the ties on the rack. Why was he making himself crazy over this? It was just Aguilar. She'd probably wear blue jeans and a tank.

Thomas swept his phone to the browser and found the number for Bernadette's flower shop. He couldn't predict how Aguilar would react to a bouquet. Now that he thought about it, she'd laugh and tell him not to get his hopes up, then grill him for the rest of the night. Yeah, stupid idea. Except he didn't feel right picking a woman up for the Magnolia Dance without flowers. Old fashioned and set in his ways, he made the call.

The phone rang. He read his mother's name on the screen. The ringer shrilled until he gave in.

"Your father expects an answer, Thomas."

"I gave him an answer at dinner."

"Don't be foolish. You'll never worry about money again."

"I don't worry about money, Mother. You do."

She sniffed.

"Shepherd Systems must stay in the family. Don't do this to your father. Not now. You'll break him if you turn down the offer."

He couldn't voice what lay unasked. How long did his father have?

"How is father?"

It took a moment before Lindsey Shepherd responded.

"He's not well, Thomas. You saw him at dinner. It won't be long."

"I'll stop by in a few days."

"Sure," she said, her voice bleeding sarcasm. "After you finish this important case you're working on. Of course, we all know you'll find another case to keep you busy, another excuse to ignore your dying father."

"That's not fair."

"When will you come to your senses and cease this foolishness? It's impossible for someone like you to survive in law enforcement."

She finally said it. Since the high school internship, she'd danced around the issue, His mother didn't believe anyone on the spectrum could be a police officer.

She let out a breath.

"That came out incorrectly, Thomas. You'll forgive me for misspeaking."

"I'll see you soon."

"Will we?"

The call ended. Thomas was running late.

He checked his hair in the mirror, considered running a brush through the snarls.

On his way out the door, he paused and glared across the road toward the tree line. A creepy sensation of being watched slid down his spine. Instinct dragged his gaze back to the house, as though he'd missed something important. He waited several heartbeats. Nothing moved except the lake breeze snaking through the tall grass. Chalking his anxiety up to the festival, he spun the key ring around his finger and hurried to the F-150.

The sun began its descent. Dying rays washed the valley in red. After picking up his order at Bernadette's, he queried the GPS to direct him to Aguilar's house. The deputy owned a burgundy ranch in a quiet neighborhood on the west side of the village. He idled the truck in the driveway, torn between honking the horn and ringing the doorbell. Aguilar or not, Thomas was a gentleman at heart, so he crawled down from the cab and pressed the doorbell.

The chimes hadn't finished ringing when the door opened. Thomas rocked back on his heels. He almost didn't recognize his fellow deputy. Aguilar wore a black-and-white floral Cami dress. Supple straps ran from her neck to the small of her back, accentuating her muscular physique. She'd braided her hair and draped the lengths over her left ear. My goodness, she looked stunning.

She eyed him in the doorway.

"What are you looking at, Shepherd?"

Same old Aguilar. Even dressed to the nines, she disarmed him with macho bravado. Yet he caught the pink on her bronze cheeks as she raised an expectant eyebrow. She glared at the flowers in his hand.

"Oh," he said, remembering the bouquet. "These are for you."

She snatched the flowers.

"Now that the formalities are out of the way, can we go?"

"After, you should put the flowers in water so they don't dry out."

No parking spots existed near the dance. Thomas abandoned the truck behind an Italian restaurant, and they walked two blocks to reach the celebration. A kaleidoscope of colors greeted them. The event planners covered the entrance with magnolia cuttings. A nineties cover band played a Weezer song, and disinterested teens watched their parents dance. Thomas led Aguilar beneath an enormous tent that lent the celebration a circus atmosphere. Card tables covered the ground, and an open circle in the center allowed for dancing and mingling.

"Where would you like to sit?" Thomas asked, scanning the crowd for familiar faces and finding none.

"How about over there?" Aguilar said, gesturing toward a quiet corner near the back.

"Perfect."

Scents of grilled chicken and burgers wafted through the tent flaps. Though the gala was Wolf Lake's version of a Valentine's Day dance, the food choices were typical of barbecue stands in July. An obese woman at the next table dug into a heaping plate of chicken and potato salad.

Desperate for a conversation starter, Thomas brought up Anthony Fisher's name. Aguilar shook her head.

"No work talk. I'm off until Monday morning, and I intend to keep it that way."

Thomas tapped his fingers to the beat and surveyed the dance floor. He wanted to tell Aguilar about Scout viewing the murder videos behind her mother's back. But his partner made it clear work talk was off limits tonight. Deputy Lambert grinned at him from across the room. Thomas waved, and the deputy burst out laughing and pointed at him. He swallowed. During his teenage years, someone laughing and pointing did so to humiliate. Thomas understood Lambert was having fun. But the gesture still stabbed at him.

"I should grab us food before the line gets too long. What do you want?"

Aguilar shrugged.

"Something that doesn't have a bun around it. Surprise me."

Thomas squeezed between patrons and searched for anything that didn't look like a hamburger. He settled on a stand selling roast beef platters with a choice of vegetables or mashed potatoes on the side. Knowing Aguilar took nutrition seriously, he opted for the broccoli.

"This is almost edible," he said, setting the plates down. "It has protein and carbohydrates."

She took one bite of the roast beef and smiled.

"Good cut. It melts in your mouth."

Finally, Thomas had done something right tonight. As they ate, he watched the dancers, most of them inebriated and teetering. Aguilar chuckled when a silver-haired man tripped and dropped his food. Thomas poured them each a cup of water from the pitcher set at the center of the table. He swallowed and coughed. Chelsey passed their table with Ray's hand locked on her wrist. Aguilar glanced up at him.

"Do I need to perform the Heimlich?"

"I swallowed down the wrong pipe."

He concentrated on his plate. But Chelsey drew his eyes back to the dance floor. His old girlfriend wore a black fit dress that kissed her mid-thigh and showed off strong shoulders. Ray spun her around, then pulled her hips against his. Two hands groped up her dress. Chelsey slapped his hands away, and Ray snickered as though he was fooling around. But Thomas caught the derision on his face. What was she doing with that creep?

"So, who's the chick?"

Aguilar's voice pulled Thomas out of his daze.

"What?"

"Don't bullshit me, Shepherd. I've seen that look before. Who is she?"

"Someone I knew a long time ago," Thomas said, refilling his water and wishing for something stronger.

"Wait a second. Isn't she the private investigator in town? Wolf Lake Consulting, right?"

Thomas scrubbed a hand down his face.

"Yes, she owns Wolf Lake Consulting."

"Yeah, her partner chased down Hugh Fitzgerald. And the

two of you have a history? This sounds juicy. Start talking, Shepherd. I want all the dirt."

"It's nothing. It was just high school stuff."

Aguilar crossed her legs and gave Thomas a *be-straight-with-me* stare.

"Don't pretend you're over this woman."

Thomas picked at his food, his appetite lost.

"I haven't seen Chelsey in a long time. Not much I can do about it, anyhow. She met somebody. It's time we moved on."

"Please. She's not serious about that gorilla. No self-respecting woman would commit to an animal like that."

He forced a laugh and chewed a piece of broccoli. As he raised his eyes, Ray stared at Thomas over Chelsey's shoulder. He danced on two left feet, the bully three sheets to the wind. Ray's face twisted, and before Thomas reacted, the man shoved through the dancers and bee-lined at Thomas and Aguilar. Chelsey rushed to catch up.

"I thought that was you, Shepherd," Ray said, dropping a meaty paw on the table. Aguilar's water spilled. "Wipe the smirk off your face. I don't appreciate guys staring at my girl."

"Hey, Ray," Chelsey said, grabbing his chin and directing his eyes at hers. "Thomas and I ran into each other on a case. Sometimes we work together. There's nothing going on."

Ray narrowed bloodshot eyes at Thomas.

"'Course there's nothing going on," Ray slurred. "Shepherd knows what would happen if he moved on my woman. Ain't that right, tard?"

"That's enough. You've been drinking."

Ray ignored Chelsey and bumped into the table. Thomas caught his cup before the water spilled onto Aguilar. Where the hell was Lambert?

"You think I'm impressed that you're a shitty county deputy? If you didn't have that badge, I'd kick your ass across the village."

Thomas held Aguilar's arm and rose from the table.

"We were just leaving, Ray. Nobody wants trouble."

Aguilar's eyes shot between Ray and Thomas.

"We're leaving?"

"I didn't mean to cause a scene. Sorry if I interrupted your dance."

Aguilar's mouth hung open. What did she want Thomas to do? He wasn't a teenager anymore and couldn't start a fight over an old girlfriend.

"Just like you, Shepherd," Ray said, leaning his arms on the table. "Running off like the yellow punk you always were. That bitch on your arm would be a better challenge. I didn't realize you dated boys. Retarded and queer."

"That's enough!" Chelsey snatched Ray's arm and yanked him away from the table.

Ray threw Chelsey off his arm and lunged at Thomas. Chelsey smacked the ground and clutched her side. Thomas pushed past Ray to get to Chelsey before Ray threw a punch at Thomas's face. Ducking under the blow, he wrapped his arms around the bully and subdued him as the dance floor cleared. Someone screamed for the police.

"Get off me, you son-of-a-bitch," Ray growled.

"I won't fight you, Ray. Stop struggling."

Ray freed one arm and swung his elbow into Thomas's temple. Pain shocked through his head. Thomas ducked another blow, then grabbed Ray's arm and twisted it behind his back. Lambert arrived as Thomas pinned Ray face-down. Aguilar stood over the fallen drunk with a smirk on her face. Thomas glanced up at Aguilar as he struggled to keep Ray down.

"You seem to be taking this rather well."

Aguilar shrugged.

"I've been called worse. Besides, this is the most entertainment I've had in years. You're all right, Shepherd. I'll never forget this act of chivalry."

"Thank you, but he's a rather large man. Could you help?"

Lambert arrived and helped Thomas hold Ray flat. Thomas watched from the corner of his eye as Chelsey brushed off her dress. Raven appeared. She consoled Chelsey and stared at Thomas as though he'd caused the fracas. Lambert removed his cuffs.

"Didn't I tell you not to cause a scene?" Lambert said, smiling at Thomas as he clipped the cuffs over Ray's wrists.

The tall deputy yanked Ray into a standing position and shoved him toward the waiting cruiser.

"You better go after your woman," Aguilar said, lifting her chin at Chelsey.

"That wouldn't be wise."

"Don't argue with me, Shepherd. Help your girl."

Chelsey swiped a tear from her eye and stomped out of the tent. Hearing her choked sob, Thomas rose to run after Chelsey. Raven set her hands on her hips and blocked him.

"What the hell was that? I thought you were supposed to uphold the law, not start fights."

"I did everything to mitigate a fight. Let me pass."

"Oh, no. You've done enough damage for tonight. Stay the hell away from Chelsey." Before strutting away, Raven whirled back on Thomas. "And leave my brother alone. You don't know what we've been through. He's not a killer."

37

Chelsey leaned against her Civic and threw her hand against the door. Tears blurred the parking lot. Around her, couples strolled hand-in-hand and cast troubled glances as she sobbed. A week ago, she'd felt like she had her life under control. Then she turned a corner and found *him* standing there. It was as if she walked into a time warp. The old feelings rushed back at her.

Thomas was the only boyfriend who treated her right and cared. And she'd loved him. My God, she'd loved him. There was no good reason for tossing Thomas out of her life. But she'd been young, confused, and terrified. When depression struck Chelsey, she blamed herself, as if she could have foreseen her mental breakdown and staved it off. Hundreds of therapy sessions and countless failed relationships later, she just wanted to forget who she'd been before her life spun out of control.

She plunged inside her purse and ripped a tissue out. Dotting her eyes, knowing her makeup was ruined, she stared at the stars and searched the heavens for answers. Why now? Why throw this man into her life when everything seemed perfect?

Heels clicked across the blacktop. Chelsey followed the

sounds to Raven. Her partner cupped her elbows with her hands and shivered. Setting her eyes on Chelsey, Raven hurried to her friend.

"What happened in there?"

"I don't want to talk about it."

Raven set a hand on Chelsey's arm. Chelsey fell forward and accepted her partner's embrace. She cried into her friend's shoulder, unaware of the whispers directed their way from people who witnessed the altercation. Beneath the tent, the band played on. Villagers laughed and danced, and the world spun, indifferent to Chelsey's frustration.

"Ray Welch is a horse's ass. I never understood what you saw in him."

Chelsey shrugged.

"He's the only guy in town who paid attention to me."

Raven held Chelsey at arm's length and met her eyes.

"Are you serious? There are hundreds of men in Wolf Lake who'd kill to be with you." She tilted her head at the tent. "Starting with that fine looking hunk of deputy."

Chelsey squeezed her eyes shut and shook her head.

"That's not a road I'm willing to go down again."

"Hold on. You know Deputy Shepherd? I thought he was new in town."

"No, he's from the village. He moved out to Los Angeles and made detective with the LAPD."

"You sure know a lot about Deputy Shepherd. What are you waiting for, Chelsey? He stood up for you, and he's ten times the man Ray is."

"Thomas and I were together a long time ago. Sometimes, you need to let go."

"From where I stand, you don't appear ready to let go."

"I don't believe in fairytale endings or second chances. What's done is done."

Raven dropped her arms to her sides and appraised Chelsey as she would a shattered mirror not worth repairing.

"All right, I won't debate you on the issue. Let's get you home and cleaned up."

Chelsey pulled the keys from her purse.

"I can drive. I only had one drink, and that was an hour ago."

"This isn't about how many drinks you had. There's no reason for you to be alone tonight. I worry about you."

"Well, don't. I've taken care of myself since I was a teenager. If you don't mind, I'd prefer to put on a pair of sweats and watch Netflix with Tigger."

With a sigh, Raven glanced toward the tent. Deputy Lambert led Ray to the cruiser in handcuffs, while Chelsey pretended not to notice. But the hurt crawled into her throat and coiled there. How had tonight spun out of control?

"Will you at least call me when you get home? I need to hear you're okay, or I won't sleep tonight."

Chelsey nodded once. Raven pulled her into another hug and patted her on the back.

"Don't fight your demons alone, Chelsey. People care about you. Let us in."

38

Distant lights sparkled inside the village as Scout watched from her bedroom window. If she used her imagination, she could hear the music and smell the sweet flower scents mingling with the smoky, greasy foods. She struggled across her bedroom floor, pulling the chair over a dirty shirt she forgot to toss in the hamper. The Virtual Searchers website filled her browser, and a document containing everything she'd discovered about the killer—his username, the times and locations he recorded the videos, and links to the websites that hosted the files, sat in the bottom right corner of her screen.

The killer used a sock puppet account, a deceptive online name. Some people used generic names like John Doe. Others hid behind celebrity names. This madman used Max Cady from the Cape Fear movie. A Google search for Max Cady yielded notes about the story. Typing at her terminal, she narrowed the search to forums and found reviews and opinions. Nothing about the man hiding behind the fictional name.

An idea occurred to Scout.

Using an internet tool, she could drag images into a search

box and compare results across the web. Excitement chipping away at her exhaustion, Scout copied an image from the guinea pig video and watched the results scroll across her screen. Her eyes scanned the images and stopped. While the killer uploaded the Erika Windrow murder videos under Max Cady, she discovered two sock puppet accounts linked to the animal torture videos—Max Cady and ScorchedEarth666. Anticipation tingled her skin. Criminals always made mistakes and left a trail of breadcrumbs. She'd found one.

Scout opened a second window and searched images uploaded by ScorchedEarth666. He'd uploaded pictures under this name for over a year. She clicked a photograph that appeared taken from an apartment overlooking a city. The disturbing image featured a skull on the edge of a desk with a cityscape at night in the background. For a moment, she wondered if the skull was real. But the skull appeared too perfect. It glimmered in the light, fake and plastic. A Halloween prop.

Why upload this picture? The image received no likes, zero comments. Was this a twisted warning, a preview of the forthcoming murders?

Perhaps she was wrong and this wasn't the same man. Then her eyes locked on a candle behind the skull. She recognized it. Squinting, she was certain this was the same candle he placed beside Erika Windrow's severed head.

Scout pulled the image into her editor and zoomed in on the cityscape. He'd photographed the image with a small aperture, throwing the background out of focus. A red sign stood amid the lights, nothing she recognized. This might be any city. Tapping a frustrated hand against the desk, she examined the EXIF data. Harmon, last December. Right before the animal videos surfaced. That confirmed ScorchedEarth666 and Max Cady were identical.

"Scout, are you still awake?"

Mom's voice. Scout shut the monitor down and wheeled back to the window. She snatched her social studies textbook off the nightstand and opened it to the middle.

"I'm awake."

A hesitant twist of the knob, then the door swung open. Mom glanced at the clock—it was after ten.

"I thought you intended to wake up early tomorrow and go to the farmer's market with me."

Scout snapped the book shut and set it on her lap.

"I'll be fine. I just want to finish this chapter before bed."

"No problem. It's not a school night, and you're welcome to sleep in tomorrow if you'd prefer to stay home."

The hopeful glimmer in Mom's eyes made Scout bristle with guilt. These days, they rarely spent time together.

"I want to go with you. It will be fun."

"All right, but don't stay up late." Mom wrung her hands in the doorway. She studied the computer monitor and desk, as if she sensed the heat pouring off the screen and knew Scout had been on the internet moments before she opened the door. "I spoke with your father tonight."

An electrical shock moved through Scout. She set the book on the nightstand and turned the chair to face her mother.

"Did he ask about me? Is he coming to visit soon?"

Mom glared at the floor.

"Dad got a new job in Ithaca. The electric company promoted him to supervisor, and he's working long hours."

"So he's too busy to see us."

"Scout, your father is dealing with the accident on his own terms. He still blames himself for what happened. Your father will come around."

Tears pressed against the backs of her eyes. She sniffled and turned back to the window.

"I don't care anymore."

"Don't say that, honey."

"Why not? It's true. He'd rather apply for promotions than be with his family. I'm not waiting for him any longer."

"Listen, let's call him together—"

"No!"

Mom bit her lip. Scout saw the injury on her face, watched her mother's back slump in defeat. Mom drew a composing breath and straightened her blouse.

"I promise everything will get better. Don't hate your father. Please be patient."

"Can you close the door?"

Mom opened her mouth and swallowed her reply.

"I love you, Scout. I'll be in my room if you want to talk."

The door closed. Quiet suffocated the room, forcing Scout to tug the window open and invite the chilly night inside. Now the music played from afar. She closed her eyes and breathed, a technique her therapist taught her during the months following the accident. Outside, a branch snapped, popping her eyes open.

She waited for the sound to come again. It didn't.

Scout shut the window and pulled the shade down. She sensed eyes on her, though nobody could see past the shade.

Calm down, she thought. This is just your imagination.

She turned the computer on and glared at the image. The skull, the cityscape, the night. What was she missing?

As she turned away, her eyes locked on an imperfection. Something on the tabletop. Scout refocused the picture and narrowed her eyes. The table reflected the man's hands as he held the camera. She swallowed. The sheriff had it wrong. The killer was white.

39

Darren Holt handed a trail map, a restaurant guide, and the keys to cabin three to the bald man at the welcome desk. The man wore thick glasses and a winter coat that wouldn't serve him well when the temperature hit sixty-five this weekend. A pigtailed girl with a thumb buried in her mouth rested in the crook of his arm. The mother, a blonde woman in dress slacks and flats, clutched the handle of her suitcase. The state park attracted all types. Darren hoped the family packed outdoor clothes, or they were in for a long weekend.

After the door shut, Darren ran a tired hand down his face and grabbed his keys. He switched the lights off on his way out. Sharp starlight threw long shadows across the gravel parking lot as he trudged to the ranger's cabin. He fit the key into the lock and flipped the lights on. His eyes stopped on the sink. The faucet dripped with hollow plunks. Confused, he wrenched the handle until the drip stopped. He swore he'd shut the faucet down before he left.

Studying the room for anything out of place or missing, he shrugged off his paranoia. Why would anyone break inside his cabin? He kept his wallet and weapon on him. There was nothing worth taking, unless someone wanted the area rug.

Darren snatched a beer from the refrigerator and popped the top, squinting at the first bitter sip. He set the beer beside the window, settled into a chair, and propped his feet on the wood stove. Coal and ash scents tickled his nose. After opening a hunting magazine, he found himself staring at pictures and words without comprehension. Why couldn't he relax?

Screw this. He set aside the beer and magazine, donned his jacket, and stepped outside. Lights shone inside cabin three. The woman's shadow passed over the shade. It was good to have company for a change, though he doubted he'd encounter the family on the hiking trails. With a grumpy, tired four-year-old, the couple would stick to the cabin grounds and use the grill.

Cold sliced through Darren's skin. He tucked his hands inside his pockets and moved down the trail, overcome by the sky. Stars stretched from one horizon to the next, unimpeded by the village lights. The trail glowed in silvers and blues, interrupted by the shadows of overhanging branches as he pushed through underbrush and stepped over a muddy trench. Below the park, Wolf Lake shimmered. His gaze automatically searched for a boat, someone on the water after dark. But it was deathly quiet. Not a soul in sight.

He descended the ridge and considered stopping by Deputy Shepherd's house. Then he remembered the village dance. Thomas wouldn't be home until late.

An unearthly howl rose off the faraway hills. He froze and listened. He might be crazy, but that sounded like a wolf. There hadn't been a wolf sighting in New York State in two decades, and the last known wolf had been shot two hours east of here. Had to be a coyote or a dog. He waited for the howl to come again, listened for a return call. Nothing.

At the ridge base, he spied the shoreline where the killer had dragged the skiff into the water. Brazen. It was as if he wanted the deputy to catch him.

The A-frame house peeked over the tree line, the downstairs lit like a runway. Water kissed the land in gentle hushes. As Darren turned away, he saw the shadowed figure behind the deputy's house. The man faced away from Darren and stared at the Mournings' house, silent as a statue.

Pins-and-needles swept through Darren's limbs. He reached for his phone and realized he'd left it on the kitchen counter.

Darren took a hesitant step forward. The gun rested on his hip. But he had no authority on private land, and he was steps away from leaving the park. The marshy ground squished beneath his boots. He stopped and held his breath, worried he'd given himself away. The silhouetted figure didn't move.

Closer now.

Darren crossed the shoreline and entered Deputy Shepherd's backyard. A hemlock tree leaned between Darren and the stranger. His heart hammered with the possibility this might be the killer, the maniac who tossed Erika Windrow's remains into Wolf Lake. Whoever it was, he was trespassing on the deputy's property and stalking the neighbor. Darren remembered the woman—a single mother with a young teenager in a wheelchair. And he had no way to contact the sheriff's office or call for help. His shoulders tensed.

Another step forward. He pressed against the hemlock and peered around the trunk. The stranger hadn't moved, didn't realize Darren had closed in on him. The ranger removed the gun. Stepped out of the shadows and onto the starlit lawn.

A twig cracked beneath his boot. Dammit.

The man darted between the houses and vanished as Darren sprinted after him.

40

Regret gathered in a ball beneath his breastbone.

Thomas stared straight ahead with his hands curled around the steering wheel, the black night flying at the windshield. He avoided discussion of what happened tonight, though he felt the interrogation in Aguilar's stare. He'd wanted the deputy to enjoy herself at the dance. They'd met less than a week ago, but already he liked Aguilar. She'd never admit tonight was important to her, but the supple dress told the story. The deputy wanted a fun night out on the town, and Thomas's drama ruined her plans.

When Thomas ducked the punch and took Ray Welch to the ground, he was an angry teenager again, sick of the bullying. It took all his reserve not to twist Ray's wrist up his back and snap the drunk's arm. He saw red when Chelsey landed hard.

"You should call her, Shepherd."

His attention drifted across the car. Aguilar leaned in the corner between the seat and door, one leg crossed over the other, deep understanding sharpening her eyes.

"Who, Chelsey?"

"Who else would I mean?"

Thomas gripped the wheel a little harder, then eased off. Aguilar judged every move he made.

"I doubt she wishes to hear from me."

"If not now, when?"

He didn't have an answer. Besides, Chelsey had no interest in discussing their past. She'd made that clear inside the warehouse. His phone hummed in the cup holder. He'd forgotten to take the phone out of silent mode. Transferring the call to the speakers, he was surprised to see Darren Holt's name on the screen.

"Ranger Holt. What may I do for you?"

"Thomas." Darren sounded out of breath. "I'm at your neighbor's house."

Thomas straightened in his seat. Aguilar leaned forward.

"The neighbor's house. Are Naomi and Scout okay?"

"I caught some guy watching their house from your backyard. He heard me coming and took off running. I lost him in the thicket across the road."

"Did you get a look at him?"

"Big, athletic guy. That's all I could determine in the dark."

"Strong enough to carry a skiff across my yard and dump a dead girl in the lake?"

"I'd say so. Sounds like we're on the same wavelength. I called the sheriff's department. Gray is on his way to Naomi Mourning's house. And Thomas?"

"Yes?"

"There's a hole in your sliding glass door. Looks like the guy used a glass cutter to break inside."

"Don't touch anything. We need to dust for prints." He kicked himself. Darren didn't require his explanation. "I'm on my way."

Thomas swung his gaze to Aguilar. He didn't need to ask if the deputy wanted him to drop her at her house. She kicked off her heels and dug two sneakers out of her bag. Aguilar caught him staring and shrugged.

"What? I come prepared."

He cut through downtown and hit the lake road. With no street lights, the blacktop drowned in darkness, and he pumped the brakes when he took the bend too fast. Sheriff Gray's cruiser slumbered in the Mournings' driveway when Thomas stopped the truck. Darren met them on the steps.

"Gray is inside taking statements," said Darren, edging the door closed. "Just so you're aware, the mother isn't taking this well."

"What did she say?"

"She needs to blame someone for putting her daughter at risk, and you're a convenient fall guy."

"I understand."

"She'll come to her senses. Follow me."

They circled the A-frame and climbed onto the back deck. Thomas scanned the boards for dirt or a shoe print as Aguilar knelt beside the deck door. Wind rustled the curtain.

"Yeah, he used a glass cutter," Aguilar said. "I'll call county forensics. Let's hope this prick screwed up and left a print."

Thomas whipped his eyes toward the neighbor's house. Lights blazed through the windows, and Naomi sobbed inside.

"We go in slow and careful," Thomas said, unlocking the door. "Just in case he's inside."

The door whispered open. Aguilar, wearing the floral Cami dress and running sneakers, took the living room while Darren eyed the staircase. Thomas swept the gun across the kitchen, then joined Darren at the stairs. The ranger's eyes locked on the wall at the top of the staircase. When Thomas looked up, he saw the red dripping letters painted against the wall.

Hero.

Darren's jaw worked from side to side.

"Bold bastard, isn't he?"

Thomas pulled his mouth tight and led Darren up the steps while Aguilar guarded the downstairs. He caught a whiff of fresh paint when he cleared the top step. Room by room, they searched the upstairs. The maniac wasn't inside the house.

"He probably broke inside before you caught him in the yard," Thomas said, standing away from the wall, not wanting to touch anything. The forensics team would arrive in less than an hour.

"He might have broken into my place too."

"The ranger cabin?"

"I worked the front desk early in the evening. When I returned to the cabin, the faucet was dripping, and I'm positive I'd shut it off. I swear something seemed out-of-place inside the cabin, as if he'd rummaged around while I was away. What the hell does he want with me?"

Thomas holstered his gun and descended the stairs.

"The same thing he wants with me. To get inside my head and prove he can reach me anytime he wants."

Gray met them in front of the Mournings' house.

"I'll stick around until forensics arrives," Gray said, working a kink out of his neck.

"Did they see anything?" Thomas asked, lifting his chin toward his neighbor's window.

"Nothing. Until Ranger Holt pounded on the door to check on them and use their phone, they didn't realize someone was in the yard."

The door creaked open. Naomi angled her head through the entrance.

"Deputy Shepherd, may I speak with you a moment?"

Aguilar glanced at Thomas. He lowered his head and climbed the ramp. When he reached Naomi, he raised two hands in placation.

"I understand you're upset. You have a right to be."

Naomi's face was red and chapped with dried tears. She swiped a tissue beneath her nose.

"Since you arrived, I've needed eyes in the back of my head to keep my daughter safe."

"I'm sorry. I don't want any of this."

"What does he want with you?"

Thomas released a breath. With Naomi's hair down and cupped against her face, it struck Thomas how much the woman looked like Erika Windrow. He searched the catalog of his memory—similar height and build, high cheekbones, inquisitive eyes.

"Naomi, it's possible he's targeting you."

Naomi's face froze in a stunned expression.

"Why me?"

"Maybe he saw you when he canvassed the lake. Remember you said someone was in the yard Sunday night?"

"So he stalked my family?"

"It's one theory. But I'm on his radar. Before Ranger Holt chased him out of the yard, he broke inside my house and left a message on my wall."

She covered her heart with her hand. Behind Naomi, Scout's wheelchair squealed.

"I need to speak with Deputy Shepherd," Scout said, imploring Naomi with her eyes.

"Not a chance, Scout. I told you to stay away from those videos, and you went behind my back." Naomi's glare flicked to Thomas. "Tell my daughter, Deputy. She's not to involve herself in your investigation."

Thomas bit his lip. Scout had tried to tell him something earlier, and he'd ignored her. Had the killer discovered Scout was investigating him? Naomi set her hands on her hips and stared at Thomas.

"You look like you have something else to tell me."

"Come outside for a second," he said, pulling the door shut.

While Gray conferred with Darren and Aguilar in the driveway, Naomi danced to stay warm on the porch.

"What do you need to say?"

"What if this guy is after Scout?"

Her face twisted, prepared for an argument.

"How would the killer know she's searching for him?" Cold realization hit her eyes, her body wracked by terror. "The sleuthing website. He's on the forum."

"That's what I'm afraid of. Let me speak to your daughter. I need her contacts, anyone she corresponds with online."

"Yes, whatever you need."

Thomas scratched behind his neck and swiveled his head toward his house as the county forensics team pulled into his driveway.

"I need to deal with the forensics team. After that, would you like company tonight?"

Naomi brushed the chill off her arms.

"What are you suggesting?"

"We don't have the resources to post a deputy outside your house all night. I keep an air mattress in the closet. Let me set it up in your living room. I'll sleep better if I know you're safe. You won't even know I'm here."

Naomi pressed her lips tight.

"All right. I'm scared, Deputy."

41

After stealing four hours of sleep in Naomi's living room, Thomas called Darren and asked the ranger to watch Naomi and Scout while he drove to work Saturday morning. Using voice commands, he dialed his father's number. No answer. Next he called his mother and got her voice-mail. He pictured them staring at his name on their screens, ignoring him until, in his mother's words, he came to his senses.

"Mom, it's me. I'm checking on Father and would like to stop and see you. If there's a convenient time, please call me." He hesitated. "I love you both."

As he pulled into the lot, he noticed Gray's vehicle. Thomas hoped he could avoid the sheriff today. Gray still insisted the Harmon Kings were behind Erika Windrow's murder, and Thomas wasn't up for an argument.

He passed through the empty lobby, coffee scents wafting through the station. Keeping an eye out for Gray, Thomas kicked his computer out of sleep mode.

"It's your weekend, Shepherd. You couldn't stay away?"

Thomas turned to find Lambert leaning in the doorway, one hand wrapped around a coffee mug.

"I'm tying up a few loose ends."

"They figure out who broke into your house?"

Thomas slumped into his chair and entered the URL for Scout's teen sleuthing website.

"Not yet."

"If I were you, I'd put cameras on the yard. Don't let this psycho sneak up on you again."

Not a bad idea. He needed to stop at the hardware store. The days were getting warmer, and he didn't want every insect in Wolf Lake to crawl through the hole in his deck door. Lambert peeked over Thomas's shoulder while he navigated the forums. Over two hundred sleuths claiming to be teenagers called the website home. Thomas wondered how many were adults. Was the killer among them?

"Gray's in a foul mood this morning," Lambert said as Thomas typed Harpy's name into the search box.

Scout had been reluctant to give up her friend's name. Naomi insisted, if Scout wanted internet access.

"Something going on?"

"Tessa Windrow was in here earlier. Now she's threatening to sue Gray and the county. As if it's our fault. If she'd paid attention to her daughter, the girl wouldn't have run away in the first place." Lambert pointed at Thomas's computer screen. "Who's Harpy?"

"A girl Scout Mourning chats with online."

"That's the teenager in the wheelchair you mentioned?"

"My neighbor, yes. Something tells me this friend of hers isn't who she claims to be."

Memories from last night stuck into his skin like prongs. Scout believed the same man who uploaded the animal murder videos killed Erika Windrow. The data proved the videos came from Harmon, so Scout might be right. He was aware serial killers progressed from animals to humans as they gained confidence. Scout linked the Max Cady profile name to ScorchedEarth666, something Thomas had failed to do. One image showed the man's hands reflected on the table top. A white guy. This wasn't LeVar Hopkins or Anthony Fisher.

But something else struck Thomas. Harpy knew too much about the killer. She located images and videos Scout couldn't find. Yet Harpy never noticed the reflected hands. Was Scout a superior investigator, or was Harpy concealing the killer's race?

Lambert pulled up a chair just as Gray's door opened. The sheriff's eyes locked on Thomas.

"Isn't this your day off, Deputy Shepherd?"

"I'll be out of your hair in a second," Thomas said as he loaded Harpy's posting history.

Gray strode to the computer. His eyebrows angled down.

"You're wasting time. You won't find a killer on a message board."

"It's worth checking."

Gray harrumphed.

"Shepherd, in my office. Now."

Lambert gave him a sympathetic look. Thomas followed Gray into his office. The sheriff closed the door, fell into his chair and leaned forward.

"Your judgment has me concerned, Deputy."

"Sir?"

"Listening to a teenage girl when the evidence points to LeVar Hopkins and Anthony Fisher."

"There's reason to believe the killer is white. If you examine the photos—"

"We have Anthony Fisher on camera mailing Erika Windrow's remains. What more proof do we need?" Gray's eyes softened. "This can't be easy on you, Thomas. The shooting, your father's diagnosis, and I threw you into a murder investigation your first day on the job. As much as I'd prefer to hand the case over to Aguilar or Lambert, I need your expertise."

"Anthony Fisher is just a kid. I don't believe he murdered a prostitute and cut her into pieces."

"That's because LeVar Hopkins did the deed. But if we prove Fisher knew what was in the box, he's just as guilty."

"This doesn't feel right."

Gray drew a long breath and set his palms on the table.

"If you insist on working on your day off, I want you focused on Hopkins. Link him to the murder. I want a search warrant for the Chrysler Limited and his mother's apartment. Get me both. That's your task for today."

Thomas wanted to tell Gray he'd peered inside the Limited with Aguilar. No bloody passenger seat. No signs of a struggle. He saw no point in arguing with the sheriff. Gray had decided.

He left the sheriff inside his office and returned to his computer. Lambert held the phone to his ear. He pointed at Thomas and snapped his fingers. A second later, Lambert hung up.

"We got an Anthony Fisher sighting. He's at the corner of Third and Main in Harmon."

Thomas hustled with Lambert to the cruiser. The deputy hit the siren and cleared traffic on their way to the interstate. With Lambert's foot jammed against the gas, they reached the Harmon city limits minutes later.

"Kill the siren," Thomas said as they descended the exit ramp into Harmon.

With the lights and siren off, Lambert slowed as they neared Third Street. The sidewalk was vacant at this time of the morning. The shops wouldn't open for another half-hour. Lambert searched the left side of the street while Thomas leaned out the window, eyes locked on the alleyways.

"There they are," Lambert said, hitting the accelerator.

Thomas swung his eyes to the corner. Anthony Fisher and LeVar Hopkins split, Anthony sprinting left as LeVar took off in the opposite direction. A tractor trailer blocked the intersection.

"Shit." Lambert requested Harmon PD support and swung the cruiser to the curb. "You up for a morning jog, Shepherd?"

Lambert ran after Anthony. Thomas slammed the door and cut across Main Street as a white SUV skidded to a stop ten yards from him. The driver laid heavy on the horn and cursed out his window. LeVar vanished around the corner at Second Street. Thomas pumped his arms and legs. With no chance to beat the teenager in a footrace, he took a diagonal angle and cut through a parking lot, gambling LeVar would stick to Second Street.

The dice roll paid off. Thomas emerged from the parking lot steps behind LeVar. The teenager ran too hard to notice, long legs widening the gap between Thomas and his target with each stride. Thomas's chest tightened, his lungs burned. An alarmed woman with a grocery bag under her arm dove back when Thomas passed. Now LeVar was half a block ahead and pulling away.

Thomas reached for his radio. Out of breath, he gave the Harmon dispatcher LeVar's position. The teenager hugged close to the storefronts, convincing Thomas he'd turn left at the corner. Thomas ran through an alleyway that opened at Lewis Boulevard. When he turned the corner, he gained a hundred feet on LeVar. The teenager glanced over his shoulder, spotted Thomas, and kicked into a hidden gear. He leaped over a hedge and bounded across a lawn. A second later, LeVar's feet disappeared over a wooden fence.

After Thomas climbed the fence and squeezed between a sports car and a garage, his lungs on the brink of mutiny, he stood upon a crumbling sidewalk. Apartment houses lined the street. No sign of LeVar.

He searched left and right. Then he spied the sign on the corner. Bethel Avenue. LeVar's mother lived in an apartment at twenty-six Bethel. He scanned the building for numbers and located the gray brick apartment complex halfway down the block. Thomas crossed the street and removed his weapon.

The outside door wasn't locked. He turned the handle and stepped inside. A hallway marred by cracked plaster led to four closed doors. A cartoon boomed from the closest apartment. As Thomas eyed the staircase, a child laughed behind the door.

Steps squealed beneath his weight as he climbed the stairs toward the Hopkins apartment. When he reached the landing, he stared at the open doorway.

"Ma...ma! Wake up!"

Thomas threw himself through the entrance. LeVar hunched over a figure on a couch. The woman's legs hung off the edge like broken oars, her arm draped against the floor. Even with the teenager blocking his view, Thomas spied the syringe on the floor.

The boards groaned as Thomas crossed through the kitchen. LeVar spun around. A mix of fury and panic twisted the teenager's face. Time froze as they glared at each other like two enemy dogs that watched one another from neighboring windows with sharp, snarling teeth.

"What the hell are you waiting for? Call an ambulance!"

Hurrying to the woman's side, Thomas dropped to his knees and raised the radio to his lips. As he requested the ambulance, Thomas snatched her wrist and searched for a pulse, shocked at the brittle frailty drizzling beneath her flesh. He found the pulse —weak and fading. LeVar glared between Thomas and his mother. The teenager appeared torn between jamming his

Taurus 9mm against Thomas's temple and scooping Serena into his arms. Shock forced the boy to do neither.

"She's alive, right? Tell me she's breathing."

"Your mother has a pulse. The ambulance is on the way."

LeVar clutched his face and squeezed. He seemed ready to tear flesh away before his arms dropped to his sides and a defeated cry poured out of his throat.

"I knew it would be the goddamn heroin. I tried to make her stop, but she don't listen."

Serena's lips turned purple, the color of gloaming. Thomas put his hand over her mouth. At least the woman was breathing.

"Put the gun away, LeVar."

"What?"

"You heard me. Find a place for the gun before the apartment fills with cops."

Thomas gave LeVar a meaningful look. Understanding smacked the teenager in the face, and he turned down the hallway, looking back at his mother. As Thomas worked, hangers clinked inside a bedroom at the end of the corridor. A box opened and snapped shut. Where the hell was that ambulance?

"Stay with me," he begged as he ground his knuckles into the woman's chest.

LeVar whipped around the corner and grabbed Thomas by the shoulder, yanking him off his mother.

"What the fuck are you doing? You're killing her."

"I'm trying to save her life. Stand back and let me do my job."

Thomas searched for a pulse again and found none. He tilted Serena's head back. As he began CPR, his eyes locked on a chemistry textbook on the end table with a notebook tucked beneath. Was LeVar or Serena taking classes? Counting the compressions beneath his breath, he pushed down on the woman's chest. Stopped and pinched her nose before delivering rescue breaths. No response. He placed one hand on top of the other and began another round of compressions when the ambulance siren shrieked around the corner. Beside him, LeVar knelt with his arms clutched around his head.

As the emergency crew clambered up the staircase, the woman gasped. Thomas met the teenager's eyes.

"She's alive."

42

Seeing all those tubes and wires snaking out of her mother punched Raven in the gut.

After the altercation at the dance last night, she'd gone into the office and worked until the adrenaline wore off. Chelsey wouldn't accept her company, claimed she needed to be alone, and Raven knew better than to argue with her friend's mule-like stubbornness. She hadn't fallen asleep until four. Then the phone rattled her out of bed at eleven. LeVar never called Raven, and she knew with dreaded certainty something terrible had happened when his name appeared on the screen.

LeVar sat beside their mother, the plastic chair drawn beside the bed. A heart monitor beeped and displayed an erratic rhythm. Outside the door, a doctor in blue scrubs hurried past.

"What happened?" Raven asked, sliding into a chair beside LeVar's.

Their mother looked too frail to be alive. Brittle bones. Skin like fading parchment paper, stretched to the point of tearing.

"She overdosed."

"Heroin again?"

He lowered his head and rested his hand on their mother's.

For a long time they watched her without speaking. There were no words. No doctor needed to tell them she was hanging by a thread. For too many years, Raven and her mother had remained estranged. After Serena threw Raven out of the house, Raven wanted nothing to do with her mother and realized Serena couldn't be saved. Seeing Serena on the brink of death, a bridge spanned the many years of regret, and Raven's anger and resentment faded away.

A nurse rapped on the door and ordered Raven and LeVar to leave. The doctor would be in shortly, and they could sit in the waiting room. The way the nurse twisted her lips in disgust made Raven wonder how the woman treated the white, wealthy visitors from Wolf Lake.

A dozen cushioned chairs girded the waiting room. A corner table held various magazines and yesterday's newspaper. Raven and LeVar were the only people in the room. He crumbled into a chair along the far wall and sat with his elbows on his thighs and his head hanging to his chest. Long dreadlocks dangled to his knees, and his hands clasped together, as though he uttered a silent prayer. As Raven slid into the neighboring seat, she realized she hadn't felt this close to her brother since she was a teenager and he was barely out of puberty. How could she ever fear him? She set a trembling hand upon his, expecting him to pull away. Instead, he reached across with his free hand and covered hers. Together, they sat in quietude while the hospital staff bustled through the corridor.

"Will she make it?"

When LeVar raised his head, tears cut down his cheekbones, his eyes washed in red. Raven needed to give him an answer, though she couldn't predict what would happen. The next few hours were crucial. If their mother survived the afternoon, she had a fighting chance.

"She's a strong woman."

He sat back, released a breath, and brushed the dreadlocks over his shoulder.

"I been trying to get her into rehab. Told her I'd pay, but she wouldn't have it."

She patted his arm.

"You can't play the role of parent."

"Why not? Someone has to."

Raven saw the accusation in his stare. She looked away.

"If she wakes up—"

"*When* she wakes up," he corrected, locking eyes until she nodded.

"When she wakes up, we both need to be there. We'll form a united front and demand changes. She has to check into rehab."

"And if she says no?"

Raven chewed the inside of her cheek.

"Then we both walk away. Tough love, isn't that what they call it?"

"Seems to me that's all you've done for the last seven years. Has it worked?"

"Mom left me no choice."

He lifted his chin and glared at the opposite wall. LeVar possessed his own stubborn streak.

"Well, it ain't right. No matter how she treats us, we gotta be there for her. She's all we got."

Raven dropped a reluctant arm over his shoulders. His muscles twitched, but he didn't pull away.

"I don't get it, LeVar. You're a smart kid with a good heart. Why do you run with the Kings?"

"I make more with the Kings than I would working three jobs."

"Is the gamble worth it?"

"Someone's gotta pay the rent and put food on the table. You think I wanna risk my head every day, or worry if Rev is gonna explode over some stupid bullshit? I do what I gotta do. You ain't helping, so don't judge me."

An idea struck Raven. Why hadn't she seen it until now?

"You're trying to leave the Kings."

He turned his head.

"What's this nonsense?"

"Don't lie to me, LeVar. For the past month, you've been sneaking into my house, sleeping on the couch, and hiding out. You're planning to leave the Harmon Kings."

He ground his teeth. But he didn't deny her accusation.

"Do it," she said. "Whatever you need, I'm there for you. But you have to get out of that apartment. You can't live with that madness another day."

"Who will take care of Mom? She can't do it by herself."

"That's why we need to get her into rehab. When she gets out, she'll be a new person." Raven tasted the lie on her tongue and struggled to hide her doubt. "Either way, you can't watch over her twenty-four hours a day. Mom has to stand on her own two feet."

LeVar rubbed his eyes.

"Everything I do...it's all for Mom. She don't thank me sometimes, but she knows."

Raven turned to face him and set her hands in her lap.

"I need you to be truthful. Because you're my brother and I'll do anything for you. But you have to tell me. All these things people say you did, all the gang violence in Harmon—"

He shook his head and leveled Raven with a glare. And in that moment, she believed him.

"Ain't none of it true. I busted a few lips, but no way I pulled the trigger on anybody. People say shit, but it don't make it fact."

"You're the most feared man in Harmon."

He laughed, but the humor didn't reach his eyes.

"I survive on rep. People believe I did these things, so when they see me coming, they step. Haven't needed to pull my gun in a long time."

A tear tracked down her face. She touched his cheek.

"I never believed the rumors. Thank you for telling me the truth. But it doesn't change what I said. You can't stay there any longer. Eventually, the city will catch up to you, and something terrible will happen. Get out, LeVar."

"You don't just walk away from Rev."

"Come stay with me. I'll protect you."

"In that tiny ass house? Not enough room."

"Could have fooled me, all the times you slept on the couch while I was on the job."

He became quiet, considering. After several heartbeats, he glanced down at his hands.

"I'm taking classes."

Her mouth froze open. LeVar had dropped out of high school two years ago.

"Wait, you went back to school?"

"I'm getting my GED at the community college."

Raven's throat constricted, and she touched her heart.

"Why didn't you tell me?"

He lifted a shoulder.

"Didn't tell no one. Thought I'd finish things up, then surprise everyone when I got my degree. My teacher says there are scholarships for people like me, that I should take a few college classes after and see if I like it."

No words sufficed to express the joy surging through Raven.

"You'll do it, right?"

"I'll give it a shot."

"This is amazing news. Everything is turning around for us, LeVar. Mom will be all right, and you're leaving the Kings and earning your diploma."

"I can't be living on no couches, though. You hate the Kings. I get it. But the money is good, and I can pay for my own apartment, if I stick it out a little longer."

"No. That's no good. Not another day with the Kings. Don't be afraid of Rev."

"It look to you like I'm afraid of anybody?"

He wasn't afraid of Rev, and that scared the hell out of her. A knock on the door pulled their heads up. Deputy Shepherd leaned in the doorway. LeVar straightened his back.

"How's your mother?"

Raven glanced at her brother. She was certain the deputy intended to arrest LeVar.

"We're waiting to hear from the doctor. But she made it through the hardest part."

"Anthony didn't kill that girl," LeVar said, rising out of his chair. "What did you do with him?"

The deputy blocked the doorway.

"Anthony Fisher is at the Nightshade County Sheriff's Department for questioning. If either of you know anything, now is the time to talk."

LeVar questioned Raven with his eyes. She nodded.

"Anthony says a big white guy approached him. Gave him a hundred dollars to mail the package. You won't arrest Anthony, right? He's just a kid."

"I can't make any promises about Sheriff Gray, but I'll relay what you said. My partner is talking to Mr. Fisher now."

"Let our boy walk," LeVar said, rising from his seat.

The deputy hesitated.

"That's not for me to decide."

43

When Thomas returned to the office, Gray stood with his arms folded outside the meeting room. Lambert interviewed Anthony Fisher while Gray watched through the window and guarded the door.

"Did I miss anything?" Thomas asked, setting his coffee on the desk.

"The kid claims some guy paid him to mail the package." Gray swiveled to Thomas and set his hands on his hips. "Where's LeVar Hopkins? I thought you drove to the hospital to see about the mother."

"He's there with his sister."

"And you didn't arrest him?"

"On what grounds?"

A vein pulsed in Gray's neck.

"We went over this. Build a case on Hopkins and get me a warrant. Now if you'll watch the door, I need to make a phone call."

A minute later, Lambert led the handcuffed boy out of the meeting room.

"You're locking him up?"

Lambert's exasperated expression told Thomas he had no choice. Thomas slid into the rolling chair in front of his desk and picked up where he'd left off this morning, clicking through Harpy's forum activity. Lambert returned and sat on the edge of Thomas's desk.

"So the kid claims a white guy paid him to mail the box."

Thomas rocked back in the chair.

"Do you believe him?"

"If he's a liar, that kid will make a fortune in poker."

"Did you get a description on this mystery guy?"

"Caucasian, an inch or two over six feet, muscular. Buzzed blonde hair, military length. Fisher described the guy's face as red and irritated. Like he shaves too close or something. He wore sunglasses and a Yankees cap."

"Anything else?"

"Fisher said the guy was quirky."

"How so?"

"After he handed the box to Fisher, the guy dug into his pocket. The kid figured he was reaching for a gun. Instead, he pulls out a bottle of hand sanitizer and disinfects his hands. Starts rattling on about germs getting under his skin."

Thomas touched a pen to his lips.

"Fisher ever see this guy around before?"

Lambert shook his head.

"Never."

"If this was Los Angeles, I'd sit Fisher down with a sketch artist."

The tall deputy chuckled.

"Good luck getting a sketch artist around here. We'll be on a two-week waiting list."

"What do we do now?"

"I'll send his description over to Harmon PD. Maybe it rings a bell with the beat cops. You heading home?"

"Not until I go through these forum posts."

Lambert patted Thomas on the shoulder and walked to the break room. As Thomas sifted through the messages, he considered the information Scout had gathered. The picture she recovered proved the murderer was white. But he couldn't prove Fisher was telling the truth, or the man in the video was the same person who paid Fisher to mail the package to the *Bluewater Tribune*. He tapped the pen against the desk and squeezed his eyes shut. The killer flaunted his murders instead of hiding. Why couldn't they catch this guy?

He picked up his phone and dialed Naomi. Her cell dumped him into her voice-mail. Next, he called the house phone. No answer.

Ice formed over his spine. Where were they?

44

Sunlight sparkled across Wolf Lake as a mild breeze played through Scout's hair. Though Deputy Shepherd —or Thomas, as he insisted she call him—hadn't poured the concrete, the carved paths allowed her to navigate the wheelchair through the bumpy, rutted yard. Trying to repay Thomas for his generosity, Mom polished the guest house windows.

"Don't leave my sight," Mom said as Scout wheeled toward the hemlocks guarding the back of the yard.

"I won't go far."

She stopped at the tree line. Though the shore lay fifty feet away, she could see the lake from here and taste winter's chill burgeoning out of the frigid water. By summer, the water would be warm enough for swimming. A dip in the lake today would cause hypothermia.

As the water breathed against the shoreline, she shielded the phone from the sun. Unable to read through the glare, she muscled the chair forward until she rested in the shadow of the hemlocks. Over her shoulder, Mom scrubbed the windows overlooking the lake. Scout called up the Virtual Searchers website and entered her password. No new messages awaited her, and she felt a pang of disappointment. With Harpy's aid, she'd discovered secrets about the killer the police hadn't known.

Scout read the latest posts on the Wolf Lake murder and found nothing useful, just hyperbole she'd expect to read in the newspaper. She was about to give up when a notification appeared. Clicking the icon, she caught her breath. Someone tagged her name in a post.

She followed the link and found a message. A forum administrator who went by the name CerealKilla had discovered a new video from ScorchedEarth666. Her heart pounded. This was the first activity from the sock puppet account in months, and the video hit the internet two minutes ago. Why had the administrator tagged Scout?

While she waited for the video to load, she surveyed the water. Despite the beautiful weather, nobody was on the lake today. Her gaze moved to the state park. Smoke curled over the trees, evidence someone grilled outside the cabins.

The video still wouldn't load. The WIFI didn't reach this far from the house, and she relied on the slow cell network to access the internet. She read through the comments.

Ms. True Detective posted: *Call the police, Scout. And please tell us when you're safe.*

Scout's hands trembled. How had the poster learned Scout's name? She never shared her name on the forum, choosing to hide behind the user name, Rokdab3lz, which referred to *Rock the Bells*, a classic hip-hop song from LL Cool J. Another poster warned Scout to get inside and call the authorities.

She could barely hold the phone by the time the video loaded. Her eyes flicked around the screen in confusion. The video title included Scout's name:

Watching Rokdab3lz aka Scout Mourning

Scout played the video. This was impossible. The video revealed Scout in the wheelchair, her mother scrubbing the guest house windows in the background.

Her eyes shot to the trees. The shore. The shadows spilling across the yard like blood at midnight. A sob wracked her chest, and she fumbled the phone into the dead leaves. She bent over and reached, but the phone lay beyond her fingertips.

A branch cracked like a bull whip.

Her head spun toward the noise.

"Mom?"

No answer.

Now she struggled to move the wheelchair over the soft ground as the wind became insistent, pressing her, filling her ears with its shrieking rage.

"Mom!"

Footsteps racing at her from behind as the damn wheel stuck in the earth.

"Help, Mom!"

Closer.

"Scout? What's wrong, baby?"

Mom pulled the wheel out of the divot and knelt before the chair. Panic fluttered like frenzied birds in her mother's eyes.

"He's watching us."

"Who? What's going on, Scout?"

The tremolo ripping through Mom's voice told Scout she knew.

"Call Deputy Shepherd. The killer is here."

45

"Explain to me what you mean by EXIF data."

Thomas shared a tired glance with Lambert. They sat across the desk from Gray, the sheriff's hands folded in his lap. Gray's face was a mix of confusion, irritation, and surprisingly, curiosity. As Lambert's legs bounced with unspent energy beneath the desk, Thomas reiterated his belief the same man behind the animal murders killed Erika Windrow. On Gray's computer, Thomas loaded the image Scout located. Gray squinted at the table top reflection.

"Appears to be a white person holding the camera," the sheriff said. "But we need more proof. All this tells me is the video came from Harmon. We have a hundred thousand people in the city. You need to narrow it down, unless you expect me to arrest every white male."

"What do you intend to do about Anthony Fisher?"

Gray rocked back in his chair.

"He delivered the box. I can't release him until we're certain he didn't know about the contents." The sheriff brushed his mustache. "This murder is gang related. I can feel it in my bones."

"The Kings don't have any white members," Lambert said.

"Then we should focus on the Royals and Troy Dean."

Thomas scratched his chin.

"Why would the Royals murder their own prostitute? A pretty woman like Erika Windrow must bring in a lot of money."

"What if she shorted the Royals on cash and owed them?"

"It's a possibility."

Gray rapped his knuckles on the desk.

"Follow that path. Link the 315 Royals to the murder and find out who had motive to kill Erika Windrow."

Thomas edged the door shut and stared at Lambert. The deputy threw his hands up in frustration.

"I'll talk to Fisher again," said Lambert. "But it seems he would have told us if a Royals gang member paid him to send the box. Why would he cover for a sworn enemy?"

"I don't understand it, either."

As Lambert wandered back to the cell, Thomas's phone rang. He was about to call Naomi again. Relief flooded his body when he read his neighbor's name on the screen.

"Naomi, I called you earlier."

"The killer is watching us right now."

With the phone clamped between his ear and shoulder, Thomas opened Gray's door and motioned the sheriff to follow.

"The killer is near your house? Can you see him now?"

Gray's eyes widened. He mouthed, "Mourning?"

Thomas nodded and held up a thumb. While Gray fastened the holster and straightened his hat, Thomas wrote everything Naomi told him. This was their chance to catch the madman before he escaped. His priority was keeping Naomi and Scout safe, but even driving at twice the speed limit, Thomas wouldn't reach the lake for ten minutes.

"Get inside, lock the house, and don't answer the door for

anyone you don't know. I'm calling Ranger Holt. We'll be there soon."

His body thrummed with tension. The killer targeted Scout and posted the video for the world to see, an open challenge to the sheriff's department. As Gray and Thomas hurried to the cruiser, Thomas phoned Darren. The ranger was at his cabin and could reach the Mourning residence in five minutes. Gray called Aguilar from the car and told the deputy to meet them at the lake.

The trip took less than ten minutes. To Thomas, it seemed like hours before the cruiser pulled into the driveway. Darren opened the door as Gray and Thomas approached.

"Did you see anyone along the lake?" Thomas asked.

"Nobody," Darren said.

Thomas found Naomi and Scout in the living room, the girl's face pallid and shocked, Naomi seated on the edge of the couch with her face buried in her hands.

"Tell us what happened," Thomas said as Gray moved from window to window, peeking through the curtains.

Naomi had been in the yard, tidying the guest house windows while Scout sat near the lake shore. The Virtual Searchers forum posted the link as soon as the killer uploaded the file. The forum administrator ran a scan which searched the internet for files uploaded under the Max Cady and ScorchedEarth666 sock puppet accounts. After the admin received an alert and noticed Scout's name in the title, he realized the killer was recording the girl.

"All right," Thomas said. "You're safe now, but I need to see the video."

Naomi retrieved her laptop. As the recording played, Thomas focused on the shooting angle. He waved Darren over and turned the screen toward the ranger.

"Does it look to you like he's shooting from Mrs. Kimble's yard?"

Darren bent closer and narrowed his eyes.

"From the trees, yes. Look at the top left of the screen. There's a blue spot where the water reflects off the lens. He was close to the shore."

Another vehicle pulled along the shoulder, and Thomas spotted Deputy Aguilar striding toward the ramp as Gray opened the front door. After they briefed Gray and Aguilar on the killer's position, the sheriff took the deputy outside to search Mrs. Kimble's property.

"Any way to track this guy from the upload?" Darren asked.

Thomas shook his head.

"The video will tell us where and when he uploaded the file. But he's using assumed names, and so far we haven't linked the sock puppet accounts to an actual person."

Outside, Gray discovered a shoe print among the trees and called the forensics team. The print location aligned with the video angle.

"It isn't safe here," Naomi said, shivering as she cupped her arms. "I'm taking Scout to her father's house in Ithaca."

Thomas eyed Gray, who shook his head.

"I don't recommend you do that," said Thomas. "You're safe with the sheriff's department watching over you."

"You can't be two places at once, and it's a small department."

"I'm off work through the weekend, and I'm not leaving you alone. Let's get you out of the house. I have a guest room upstairs at my place. No sense in you being alone now that the killer recorded Scout."

"I don't know," Naomi said, dropping her gaze to the floor. She sniffed and brushed a tear off her face. "We outfitted our house with ramps, and you can't get Scout's wheelchair up the stairs."

"That's nothing we can't work out. The important thing is I move you to a different location and protect you. My house is defensible."

"Is it? He broke into your house too."

He tapped his holster.

"I'll be ready if he tries again."

46

Savory scents wafted through the A-frame's kitchen as Naomi stirred a pot of beef stew. Thomas offered to cook or order food. Naomi refused and said she'd lose her mind if she didn't stay busy. Now Uncle Truman's former house smelled like the good old days, Aunt Louise and Uncle Truman hosting Thomas for the weekend, the boats passing by outside the windows. Then he'd felt secure, shielded from the world. Thomas didn't trust the memories. Nobody was safe until they caught the killer.

The last rays of the sun vanished behind the western hills. Red spilled across the lake's placid waters.

Thomas lowered the phone and leaned against the counter while Naomi added a dash of salt. He'd just talked to Gray at the office. The forensics team confirmed the shoe print matched a print taken behind the A-frame. Meanwhile, Lambert worked overtime and studied the video for anything they missed. Aguilar was in Harmon, coordinating with the city police department and questioning the prostitutes again.

Scout sat in her wheelchair beside the kitchen table. The girl hadn't spoken in hours, and Thomas could see the terror scuttling on spider's legs beneath the girl's skin. With Darren's help, he'd carried Scout and the wheelchair up the deck stairs and into the house. When this nightmare was over, he'd knock down the steps and add a ramp. He wanted Scout and Naomi to visit and never worry about accommodations.

After the frantic afternoon, Scout had forgotten her phone charger inside her bedroom. Now her phone battery was dead, and it was obvious the girl wanted to access the internet and read the Virtual Searchers forum.

"Take it as a blessing," Naomi told Scout as she lowered the burner flame. "The last thing you should do is read the sleuthing website. That's how all this trouble started."

Scout turned her head and bit back an argument as an idea occurred to Thomas. By studying the killer's videos, they'd discovered he was Caucasian and lived in Harmon. The killer was careful, but he'd slipped up more than once. This was their best chance to catch him.

"Naomi, I'd like your permission to bring Scout into the investigation."

Suddenly awake, Scout glanced between Thomas and her mother. Naomi's mouth dropped open.

"I don't like the sound of this. How would Scout assist you?"

Thomas studied the girl, astonished by the inquisitiveness lighting her eyes.

"Scout drew the killer's attention because she came so close to catching him. She has ways to track this guy we haven't thought of."

"I'm not comfortable with Scout talking to people she's never met. Do you really believe half the members on that forum are teenagers? They might be adults...or anyone."

"Exactly." When Scout glanced at Thomas, he folded his arms. "What do you know about this friend of yours?"

"You mean Harpy?"

"Tell me about her."

Naomi set the spoon down and turned her attention to her daughter. Scout shrugged.

"There's not much to say. She's about my age, and she's the most active member on the forum."

"Where does she live?"

"I never asked. She mentioned snow in January the same weekend we had a storm, so I figured she lives in the northeast."

"Does Harpy know you live in Wolf Lake?" Scout licked her lips. "Be honest."

"Yes."

Naomi exhaled and said, "I told you never to divulge your name or location on that forum."

"It was only Harpy," Scout said, picking at her shirt. The girl couldn't decide what to do with her hands. "And I didn't give her my name."

Thomas tapped his foot and considered his options.

"Sheriff Gray is useless with technology, and Deputy Aguilar hasn't returned from Harmon yet. But Deputy Lambert knows his way around computers, and he's searching the forum now." Thomas glanced at Naomi. "What if we contacted the Virtual Searchers website for Harpy's identity?"

Naomi scrunched her brow.

"Do you have the technology?"

"If the sleuthing forum provides Harpy's IP address, I can trace her location."

They were both staring at Scout now. The girl's fingers curled around the chair arms.

"You're asking me to betray a friend. She'll never forgive me."

"The greater risk is Harpy isn't who she claims to be."

Thomas bore his eyes into her until Scout recognized the danger.

"All right. Do what you need to do."

"I'll call Lambert and have him track down the forum's contact information. In the meantime, I'd like Scout to show me how she tracked the killer's sock puppet accounts." Thomas stared at Naomi. "If you approve."

Naomi chewed a nail.

"I'll allow it."

Thomas retrieved his laptop from upstairs and set it on the kitchen table. Pulling a chair beside Scout as Naomi stood on tiptoe and peeked over their shoulders, Thomas unlocked his screen and turned the computer to Scout. The girl's fingers raced across the keyboard as Thomas studied her technique. She opened an application unfamiliar to Thomas. After she retrieved images from the animal murder recordings, Scout dragged the pictures into the application. Similar images filled the screen. Most were false positives, but three originated from the guinea pig video. Half the images came from Max Cady, the remaining portion from ScorchedEarth666.

"This is how I linked the sock puppet accounts," Scout said, pointing out matching images.

"How did you determine the second account wasn't just a fan uploading the killer's pictures?"

"The EXIF data. All these images came from Harmon around the same time. Basically between December and February."

Thomas rested his chin on his fist.

"What if you searched for images from ScorchedEarth666?"

"I already did that. That's how I found the table top reflection of his hands."

Thomas figured the killer hid behind additional user names.

"And did you pull that picture into your application?"

Scout scrunched her face.

"No, I didn't think of that."

"Give it a try."

Naomi pulled a chair beside the table and watched her daughter work. She appeared taken aback by Scout's knowledge. Until now, she'd seen the investigations as a hobby. Now she appreciated Scout's knowledge, recognized what her daughter could become with the proper guidance and training.

Five rows of six images, thirty photographs in all, filled the application's window. Thomas leaned forward and studied each image. Most were Halloween-themed pictures of skulls, not identical to the original image. Three rows down, his eyes stopped. Scout tapped her finger against the screen.

"It's the same skull image," Scout said. "But Scorched-Earth666 didn't upload this photograph."

"Who did?"

Scout clicked on the picture. The right side of the screen filled with data.

"RoyalsNY2. Does that mean anything to you?"

Was the killer a member of the 315 Royals as Gray theorized?

"Maybe. Search his account. What else has he uploaded?"

Scout's fingers flew across the keyboard, her eyes alive from the hunt.

Three pages of pictures loaded. Scout handed Thomas the mouse, and he scrolled through the rows.

"What are you looking for?" Naomi asked, her hand set on the back of his chair.

"These photographs date back two years." Thomas loaded a second page of pictures. "I'm searching for anything that tells me who this guy is."

"They're just random photos. It's like he got bored in his apartment and recorded anything he saw."

Thomas recognized the desk. This was the same room where he'd photographed the skull and surrounded Erika Windrow's head with candles.

A random photograph of the door and wall, taken at a sharp,

tilted angle. A cracked and stained ceiling, photographed from carpet level.

"Wait, what's that," Scout said when Thomas enlarged another wall shot.

She tapped her finger against a curtained window. In the distance, red letters glimmered atop a high-rise. Thomas couldn't read the blurred letters. But he knew what they spelled.

Thomas copied the photograph and sent it to Lambert at the office.

"That's the First National Bank of Harmon."

47

Full dark bled down the bedroom window. Thomas was uncomfortable leaving Scout and Naomi alone downstairs. But he couldn't coordinate with Harmon PD with his neighbors in the same room and eavesdropping on the investigation. Fifteen minutes from now, Deputy Aguilar, who'd worked since late morning and needed a break, would arrive to watch over Naomi and Scout. Thomas would take her place in the field.

His laptop displayed a Google Maps view of Harmon, centered on the First National Bank. Detective Barnes, a gruff sounding man with a baritone voice, worked on the other end of the line. Thomas heard the man typing at his terminal.

"He shot the picture from at least ten floors up," Thomas told Barnes.

"I've got four high-rise apartment buildings within a one-mile radius of The First National Bank."

Thomas scribbled the addresses as Barnes read them off. He plugged each into the search bar and viewed the bank from their locations. The first three apartment buildings had six, five, and eight floors, respectively.

"No, he's higher up."

Barnes exhaled.

"All right. Try Bellview Apartments on Main."

Thomas entered the location. Bellview Apartments had sixteen floors, tall enough to match the angle in the photograph. But something was wrong. He switched the view to a three-dimensional image. Panning around the screen, he located the bank. The red letters shone atop the building, but they were backward.

"No good. This view is on the west side of the bank, but the picture was taken from the east."

"Those are the apartment complexes within a mile of the bank that meet your criteria."

"Expand the radius. Give it another half-mile."

An irritated groan. Barnes went quiet as he pulled up a new list of apartment buildings.

"Try the complex at 46 Tasker Boulevard. The building sits east-southeast of the bank."

Thomas entered the new coordinates. The angle and distance looked right.

"That has to be the building."

"Trouble is, the complex has fourteen floors and two hundred tenants. How in the hell will you narrow it down?"

Shuffling his papers, Thomas grabbed the description of the man Anthony Fisher met. He read it back to Barnes.

"That sound like anyone you know?"

"It doesn't ring a bell."

"Which of your detectives covers the 315 Royals?"

"We all do." Barnes grumbled. "But Detective Edwards knows the Royals better than anyone."

"Is Detective Edwards in tonight?"

"She's out on a call."

"Patch me through to her. It's urgent."

Barnes wasn't happy. He hadn't met Thomas and didn't appreciate a county deputy acting like he ran point on a Harmon gang case. Thomas waited on hold for three minutes, the phone dead quiet as if he'd lost the connection. He was ready to hang up and call back when Detective Edwards answered.

"Good evening, Detective Edwards. This is Deputy Thomas Shepherd with the Nightshade County Sheriff's Department. I understand you cover 315 Royals activity."

"Among other things, including the Kings. What are you looking for?"

"I'm searching for a Royals member who meets the following description. It could be a former member, someone the new recruits wouldn't recognize."

Thomas read the description.

After a pause, Edwards said, "Shit. That sounds like Jeremy Hyde."

Thomas tore a sheet off his memo pad and wrote the name.

"Is Hyde currently in the Royals?"

"No. Hyde ran with the Royals two years ago, but didn't stick. The guy was a loose cannon. He did six months for assaulting a woman in the Target parking lot. Grabbed her by the throat and pinned her against a car. Two workers pulled Hyde off the woman and phoned the police after he ran off."

"When did Hyde get out?"

Edwards hummed as she thought.

"Last September or October. Is this related to the murder in Wolf Lake?"

"I believe so."

After thanking Edwards, he phoned Lambert.

"I got him," Lambert said. "Jeremy Hyde. Apartment 1224, forty-six Tasker Boulevard."

"That's our guy."

Thomas rocked back in his chair and caught his breath. His pulse raced, fingers tingled. He wanted to be in the field when the police and sheriff's department converged on Jeremy Hyde's apartment. What was taking Aguilar so long?

Voices carried from downstairs, soft and muffled. He dug his fingers into his scalp and forced his brain to slow down. No way he could think straight with a million images flying at him—Erika Windrow's headless corpse washing ashore, the serrated hunting knife sweeping across the woman's throat, a shadowed figure staring at the Mournings' house from his yard. How close did Hyde come to capturing Scout and Naomi? Had the killer been inside the house while Thomas showered before the Magnolia Dance?

He closed his eyes and breathed. Set his hands on his thighs and pictured the negative, frantic energy whirling inside him. In his mind, he directed the energy toward his fingers, a relaxation trick his therapist taught him after the shooting.

After a moment, his eyes popped open. Keeping his gun on him, he arranged his notes into neat stacks and clicked the papers against the desk three times, ready to leave as soon as Aguilar made it back from Harmon. Checked the time. If Aguilar didn't arrive soon, Thomas wouldn't make it to Harmon before the police took Hyde down. He'd promised to keep Naomi and Scout safe, and he meant to keep that promise.

But as he moved to the staircase, someone pounded on the door.

48

Thomas descended the stairs. In the living room, Naomi stood protectively in front of her daughter, the woman's eyes full moons of terror.

From this angle, he couldn't see the front steps, only a black shadow mirrored against the planks. Peering out the window, he searched the shoulder and driveway for Aguilar's cruiser. A green Honda Civic lingered behind his truck.

Chelsey.

"It's okay," he told Naomi. "I know her."

When he opened the door, Chelsey barreled past and set her hands on her hips.

"You told me we'd work together on the LeVar Hopkins case," she said, fire burning in her eyes. "Now I find out he's been at the hospital all this time."

Chelsey's gaze swung to Naomi and Scout. Confusion twisted her face.

"These are my neighbors," said Thomas. "Naomi Mourning and her daughter, Scout. You may speak in front of them."

Chelsey shook her head as though clearing away cobwebs.

"Serena Hopkins overdosed, and you never called me like you promised."

"I'm busy tracking a murderer, and there's no reason to pursue LeVar Hopkins. He didn't kill Erika Windrow."

"And who's Jeremy Hyde?"

Thomas did a double-take. Chelsey must have a contact inside the Harmon PD.

"Let the police handle it."

"If he murdered Erika Windrow, I need to be in the loop."

Another knock stopped Thomas from arguing. Finally, Aguilar had arrived. He pulled the door open and made introductions. Aguilar's brow quirked up when she saw Chelsey. Thomas threw a jacket over his shoulder.

"What did you find out in Harmon?" Thomas asked. When Aguilar glanced at the three guests inside his house, he held up a hand. "They've heard everything already."

Aguilar gave a hesitant nod.

"I received Lambert's call before I left, so I interviewed the women again. None of them recognized Hyde's name. But when I showed them Hyde's mugshot, they all claimed they'd seen the creep hanging around. Said he watched them from the alley near the adult video store."

"Did he ever approach the women?"

"No, but one swore she spotted him inside a white SUV last week. He slowed down beside the curb like he wanted to proposition her, then he sped off when she moved toward the window. I fed the information to the department. Turns out Hyde drives a white 2017 Chevrolet Trax."

"They have his address. How long before the police go in?"

"Soon. Hurry, or you won't make it in time."

He buttoned his jacket and checked his pocket for his wallet. Aguilar tossed him the keys to the cruiser.

"You'll stay until I return?"

"I've got you covered," Aguilar said.

"Expect Ranger Holt to stop by. He's watching the house from the state park."

As Thomas turned, Chelsey threw herself in front of the door.

"If you're going after Hyde, I'm coming too."

"Absolutely not. Your investigation is over, Chelsey."

"I'm under contract with Tessa Windrow. You can't stop me from following."

"As a sworn deputy for Nightshade County—"

"Come on, Thomas. I need to be there." When he narrowed his eyes, she raised her palms in placation. "I swear I won't interfere. The police will arrest Hyde. But I want to see the bastard's face when they take him out. Erika Windrow was only eighteen."

An unbidden memory flickered in Thomas's head—Chelsey at eighteen, crippled by depression, a girl with boundless promise crawling into a shell. Why hadn't he seen it before? Chelsey identified with Erika and needed to avenge the murdered girl.

"I don't have the time or patience to fight you," he said, jangling the keys. "You may come. But stay out of harm's way."

THOMAS SWUNG the cruiser into Harmon when Lambert called him with the news. He'd matched Harpy's IP address to Jeremy Hyde. Since winter, Scout had been messaging with a madman disguised as a teenage girl. He pressed the gas. Another five minutes until he reached Tasker Boulevard. When he hit a traffic glut, he scrolled through his contacts and located Naomi's number.

"Thomas, did the police catch him already?"

"Not yet. Naomi, do not let Scout visit the Virtual Searchers forum."

"I didn't plan to. Your voice sounds different. Is something wrong?"

"The girl she talks to, Harpy, is Jeremy Hyde."

Naomi didn't respond.

"Did you hear me?"

"I understand. But I can't tell my daughter. Not yet."

"We know who he is now. Hyde won't hurt anyone again."

Six minutes after the clock struck ten, Detective Edwards gave the order. An officer with black eyes to match his hair used a Halligan bar to breach the door. He could have kicked the flimsy barrier off its hinges had he chosen.

Two pairs of police officers swept inside the darkened apartment. The lights atop their weapons picked out the bed and kitchenette before Edwards flicked the wall switch. Thomas followed Edwards inside. He recognized the table, the marred ceiling and walls, the candles on the shelf. A death scent pervaded the room. It reminded Thomas of roadkill collecting flies in the heat of summer.

Two officers swung around the kitchenette counter and angled their weapons into the shadows.

"Clear!"

Fingers wrapped around his gun and poised on the trigger, Thomas struggled to focus. Too many people, too much shouting. A sharp pain bit into his back. One hand moved to the small of his back and touched the old wound as metallic sulfur scents tickled his nose. Impossible. No one had fired a weapon yet. The flashback spun his head.

"You with us, Deputy," Edwards asked, her stare penetrating.

He swallowed and nodded, a sheen of sweat crawling into his eyes.

One room left to search. The bathroom. With no hiding

places remaining, the police converged on the door and stood aside. On the count of three, the officer who'd used the Halligan bar kicked the bathroom door ajar. Thomas followed them in. One officer swept the shower curtain aside with a hiss. A blood splotch dried in the tub.

"He's not here," Edwards said, holstering her weapon. "If Jeremy Hyde has half a brain, he hit the road hours ago."

"He wouldn't leave," Thomas said. "Not yet."

"How can you be certain?"

Thomas pushed his tongue against his cheek.

"Because his work isn't finished."

The BOLO was already out for Jeremy Hyde when Thomas descended the long staircase and exited the building. Officers stationed in unmarked Harmon PD vehicles would watch the apartment and street corner where the prostitutes congregated. By now, the television news stations were running Hyde's photo. Someone would spot him before the night ended.

Chelsey leaned against Thomas's cruiser as he crossed the sidewalk.

"He's still out there," she said, shoving her hands inside her jacket pockets.

"We'll catch him, Chelsey. The entire county is looking for him now."

She stared into the belly of the city. Harmon's gang lands looked black and heartless, solitude and strife embellished by the bright lights of fast-food restaurants and porn shops.

"I'm sorry for losing it earlier."

"You want to catch him as much as we do. I understand."

"It's not my case, and I overstepped my bounds. I just wanted to do right by Erika. What the heck was I thinking, coming here like I was an official part of the investigation? I was wrong about LeVar Hopkins, didn't even choose the right gang. I'm not cut out for this."

He wanted to lay a hand on Chelsey's shoulder, tell the woman he once loved he believed in her. Instead, he stood frozen on the concrete walkway as officers streamed past. A CSI team pulled to the curb.

"The important thing is we know who he is now. We'll catch him."

"It won't bring Erika back to her mother."

"Are you certain Erika would have gone back to her mother had she lived?" The question hit too close to home. In the throes of depression, Chelsey had fled her home and ran from demons she couldn't escape. Thomas read the hurt on Chelsey's face and wished he hadn't spoken. "I should get back to the house."

"It's good you're looking after your neighbors, Thomas. You always had the biggest heart in Wolf Lake. The woman...Naomi?"

"Yes."

"She's quite pretty."

Thomas rolled a knot out of his neck.

"I hadn't noticed. Look, Naomi and Scout are in this mess because of me. I'm obligated to keep them safe. I'd better get back to them." He removed the keys from his pocket. "I'll see you around, Chelsey."

"Wait." She grabbed his arm before he stepped off the curb. Across the street, two women whispered and pointed at the police cars. "I want to help."

"There's nothing you can do to—"

"Your neighbors are in danger because of my incompetence. Had I recognized Raven's brother wasn't the killer, maybe this guy wouldn't be running free. I'll follow you back and park down the road. You could use an extra set of eyes."

"The temperature will fall to forty degrees overnight. You'll freeze sitting in the car."

"I'm used to stakeouts."

He pushed the mop of hair off his forehead.

"You don't understand the meaning of *no*, do you?" He stepped off the curb and circled around the cruiser. When he reached the door, he peered at her over the roof. "Well, are you coming?"

49

The moon crawled beneath the hilltops, the unearthly glow haloing the peaks. Outside the window, the lake road glowed in silver and blue tones. No vehicles had passed in the last hour. The suffocating quiet made Thomas wonder if he was the only person alive in the world.

Thomas yawned and peeked at the clock. Three in the morning. He'd sent Aguilar home after midnight. Hunkered down in an unoccupied guest room on the upper floor of the house, he stared through the glass frontage overlooking the road, keeping the lights off so prying eyes couldn't see inside. In the next room, the door stood closed with Naomi and Scout asleep. Earlier he'd carried the girl upstairs, then folded the wheelchair and set it beside their bed. Since Naomi rose to use the bathroom an hour ago, there hadn't been a peep inside the house.

His walkie-talkie squawked. With his gaze fixed to the shadows curling around the house, he raised the radio to his lips.

"Thomas here."

"It's Darren. Just checking if you're still awake."

Thomas eyed the thermos of coffee. He'd consumed half a pot already, and his body buzzed as fatigue lay heavy on his bones.

"Hanging in there. You see anything?"

Darren had driven to the top of the ridge and parked his truck, watching Thomas's property through a pair of binoculars.

"Nothing. You really think Hyde will come tonight with half the county searching for him?"

"I admit I'm losing faith. If you want to turn in, I won't keep you up. I have the house covered."

"I'm in it for the long haul. Heck, I kinda miss stakeouts. All I need now is a submarine sandwich with extra onions. The smell used to drive my partner crazy."

Thomas chuckled.

"It was always tacos for me. Can't get a good taco in Wolf Lake." Down the road, hidden between two pines, Chelsey's car slumbered in silhouette beneath the shoulder. He brought his own binoculars to his eyes and searched for her. Shadows blanketed the car. "I appreciate you hanging with me all night. I owe you one."

"And I'll collect when the time is right." After a second of radio silence, Darren said, "Tell you what, Thomas. I'm not helping you by sitting on this hill. Gonna circle around and check out the lake road."

"Gotcha. Be careful."

Darren ended the conversation, and Thomas sipped from the thermos. A ground mist crept out of the trees and spread toward the road, the windows beginning to fog. He wiped the blur away with his shirt and pressed the binoculars against the glass. Chelsey's car hadn't moved since midnight. He pictured her alone in the Civic, shivering and toughing it out. She didn't have a radio, and he didn't have her cell number. He'd been too uncomfortable to ask.

This was ridiculous. It was lunacy for her to sit alone all night.

"Darren," Thomas said into the radio. "I'm heading across the road to check on Chelsey."

No answer. If the ranger had the volume low, he wouldn't hear Thomas over the engine.

He stopped outside Naomi's door and listened. The peaceful susurration of their breathing carried beneath the threshold. Descending the stairs, he grabbed a second thermos from the cupboard, filled it with coffee, and started another pot. Edging the front door open, the cold sharp enough to scour away his fatigue, he stood on the deck and peered across the road. Still couldn't find Chelsey, only the Civic's indistinct outline amid the pines. After he locked the door, he jogged across the blacktop and high-stepped through the dewy weeds. His breath caught in his throat. The car appeared empty. Then he saw her face staring at him through the windshield.

She lowered the window and glowered at him.

"What are you doing?"

"Enough is enough. It's too cold to sit outside all night. If you won't go home and sleep, at least come inside."

Her gaze cut toward him. She sighed.

"That won't make you uncomfortable?"

How could he be less comfortable? His heart hammered into his throat. It was illogical to have feelings for her after fourteen years.

"I'll worry if you don't come inside. Here," he said, handing her the thermos. "This should cut through the chill."

She stared at him through the open window for several heartbeats.

"Fine."

Chelsey raised the window and locked the car. Together, they followed his path through the weeds and climbed to the shoulder. In the five minutes he'd spent outside, the fog had spread to the median. Soon it would blanket the house. How would he know if someone was sneaking through the yard?

His hands trembled as he inserted the key into the lock. A fusion of cold and nerves. Chelsey shivered when she stepped inside the house and rubbed the goosebumps off her arms.

"Would you like something to eat?"

She shook her head.

"I can't eat this late. Upsets my stomach."

He nodded.

"Tell me if you change your mind."

Her eyes swept around the interior.

"This is a beautiful place."

"Do you remember it?"

"How could I forget? All those times you stayed with your aunt and uncle, and they invited me to eat dinner with you." She leaned against the counter. "Where are your neighbors?"

"Upstairs. You're welcome to take the empty guest room. I put fresh sheets and a comforter on the bed."

"I wouldn't sleep," she said through chattering teeth.

Thank goodness he invited her in. She teetered on the edge of hypothermia. From the pantry, he removed a loaf of raisin bread and dropped two slices into the toaster. While the bread toasted, he dug the butter out of the refrigerator. The toast popped after a minute, and he snatched the scalding-hot slices and placed them on a plate, licking the burn off his fingertips. After he buttered the toast, he raised the dish.

"Last call."

She shrugged.

"Why not? I'll be up all night, anyhow."

They took their toast upstairs to the unoccupied guest room. The chair he'd hauled out of the kitchen sat beside the window. He rolled a desk chair across the carpeted floor and gestured for her to sit down. She no longer trembled, but anxiousness coursed through Chelsey in waves.

Thomas grabbed the radio.

"Darren, you there?"

Several seconds passed without a reply. Chelsey glanced at Thomas before the ranger's voice boomed through the speaker.

"I'm back, Thomas. Had to relieve myself in the ditch."

Thomas stifled a grin.

"I brought Chelsey Byrd inside the house. You'll see her car off the shoulder if you come down this way. It's a green Honda Civic."

"Roger that. I'm a mile east of your place. You might catch me driving past in a few minutes. Gonna check the road and make sure I'm the only person out tonight."

The radio fell silent. Through the window, Thomas interrogated every shadow, every wisp of fog, ready for whatever devilry the night would bring. He felt Chelsey's stare, though he made it a point to concentrate on the darkness closing in on the house.

"Maybe this was a mistake," she said behind him.

He turned his head as she rose. As she reached for the knob, he placed his hand against the door.

"There's no reason to leave."

"This is happening too fast. It's better if I stay in my car. I'm warm now."

Lowering his arm, his fingers twitched at his sides.

"Don't go."

Just two words. He'd held them inside for fourteen years. She turned her head away, and an injury he didn't believe still existed tore open inside him. He took a shuddering breath. Stepped away from the door and held an open hand toward the chairs.

"Please," he said.

She gave him a doubtful nod and followed him back to the window.

Chelsey slid into the rolling chair and crossed one leg over the other. She sipped her coffee. He turned his chair backward and faced her.

"When you first saw me outside the grocery store," he said, setting his forearms on the chair back. "You asked me if I was okay."

She took another sip without blinking.

"I remember."

"I've wanted to ask you the same question for fourteen years."

Her lip quivered, and she bit down to redirect the pain.

"You don't have to ask. I'm better now, Thomas. I have been for a long time."

"Good, because there's something else I need to ask."

"Okay."

His fingers twined.

"Was it my fault?"

She turned her face toward his. Confusion crinkled her brow.

"Was *what* your fault?"

"The depression. Because of the pressure you were under dating someone...like me."

Her eye twitched. Now she swiveled her chair to face him.

"Is that what you thought?" When he didn't answer, she reached out and touched his arm. "No, it wasn't you. You were the only person keeping me sane."

"Why wouldn't you talk to me?"

She dropped her face into her hands.

"Because I was young and stupid. And scared. And I was too blinded by my own pain to see what I was putting you and everyone through. My family, friends. I wish I could go back in time and tell my eighteen-year-old self that the darkness will pass, that I should let people in." He handed her a Kleenex, and she dried her eyes and curled her hand over the tissue. "Leaving you ripped my heart out. But you would have gotten hurt if I'd stayed."

Thomas swallowed.

"I wanted to help."

She leaned her head on his shoulders and cried. His body went rigid. He didn't know how to react. Cautiously, he brushed the hair off her face.

"I'm sorry," she said.

"Never apologize for crying. From the time we were born, it has always been a sign that we are alive."

She raised her head and stared.

"What was that?"

He shrugged.

"A proverb. It felt appropriate, given that you were crying."

She snorted and wiped her eyes on her forearm.

"I love that you're always so literal."

Her lips tightened. She regretted her choice of words.

"I understand what you meant."

"I'm sorry I hurt you," she said, lowering her head. "That I hurt *us*."

50

Four o'clock. Fog poised over the lake road.

Thomas rubbed his eyes and slapped his cheek when he drifted off. He sat at his post beside the window, a bloody strip on the horizon foretelling the coming day. He wouldn't let his guard down until the sun rose.

Chelsey fell asleep on the bed. She curled up, childlike with her arms wrapped around a pillow, as though it were a favorite stuffed animal. Careful not to wake her, Thomas left Chelsey alone and paused beside the bedroom where Naomi and Scout rested. Everybody sound asleep except him.

Darren hadn't radioed during the last hour. Thomas wondered if the ranger had parked on the shoulder, closed his eyes, and fallen asleep. Thomas padded into the bathroom. Checked the window overlooking the backyard and lake. Nothing moved except the fog.

Maybe he should give up. With the sheriff's department and the Harmon PD searching for Jeremy Hyde, the killer might be in hiding. Detective Edwards believed Hyde fled the county. But the theory didn't sit right with Thomas. Egotistical madmen didn't expect the police to catch them.

He turned on the faucet and splashed cold water against his face. Towel-dried his cheeks and brushed his hair back. The man staring back from the mirror appeared ten years older than he'd been twenty-four hours ago, eyes drooping, face lined and pallid.

As he crossed the landing to make one more round through the house, his phone hummed inside his back pocket.

Darren.

Groggy, he fumbled the phone and picked it up after it slapped the hardwood. Still ringing.

"Good morning, Darren. The walkie-talkie run out of battery life?"

"Where are you?"

He took one step down the stairs and froze. Felt the chill of night crawling up the staircase like rising flood waters and sensed something was terribly wrong. Quickening his pace, he crossed the living room and set his back against the wall.

"I found his vehicle, the Chevrolet Trax."

Thomas's mouth went dry.

"Where?"

"A half-mile west of your place. It's behind a grove, about fifty feet off the road. I wouldn't have seen it except..."

Thomas didn't hear the rest. The lake breeze was inside the house. He glanced up at the landing. Shadows spread across the hardwood and clawed down the stairs. As he stepped away from the wall, he knew Hyde was already inside the house.

The floor groaned.

Jeremy Hyde stepped out of the shadows. The madman towered over the deputy. He held the hunting knife with the tip angled toward Thomas's stomach. Thomas discerned the wicked grin curling Hyde's lips, the lunar glow of his teeth. His hand inched toward his shoulder holster. No chance to retrieve the gun, aim, and fire before the killer closed in on him.

"It's over, Jeremy. Drop the knife."

No response.

Over the killer's shoulder, Thomas spied the deck door open. The curtains fluttered. Somehow, the madman had dislodged the lock without alerting Thomas.

"The police know you're here. Set the weapon down and step back. I don't want any trouble."

Hyde lumbered closer. Six feet away now, close enough for Thomas to smell the rank of the man's breath. It was then Thomas realized Hyde was the man who knocked him down outside the sheriff's department. He couldn't let the psychopath pass. Thomas would die defending the women. As he shifted his feet, determined to beat Hyde to the stairs, the killer read his intentions and blocked him.

"Go away," Hyde said.

"Why would I do that, Jeremy? This is my home."

"It's my home now. Leave, and I'll let you live. You know what I came for."

His heart was an auger inside his constricted throat. Thomas inched his hand closer to the gun. Hyde thrust the knife in warning, and Thomas took an involuntary step backward. Darren must have called the police. Why didn't he hear sirens? He needed to buy himself another five minutes. Keep the killer occupied until Harmon PD and the county sheriff's department stormed down the lake road.

"Why did you upload the videos, Jeremy?"

The killer's head tilted over. His eyes narrowed.

"Because I wanted the world to see what I've become."

"And what's that?"

"You wouldn't understand."

"Try me."

Hyde licked his lips.

"Ask Erika Windrow. I am the darkness, Deputy. The nightmare that wakes you in a cold sweat."

Good. He'd coerced Hyde into talking. Every second was crucial.

"By sharing the videos, you allowed us to find you."

Hyde cackled.

"That's not correct, hero. I found *you*."

The cold licked at Thomas's flesh as Hyde closed the space between them. He had no choice but to go for his gun. But Hyde was too fast. The knife sliced at Thomas's face. He lunged backward and tripped, stumbling until the kitchen counter dug into his back. White-hot pain blinded his eyes. He grabbed the first thing he saw—a kitchen chair—and whipped it at the killer. The chair bounced off Hyde's chest and crashed against the floor.

If the killer turned, he had a free run at the stairs. But that would give Thomas time to pull the weapon and fire. Hyde sprang forward. Pivoting, Thomas drove his heel into the killer's belly and knocked him backwards.

Then a silhouetted figure appeared over Hyde's shoulder. Thomas squinted and recognized Chelsey amid the darkness. Inside, he screamed for her to run before Hyde spotted her.

"Are you looking for me?" she asked.

Hyde whirled with the knife. Arrowed out of the kitchen toward Chelsey with the blade sweeping at her face.

"Get down!" Thomas screamed.

Chelsey dove out of the way as Thomas removed the weapon and fired. The shot burned a hole through the killer's shoulder and whipped him like a deranged marionette. Thomas rushed forward. Finger pulling the trigger. One shot to the chest as Hyde turned to face him. Gunshot to the neck, clipping the carotid artery and raining blood against the floor, Thomas still advancing and firing like a train off its tracks as Chelsey lay against the couch with her hands clutched against her ears.

Squeezing the trigger, filling the A-frame with black thunder, until...click...click...click...

HYDE CRASHED against the hardwood while Naomi stared down from the upper landing.

With the gun trained on the fallen killer, Thomas stepped around Hyde and kicked the knife away. Hyde's labored breathing filled the downstairs as the swirling reds and blues of the cruisers lit the windows.

Something broke inside Thomas.

When the police and deputies entered the house, Thomas dropped to his knees in the living room, grasping a pile of cleaning rags he didn't recall obtaining as he soaked up the blood seeping into the hardwood.

"I have to restore it," he said as Chelsey snatched his arm and failed to pull him away. "To the way things were before. It has to be perfect."

Then he fell into her arms, and they knelt together, Thomas weeping into Chelsey's shoulder as the officers milled around them.

51

Gray was at the hospital when Thomas strode down the antiseptic-white corridor on Sunday afternoon. He didn't remember the sheriff stopping him from cleaning Hyde's blood off the floor—it remained a crime scene until the forensics team finished their work—and his head throbbed after two hours of restless sleep.

The sheriff leaned beside the elevators, his hat tilted low and both hands stuffed into his jacket pockets.

"I told you to stay home until your psych evaluation," Gray said, glowering at Thomas.

"I'm not on the clock. How's Serena Hopkins today?"

"She had a rough night. But she's awake and out of intensive care. You heading up to check on her?"

"Yes."

"You did good, Thomas. Your quick thinking is the only reason that woman is alive, and you were right about LeVar Hopkins and Anthony Fisher."

"Where are they?"

"We released Fisher this morning. LeVar Hopkins is upstairs with his sister." Thomas nodded and pressed the button. Gray touched his arm. “We need to discuss what happened this morning.”

“Nothing happened.”

The doors slid open. Thomas stepped inside. Gray shoved his thumb against the hold-door button and blocked the entrance.

“You attempted to soak up Jeremy Hyde’s blood like you spilled soda pop on the floor. I’m worried about you.”

Thomas glared at his shoelaces and pinched the bridge of his nose.

“The situation overwhelmed me for a moment, but I’m okay.”

“First the gang shooting, now this. Don’t tough it out. Everyone will understand if you need time to process what happened. Don’t turn into a recluse and hide inside your house until the evaluator clears you.”

“I don’t intend to be alone.”

Gray gave him a confused stare.

“You have my number.”

Gray released the button and stepped into the hallway. The doors swept together like curtains closing on a tragic play, and the elevator pulsed and thrummed as it lifted him to the fourth floor.

When he entered the corridor, he spied Raven Hopkins outside the waiting room. The woman held a phone in her palm, her thumbs racing to send a text message. She didn’t notice Thomas until he stood before her. The private investigator lowered the phone and folded her arms.

“Deputy Shepherd. I didn’t expect to see you today.”

“I understand your mother is doing better.”

“She’s out of the woods. I sat with her all morning and made sure she ate. She fell asleep five minutes ago.”

“I’d hoped to say hello. Please send along my regards.”

He gave a quick bow of his head and turned.

"Thank you for what you did." He stopped. Her eyes penetrated Thomas as if seeing him for the first time. "You cleared LeVar's name, and you saved our mother. And from what I understand, you shot the maniac who murdered Erika Windrow." He didn't reply. Just stood like a rudderless boat with a storm sweeping across the ocean. "Anyway, you'll always have a friend in me."

"There's no reason to thank me for defending an innocent man."

She clasped her hands at her hips and glanced toward the waiting room.

"My brother made his share of mistakes. But he's a good person, and he's doing everything he can to get out of gang life and help our mother. LeVar even enrolled in community college classes to get his GED. But there's so much on his plate. He needs an honest job and a place to stay, somewhere far from the city."

"Is there anything I can do to help?"

She shook her head.

"This is our problem to solve. He's a product of his environment. As long as he remains in Harmon, the temptation will always be there to stay with the Kings."

"And your mother? Won't the temptation be there for her, as well?"

"We talked her into rehab. Provided her doctor clears her, she'll enter the facility before the weekend. I can't predict how long the process will take. But we'll do whatever it takes to move her out of Harmon."

He wanted to ask Raven about Chelsey and if Raven had heard from her since this morning. After the police secured the house, Chelsey took her keys and drove home. She'd almost died. Thomas wondered how she'd handled the traumatic event.

Over Raven's shoulder, LeVar exited the waiting room and strode toward the bathroom at the end of the hall.

"I should get back to my house," Thomas said. "You know where my place is on Wolf Lake?"

"Yes. I see your truck parked in the driveway."

"Send your brother to my house tomorrow morning."

"LeVar?"

"I can help."

An extension ladder leaned against the guest house. Perched atop the roof, Thomas tore shingles off and tossed them into a wheelbarrow. This was the original roof. He remembered Uncle Truman putting the shingles on, could picture the radiant summer day as if had happened yesterday, his bike tossed in the grass with Thomas sitting cross-legged and watching the roof take shape.

When Thomas smiled, it was usually inside. He'd worked on expressing his emotions since he was a child. This time the happiness met his lips. He yanked the last of the shingles off the roof and flung it over the side. As he dabbed the sweat off his face, he saw LeVar crossing the yard. He wore blue jeans with tears across the knees, a red t-shirt that showed off his arms, and a baseball cap backward on his head. He'd tied the dreadlocks. Sunglasses concealed his eyes.

Thomas crawled down the roof and searched for the ladder with his foot. This was the tricky part. You had to find the perch and descend at a slow, even pace, or the ladder would wobble. Grasping the roof for purchase, he set one foot on the rung and glanced over his shoulder. LeVar held the ladder steady, the teenager's face unreadable.

"I got ya, Deputy Dog."

Thomas climbed down and removed his gloves.

"Appreciate the help," Thomas said, grabbing his water bottle and taking a long drink.

He offered it to LeVar. The boy held up a hand and shook his head.

"Why did you call me over here?"

"Please remove your sunglasses."

"Why?"

"Because I want to see who I'm talking to."

LeVar folded the sunglasses and dangled them off the collar of his t-shirt. He lifted his chin. The Harmon Kings enforcer had four inches on Thomas.

"All right. I'm listening."

"You're strong."

"I need to be."

"Are you experienced in construction and remodeling?"

"Like houses?"

"That's what I'm talking about."

"I don't know shit about either. Don't you remember? I live in a city apartment."

"How would you like to learn?"

LeVar twisted his face.

"You offering me a job or something?"

"Not a job. A way out."

"I don't follow."

"Come with me," Thomas said.

He unlocked the guest house and stepped aside, motioning LeVar to enter first. The boy bobbed his head as he took in the interior.

"This is sweet."

"I stayed here when I was a teenager. This was my uncle's guest house."

LeVar stepped beneath the water stain and stared at the ceiling.

"You got a leak in the roof."

"Not for long." Thomas leaned against the wall and crossed his ankles. "I thought you didn't know anything about construction."

"I recognize water damage. We have a permanent stain over the living room. Lady's sink upstairs leaks all the time. Last week, the damn thing dripped on me while I laid on the couch."

"*Lay* on the couch."

"What?"

"Laid implies you...never mind." He ruffled his hair. "Someone told me I'm a literal person. I'm trying to change. But you'll get used to me."

"You're a strange one, Deputy Dog. I still don't get what you're talking about. You're not offering me a job, but a way out?"

"Follow me."

Thomas led LeVar to the window. The teenager feigned disinterest, his chest puffed out, a swagger to his step. Until he saw the view. Then his chin dropped to the floor. A speedboat motored across the lake, churning waves which spread to the shoreline.

"This is your view? How much they pay at the county sheriff's department? I need to get me some of that."

"It's yours, if you want it."

LeVar glared at Thomas.

"You selling me your guest house?"

"No, I'm offering you a place to stay. No rent, no utilities. All I ask is you help me fix it up, restore it to the way it was. Scratch that. Let's make it better."

"Like I told you, I don't know nothing about construction."

"I'll teach you."

LeVar gave Thomas a side-eyed glare, the stare he'd shoot someone handing him a three-dollar bill.

"It's an honest trade," Thomas said. "Help me with the roof and floors, and the house is yours. Purchase your own groceries. There's no kitchenette, but you're welcome to use my stove anytime you like. I'll cut you a spare key."

LeVar folded his arms over his chest.

"Why are you doing all this for me?"

"You're not interested?"

"I didn't say that. No one ever did nothing for us, so why you wanna help?"

Thomas strode to the window and set his hands on his hips. The lake reflected the pristine sky, aqua-blue and full of possibility.

"This is more than a house. It's a place of healing." When LeVar narrowed his eyes, Thomas grinned. "This place helped me escape from a dark place. I'd like to do the same for you."

"Why me?"

"You're a good person, LeVar. Your sister tells me so. I see how much you care about others, how you dropped everything to help your mother. But there's one rule you have to follow, if you live here."

"What's that?"

"You leave the Kings, and you never go back."

LeVar took a cautious step forward and stood beside Thomas, peering out at the idyllic view.

"I could get used to this." He turned to Thomas. "What happens when we finish this project? You kicking me out after?"

"No, this place is yours as long as you need it. But there's something you need to learn. After I finish a project, I start the next."

When Thomas exited the guest house with LeVar, he found

Naomi and Scout watching from the property line. Naomi cast a skeptic eye at LeVar. Scout set her phone in her lap.

"LeVar Hopkins, these are my neighbors, Naomi and Scout Mourning." Naomi gave the boy a careful wave. Thomas nodded at LeVar. "LeVar's sister works for the private investigation firm that helped us track Jeremy Hyde. He'll be living in the guest house."

"I'm considering the offer," LeVar corrected.

"Welcome to the neighborhood," Scout said.

"I figured it would be nice to have an extra pair of eyes monitoring the lake," Thomas said, holding Naomi's gaze.

Naomi waited a heartbeat before nodding.

"That would make me feel safer. Are you from Wolf Lake, LeVar?"

"From Harmon, actually."

"I heard your stereo when you drove up," Scout said. LeVar lifted his chin again, expecting criticism. "That's the new Freddie Gibbs project."

LeVar glanced at Thomas in astonishment. Thomas shrugged.

"You listen to Freddie Gibbs?"

"He has the best flow in the rap game. But I'm old school at heart. LL Cool J, Public Enemy, Run DMC. All the classics."

"What did you say your name was again?"

"Scout."

Thomas touched his nose to cover a laugh. LeVar would have to get used to it—Scout was full of surprises.

52

Maggie was on her lunch break when Thomas entered the station. Aguilar had just left. Thomas's date for the Magnolia Dance had responded to a call on the west side of the lake. Something about a man running over his neighbor's flower garden with a lawn tractor. Normalcy returned to the village, though the specter of the Erika Windrow murder would be difficult to exorcise.

Inside his office, Gray looked up when the doors swung shut.

"You're not supposed to be here, Deputy. Not until you clear your evaluation."

"I left something in my desk."

The sheriff grunted.

"Come back to my office. Since you're here, there's something I need to speak with you about."

Gray rocked back in his chair, swiveling from side to side, as though searching for the right words.

"Is there a problem, Sheriff?"

"Have you spoken to your father since yesterday?"

"No. Why?"

"He phoned the office this morning. Maggie took the call before I arrived."

"What did he want?"

Gray tapped his hand against the desk.

"Your father is quite philanthropic, Thomas. No one has donated more to the Nightshade County Sheriff's Department since I held your position."

This was news to Thomas.

"I never knew he supported the department."

"I'm sure it's a writeoff for Shepherd Systems, but it isn't chump change. His donations bought us a fleet of cruisers two years ago."

"Why are you telling me this?"

Gray set his hat on the desk.

"Your father implied the donations would stop, if we didn't make certain personnel changes inside the department."

So this was Mason Shepherd's angle.

"Did he tell you to fire me?"

Sheriff Gray held up a hand.

"Not in so many words." Gray eyed the memo pad. Thomas recognized his father's number scribbled on the paper. "I'm to call your father back before five o'clock with an answer."

"What will you tell him?"

Gray sighed and rubbed his eyes.

"That the county appreciates everything he's done for the department, and we'd like him to reconsider."

"And if he demands you cut his son from the payroll?"

The sheriff straightened his shoulders and met Thomas's eyes.

"Then I'll tell him to pound salt. Nobody tells Stewart Gray how to run his department."

~

THOMAS SHIELDED his eyes from the dusty wind and crossed the parking lot to his truck. He called his mother's cell. No answer. This was the third consecutive time he'd reached her voice-mail. The silent treatment was straight out of Lindsey Shepherd's playbook. Until he knocked on their front door and agreed to resign as deputy, she would ignore him.

A car door closed, and he swung around to find Chelsey strutting toward the building. She wore her leather jacket unzipped, the sun washing orange highlights through her hair. Chelsey pulled up when she spotted him.

"I didn't expect you to be here today."

"Technically, I'm not. What are those?" Thomas asked, tilting his chin at the papers in her hand.

"Notes from the Erika Windrow case. Gray needs my statement. Hey, Raven told me you invited her brother to stay with you while he searches for a new place."

"In the guest house, yes."

"That's kind of you. LeVar needs people on his side, especially after I accused him of murder. Guess you fixed my mess...I always make a mess of things."

An uncomfortable silence fell between them, and in that quiet, Thomas sought words to bridge the gap. The right words remained elusive, like catching will-o-wisps in the darkness. He shuffled his feet. She stood a healthy distance away, her eyes shifting to her sneakers as she spoke.

"About last night," she said. "I laid too much on you, and I'm sorry."

"We waited a long time to voice our feelings. You need not apologize."

She looked toward the building, the parking lot reflected in the windows.

"I lost control of my emotions. That's something I'm working on. I'm afraid I gave you the wrong impression, and for that, I can't forgive myself."

He squinted into the sunlight, his throat tightening. Had he the courage to speak from the heart, he would have invited her to the house, told Chelsey he wanted her in his life. Instead, he held his tongue as she erected another wall between them.

"I want you to know...I ended things with Ray. Why I was with that meat head in the first place, I don't understand. But after the way he acted at the dance, and how he treated you, I didn't want him around."

"A wise move."

Something unsaid hid behind her lips. Chelsey straightened her jacket and brushed her hair back.

"Well, I better get inside before Gray sends a cruiser to my house. Be well, Thomas. I hope we cross paths again someday."

She strode into the sun and disappeared through the doors. He swallowed the burn in his throat and slipped his hands into his pockets. Alone in the parking lot, the wind blowing the remnants of last autumn's leaves around his ankles, he found the words he'd longed to say.

"I can't live without you, Chelsey."

~

Thank you for being a loyal reader!
Ready to read the sequel, Fatal Mercy?
Read Fatal Mercy today!

GET A FREE BOOK!

I'm a pretty nice guy once you look past the grisly images in my head. Most of all, I love connecting with awesome readers like you.

Join my VIP Reader Group and get a FREE serial killer thriller for your Kindle.

Get My Free Book

www.danpadavona.com/thriller-readers-vip-group/

SHOW YOUR SUPPORT FOR INDIE AUTHORS

Did you enjoy this book? If so, please let other thriller fans know by leaving a short review. Positive reviews help spread the word about independent authors and their novels. Thank you.

Copyright Information

Published by Dan Padavona

Visit my website at www.danpadavona.com

Cover Design by Caroline Teagle Johnson

ABOUT THE AUTHOR

Dan Padavona is the author of the The Darkwater Cove series, The Scarlett Bell thriller series, *Her Shallow Grave*, The Dark Vanishings series, *Camp Slasher, Quilt, Crawlspace, The Face of Midnight, Storberry, Shadow Witch*, and the horror anthology, *The Island*. He lives in upstate New York with his beautiful wife, Terri, and their children, Joe, and Julia. Dan is a meteorologist with NOAA's National Weather Service. Besides writing, he enjoys visiting amusement parks, beach vacations, Renaissance fairs, gardening, playing with the family dogs, and eating too much ice cream.

Visit Dan at: www.danpadavona.com